Dec '97

xxx

love from AL.

DOLLY'S WAR

By the same author

A TOUCH OF DANIEL
MOG
I DIDN'T KNOW YOU CARED
EXCEPT YOU'RE A BIRD
THE STIRK OF STIRK
SHEMERELDA
TALES FROM A LONG ROOM
MORE TALES FROM A LONG ROOM
COLLECTED TALES FROM A LONG ROOM
THE BRIGADIER DOWN UNDER
THE HOME FRONT
THE BRIGADIERS IN SEASON
CALL IT A CANARY
THE BRIGADIER'S TOUR
THE BRIGADIER'S BRIEF LIVES
UNCLE MORT'S NORTH COUNTRY
TALES FROM WITNEY SCROTUM
UNCLE MORT'S SOUTH COUNTRY
HAYBALLS
WINSTON
WITNEY SCROTUM

DOLLY'S WAR

Peter Tinniswood

HarperCollins*Publishers*

HarperCollins*Publishers*
77–85 Fulham Palace Road,
Hammersmith, London W6 8JB

Published by HarperCollins*Publishers* 1997
1 3 5 7 9 8 6 4 2

A catalogue record for this book is
available from the British Library

ISBN 0 00 225410 7

Set in Postscript Monotype Baskerville
and Bauer Bodoni display by
Rowland Phototypesetting Ltd,
Bury St Edmunds, Suffolk

Printed and bound in Great Britain by
Caledonian International
Book Manufacturing Ltd, Glasgow

DOLLY'S WAR

PART ONE

I

The German bomber circled the marsh timidly. Its engines sputtered. The sun glinted wanly on the gun turret. It seemed bewildered. The eyes of its cockpit were weary.

And then without warning and rather diffidently it dropped a bomb smack in the middle of the playing fields of Lygon House Private School for Progressive Young People.

Dolly Bradman, the headmistress, stood at the window of the hunched, pinch-shouldered common room, surveying the damage.

At length she turned to face the assembled staff and said: 'Right. That's it. The shits will have to be evacuated.'

Later that evening:

'We were always on the move in my army days. I couldn't keep up with it. I sometimes think the generals did it on purpose.'

Major Pickavance to the senior master, Mr Dugdale.

The peat block slumbers fitfully in the common room fire grate. Major Pickavance polishes his collection of tiepins assiduously. Mr Dugdale thinks wistfully of Borodino, and swallows.

'There's absolutely no need to worry, my dear Dolly. You know what Papa's like. He'll make all the arrangements. If he can't fix it, then no one can. *Quel* bastard!'

The head boy, Lance Egerton, talking to Dolly in her study.

She opens the last box of her slant-eyed Egyptian cigarettes and offers it to Lance. He shakes his head testily. She lights a cigarette and presses it between his lips.

The rain leers on the windows. She sighs and thinks of bicycle holidays in the Charente.

The old house slumbers weary of its denizens.

'Oh, go to sleep,' it croons. 'Please, please, go to sleep.'

Bats flutter in the eaves of its gatehouse. The ivy tangles the cracks

3

of the demesne wall. Mists trail the skirts of the woodland. The roses nod in their arbours. The lilies pad softly in their ponds. The ancient sandstone pediments, porches and parapets drowse in the dusk. There are no bees. There is no milk from sour goats.

'Please, please, go to sleep,' it groans. 'Please, please.'

'Go to sleep, you little cows. Oh, please, please, go to sleep.'

The head girl, Natasha, to the girls of the giggling snickering junior dorm.

Perdita has ginger hair and pink eyelids. Louise is plump. Jassy is shy. Fanny has large green eyes and trim ankles. Polly is simply Polly.

Autumn waders sated with summer brood on the saltings. The marsh sheep munch. The short-eared owl ponders the tide.

'But where's the old bitch going to cart us off to?'

Celia, Dolly Bradman's niece, to Mamselle.

The clock ticks. The clock tocks.

Celia is the matron. Mamselle teaches French and Pertinent Studies. Celia's age is twenty-nine. Mamselle's is somewhat more obscure. She has small, spike-tipped breasts, of which she is exceedingly proud.

The two ladies sit in the sanatorium drinking Bombay gin.

Mrs Otto snores solidly. She has watery teeth and she clutches to her sleeping bosom a scuffed but solemn briefcase stuffed with morsels of rotting food. She calls it her *Speisewagen*.

The trawlers dare not trawl. The drifters dare not drift. E-boats prowl and colliers hug the skulking shore. Far out to sea a star shell languorously breaks its back against the mouth-black sky.

'I've just farted.'

'Have another slug of Bombay gin.'

'Go to sleep, you cows. Go to sleep.'

'Don't think of Papa now. Think of me. For Christ's sake, boy, think of me.'

'I never got the hang of moving. Never. Never.'

The tortoise roots in its straw. The white mice whirr in their wheels. Whelks rasp. Deep in the pit of his bed Mr Dugdale twitches and thinks wistfully of slender necks.

It is the late autumn of 1941.

4

2

Next morning Dolly called a staff meeting.

'I hate staff meetings,' said Major Pickavance. 'I hate anything that disturbs one's routine. That's why this war is such a confounded abomination.'

Mr Dugdale smiled to himself.

A parcel had arrived from his wine merchant. It had been much pilfered. Three bottles were broken. Yet miraculously a clutch of bottles of Montrachet had survived the perils of the railways. Years earlier one sharp winter's evening in Budapest he had drunk the wine in its prime. This morning before breakfast he had supped it again. It had softened and faded with age, but still it whispered in the pure, authentic voice of hope of the days of its pomp.

He tittered as they made their way to the common room.

'Are you drunk?' said Major Pickavance.

'Certainly not,' said Mr Dugdale. 'Why do you ask?'

'Because your breath smells most damnably peculiar.'

'Ah,' said Mr Dugdale. ''Tis but the reek of corruption and the stench of remembered joys. I smell like a grass fire.'

'You're drunk,' said Major Pickavance firmly.

'I know,' said Mr Dugdale.

Dolly scowled at them as they entered the common room. The rest of the staff were already assembled. Mamselle pulled up the hem of her skirt above her knees and licked the lipstick from her teeth. Celia inclined her head to the left and smiled vaguely. She liked inclining her head to the left. Mrs Otto scratched in the deep, echoing caverns of her ears with a spent match.

'Good,' said Dolly. 'We are all gathered.'

She was forty-six years of age. She had white skin. Her hair flustered and flowed round her neck and shoulders like the tumble of ravens. Her body was munificent. She had sumptuous eyes and faint wrinkles above her upper lip.

She was wearing a maroon, ankle-length velvet frock and fur boots.

5

'Right,' she said. 'Last night I had a long and earnest chinwag with the Head Shit. And he agreed with me that we have to evacuate ourselves. The question is, where to? Mr Dugdale, your thoughts, if you please.'

Mr Dugdale's thoughts?

At that precise moment he was on his travels once more. He was thinking of bottles of Chablis chilling in a mountain stream, of an old man hosing down the coughing, rough-nosed dust of the village square where he had drunk absinthe and waited for the bulls. He was thinking of bleak-backed skerries and the hollow chug of the winter steamer and the scream of kittiwake and the osprey's skidding plunge.

'I?' he said. 'My thoughts?'

Dolly clucked her tongue. The cigarette, stuck to her lower lip, shed its ash onto her broad collar of Macclesfield lace and nestled in the ridges and runnels of her bombazine brooch.

'Hopeless,' she said. 'Absolutely hopeless.'

And she turned to Celia and riddled her with the coal black of her sumptuous eyes.

'Oh Lor',' said Celia. 'You want my thoughts?'

Dolly nodded.

'How about the North West coast?' she said. 'I've heard some extremely good reports of the hinterland round Fylde.'

Once she had met a sublieutenant in the Royal Naval Reserve who had a widowed mother residing in Fylde. He had worn gauntlets and told her of happy days spent in Lytham St Anne's.

'Yes,' she said. 'I think the North West coast could be most suitable.'

Dolly hurled the hard-sucked butt of her cigarette into the fire and boomed: 'My dear Celia. I am not talking about moving into another nook of our own back yard. I am looking for vistas new. I am searching for ungrazed pastures far beyond the distant horizon. I seek exotic climes where minds will be stimulated, the body juices will wax and fructify and the shits will prosper mightily.'

'How about Nyasaland?' said Major Pickavance. 'They tell me it's in Africa.'

'Ah. Nyasaland! Africa!' exclaimed Dolly. 'Staff, let us forthwith discuss the merits of the Dark Continent.'

They commenced to do so.

But all the time Mamselle thought of gold teeth and toothbrush moustaches and police clinging to the running boards of snarling limousines and the crack of their handguns and the wind beating at the brims of their dove-grey fedoras.

Meanwhile in the junior common room Lance Egerton held court. The whole school was assembled before him and he gazed at them distant and aloof through the fulsome smoke of his Russian cigarette.

The small girls giggled and squabbled and pinched each other's bottoms.

Natasha gazed at Lance with adoring, hungry eyes. Her neck was wistful and slender.

Linda sat on the floor clamped tightly between Margot's thighs. Swish, swish, went the brush as it plundered the booty of her long roast-red hair. She grunted. She turned her head to Margot, opened her mouth and let the tip of her glistening pink tongue smooch softly over her lower lip.

'Oh God!' said Margot. 'Must you be so banal?'

Delphine, dowdy and dumpy, sat alone reading. Gosh, how those hussars caroused. How those Polish ladies fluttered their eyelids and heaved their bosoms. The greyhounds quartering the stricken hare. The ox carts laden with wounded gunners.

Samira sat on a prim-backed sofa.

She smiled to herself and thought of home and the purple, clove-scented nights and her father stacking his contraband under waterproof sheets.

'Doesn't anyone want to know why I've called this meeting?' said Lance.

The three boys shrugged their shoulders.

Burnaby continued to apply yellow ointment to his facial pustules. The Doucemain twins, unidentical to a man, continued to plot revenge on their parents.

Lance sighed.

How he longed for quails' eggs and blinis.

He felt Natasha's eyes, brown as moles, burrow into his groin.

He sighed again and spoke slowly and clearly.

'I shall tell you why I have called this meeting. Last night I had a long confab with Dolly and we came to the conclusion that we must evacuate this school immediately.'

There was silence. Then Burnaby looked up from his ablutions activities and said: 'Where to?'

'That's the whole point, Burnaby,' said Lance. 'We haven't made up our minds. We're open to your suggestions.'

'I hate suggestions,' said Margot. 'In my experience they always lead to unsavoury unpleasantnesses.'

She nipped Linda sharply on the neck.

Polly giggled and whispered to Perdita: 'I've just farted.'

Lance slapped his thigh with irritation.

'For God's sake,' he snapped. 'Hasn't anyone got a suggestion?'

There was silence.

Natasha knew she had to speak. It didn't matter what she said. For the sake of her beloved she had to say something.

And so she raised up her head to him and said huskily: 'What about the West Indies?'

'Right,' said Lance Egerton. 'I'll see if Papa can fix it.'

He could.

3

The day of the embarkation dawned.

Herring gulls skeined the gaunt ribs of the Channel. The sandbanks heaved their flanks at the rip race. Black mountains glowered.

They were to travel by banana boat from Cardiff.

Six weeks had elapsed since the bombing of the school. During that period Fanny had fallen from her pony and broken her back and Linda had been murdered by hand unknown.

'Women!' Dolly had said. 'Isn't that bloody typical?'

She and Celia had stayed on at the school until it had finally succumbed to the advances of the army.

'Are you two ladies part of the fixtures and fittings?' the quartering commandant had said.

Dolly had drawn in her breath sharply, pursed her lips and then slowly inflated her bosom.

In a low, sultry voice she had said: 'For tonight, *mon commandant*, I am at your disposal.'

The soldier had chuckled and spluttered.

He was an ancient, retired, reappointed lieutenant colonel with opaque silver-grey eyes and a girth the size of a brewer's piano.

'By gad, ma'am,' he had said, slapping his leather glove on the palm of his left hand. 'By gad!'

Dolly and Celia had watched the army moving in.

The fatigue party with barren mops and cans of disinfectant. The officer with the sallow cheeks and the thin, grease-slicked hair combed back without parting.

'Righty-ho,' he had said when given an order by his company commander.

'For Christ's sake, don't say righty-ho.'

'Sorry. I do try to remember. It just slips out.'

Snow sniding in from the marsh. The elms shaken free from rooks. The first snarls of winter.

'Come on, Celia, time for the West Indies.'

9

They had paused by the gatehouse and looked back at the school.

Take me with you, it had seemed to scream at them. Don't leave me. You can't leave me now. I've been your friend. I've been your faithful servant. I've been loyal and true. Catch me spilling the beans about what's gone on here. Catch me blabbering about that time you found Father McNulty in bed with –

'There's only one thing I shall miss about this place, Celia.'

'And what's that, Dolly?'

'The pub.'

Mamselle spent her embarkation leave with her mother in Altrincham in the fair county of Cheshire.

Her mother lived in a terraced cottage overlooking the cut.

From her bedroom window Mamselle could see the narrow boats laden with coke and salt. She could hear the midnight crunch and slur of clinker on the tow path. She could smell carbolic soap and damp wallpaper.

'You'll not like it where you're going, our Clara,' her mother said.

'Course I will, Mam. Don't be daft. It'll be grand, will the West Indies.'

She went to the covered market and bought ticking and elastic for her mother and second-hand gramophone records for herself.

She visited friends in Broadheath and Eccles.

'It's all right for you, Clara – us poor buggers are working in munitions.'

'And doing fire watching at night.'

'And working the switchboard for the ambulances.'

'We're working our socks off.'

She visited Mr Mazarene in his wary mansion on the lonely Moss.

'You've done extremely well for yourself, my dear Clara,' he said.

She clasped him behind the knees and rested her head on his lap.

He stroked her hair.

The threadbare carpet. Expectant.

The spike-tipped breasts. Expectant.

The angry ratatat-tat of the stick on the parlour ceiling.

He sighed.

'It never changes, my dear Clara. It never changes.'

In a small, discreet basement restaurant in London Lance Egerton dined with his father and a thin-shanked woman with tight-frizzed hair.

'Do you approve of Mrs Simister, my boy?' said Sir Graham.

'Decidedly not,' said Lance. 'Another bottle of Clos de Bèze?'

'Cheeky little sod,' said Mrs Simister. 'What he wants is a bloody good kick up the flap.'

They dined off *caviar aux blinis*, soup of *oseille*, a sole simply cooked in white wine sauce, a *caneton à la presse* and a lemon soufflé.

'Yum, yummy yum yum. How on earth do you manage it, Papa?'

'My dear boy,' said Sir Graham, taking hold of his son's wrist and squeezing it lightly. 'You are so young. So innocent.'

'Innocent? Him?' said Mrs Simister. 'And my arse. You want to see the cow eyes he's been making at the waiters.'

They parted in St James's.

'Mrs Simister and I have pressing business of a somewhat carnal nature to attend to,' said Sir Graham.

He withdrew a doeskin notecase from the inside pocket of his jacket and took out three crisp £100 banknotes.

'I do hope you'll find these useful during the course of your voyage into the great unknown, my dear,' he said. 'I wish you every success in your enterprise. Do remember to get in touch when you return.'

He kissed Lance on the lips and then withdrew with Mrs Simister clinging snitchily to his arm.

A sneer slithered across Lance's face.

The totter of her tight and tiny bottom.

The teeter and the strut.

She had winked at him during luncheon and he had felt her hand on his thigh.

Major Pickavance spent eleven days walking in the Peak District of Derbyshire.

The weather was clement and the inns welcoming.

He supped half-pints of clear, sparkling mild bitter beer and communed with dipper, pipit and gritstone sheep.

Then he repaired to the Lake District to spend a week with a cousin of a clerical bent.

They sat in his study drinking Madeira and looking out onto the lake slinking with sail boats and sinuous with the early evening's mists.

'The West Indies, eh?' said the cousin. 'You're going to the West Indies then?'

'That is correct.'

'And you are travelling by boat?'

'That is correct.'

'You'll be torpedoed.'

'What?'

'Nothing is more certain, my dear old chap. You'll be torpedoed sure as eggs are eggs. And dive-bombed by Stukas. And I've not the slightest doubt that you'll be shelled by surface raider, too.'

The cousin cracked his knuckles. His shoulders creaked. He thrust a paper spill into the fire and applied it to his pipe. He sucked. The pipe slucked.

'I wonder how you'll cope with those endless days and nights in an open boat,' he said.

'I beg your pardon, Esmond?' said Major Pickavance.

'You'll probably go mad. Drinking all that sea water, you see. It makes people go stark raving bonkers. And having to eat each other won't help matters.'

His cousin's elderly companion entered the room silently. He sat demurely in a straight-backed rocking chair in the lee of a drowsy display cabinet.

He wore a musty, ginger toupee.

The cousin sucked once more at his pipe and a dribble of brown spittle ran down his chin.

'Are you able to swim?' he asked Major Pickavance.

'Yes,' said Major Pickavance.

The cousin nodded his head slowly.

'Well,' he said. 'That is at least some small consolation for me.'

Natasha's guardian said: 'You know, Natasha, there's not the slightest need for you to go to the West Indies, if you don't want to.'

'But I do want to. Very much. Very much indeed, as a matter of fact. I'm aching for it. I'm longing for it. If you won't let me go, I'll kill myself. Do you hear that? I'll kill myself. Kill, kill, kill.'

And then she fled upstairs to her bedroom overlooking the hard-fought downlands and commenced to write a letter on her springy, lime-green, scented notepaper.

It went thus:

> My gorgeous, darling Lance,
>
>   I love you. I love you, love you, love you, love you, love you, love you, love you, LOVE YOU.
>
>   My body yearns for you. If you've never had chicory before, don't be tempted to try. It's horrid.

I love you, love you, love you, love you, love you, love you, love you.

As the poet says: 'I would love you ten years before the flood.'

I long to be with you, my precious darling. I can't wait for the day when first we kiss. Oh, Lance, say you'll kiss me, kiss me, kiss me, kiss me.

As the poet says: 'Gather the flowers, but spare the buds.'

Roll on the West Indies.

I love you, I love you, LOVE YOU, LOVE YOU.

Natasha.

PS: I love you.

In the evening her guardian shot a rabbit.

'We'll have it for supper tomorrow,' he said.

Natasha flung her arms round his neck and cried: 'I love you, love you, love you, love you.'

Delphine, plump and dowdy, sat at a stern-legged table in the high-domed, galleried library of her father's house.

It was late afternoon and the first straggle of the winter's fieldfare and redwing was already long aroost in the hedgerows.

She heard the soft, sly click of the opening door.

Her father entered and shuffled towards her with his mandarin tread and his crow-hunched shoulders. He wore a black poncho cape, a maroon and mustard-yellow check suit, a silk stock tie and dove-grey sombrero.

'You are alone, Delphine,' he said, and in his voice there was a snicker of relish.

'No, Father,' said Delphine with a gentle smile, 'I am not alone.'

And indeed she was not.

Cossack horsemen guarded her. Officers of the hussars flattered her and hung on her every gesture. The little princess with the faint-downed upper lip short over her teeth fluttered her eyelids at her. And at her side the love of her life, the prince home from the wars, lay dying.

Her father ground his teeth and turned away. As he slut-sluttered to the door he muttered to himself: 'My God, how I hate that girl. How I loathe her.'

Delphine watched him sidle out of the room and her eyes were filled with love and tender, boundless compassion.

And what of Mr Dugdale?

How did he fare?

4

Since he had received a modest legacy three years previously at the age of sixty-two Mr Dugdale had been accustomed to spending his vacations, both long and short, at The Marine Hotel.

It was a small establishment situated on a cliff top overlooking the Bristol Channel.

It was in Wales, a few miles distant from Cardiff.

From his bedroom window Mr Dugdale could see the hulks of Steep Holm and Flat Holm.

Both fare and charges were modest. The service was efficient and friendly. He was treated with courtesy.

The proprietor, he had discovered, had betimes served in his regiment in Palestine. Often they would talk of matters military and each morning Mr Dugdale would take the hotel's golden retriever, Felix, for a brisk walk along the cliff top.

Each time he arrived for his sojourn the dog would bound up to him, grinning and slavering and greeting him with the red carpet of his tongue.

'I told him you were coming,' Mr Cuthbert, the proprietor, would say. 'He's been waiting in the window all day for you.'

Mr Dugdale would smile, bend down, chucker Felix under the chin and present him with one of the biscuits he had brought especially for his delight.

Mr Dugdale looked forward to the dog's greeting.

Sometimes he felt it was the only thing that kept him going during the weary fag of term at Lygon House Private School for Progressive Young People.

The dog's company was infinitely preferable to that of the pupils or his fellow members of staff.

It was undoubtedly more intelligent, too.

This time, however, when he arrived after the closure of the school and its impending takeover by the military he had noticed a change in the dog.

There was a certain stiffness in its gait. The eyes were not so sharp. There was a hint of sadness in its smile.

Mr Dugdale heard faint murmurs of his own mortality as he massaged the flop of Felix's ears and heard his bronchial grunts of pleasure.

He was given his usual bedroom. He was given his usual table and at the end of dinner Mr Cuthbert fetched him port from the scanty stock he kept for safety in the hotel's cellars.

Yet there were other changes apart from the dog.

Two of the permanent residents, Miss Broome and Mr Box, had left. Poverty had overtaken Miss Broome, and Mr Box had moved from fear of German investment from the sea.

An RAF flight lieutenant with big ears, small feet and a desultory involvement with meteorology had taken Miss Broome's bedroom. And Mr Box's old quarters of bedroom and sitting room had been converted into separate units currently occupied by two gloom-laden naval officers. One of them wore mittens. The other went to bed immediately after dinner and could be heard at dead of night stropping his razor.

None the less Mr Dugdale was content.

His old routine was not disturbed by the changes.

In the morning the walk with Felix. Later before lunch the slow saunter into town for two whisky and sodas and the purchase of *The Times* and the *Western Mail*.

After luncheon the snooze.

Lundy far out smudged in the hazy Channel. The massed shipping held by contraband control. The mew of seabirds. The clank of dredger.

Another walk with Felix. Gin before dinner.

A chat with Mr Cuthbert in his pantry. A bottle of light ale in the bar. The slow, languid uncorking of claret in his bedroom. The slow, languid filling of his pipe. The flare of match. The smoke drift and palate thrill and croon.

Random memories of an old and handsome man: the Nansen passport. Ice grip of Stockholm winter. The soldier's scream. The horse kicking and thrashing in its traces. Screech of shell. Blackness. Silence. The earth moved beneath him.

Mr Dugdale decided it was high time he took a woman to himself.

5

She was not a banana boat.

Dolly said she was. But that was her way of coping.

The SS *Drayman* was, in fact, a portly and elderly cargo liner of a gross tonnage of 8,196, a draught of 27 feet 6 inches and an age of twenty weary, salt-sagged summers.

She had spent her entire working life pottering benignly in the Caribbean, visiting islands both large and small, venturing occasionally into fetid, mosquito-sotted mainland creeks and returning to her home port somewhat smugly with cargoes of sugar, coffee, cotton, tobacco, and on occasions objects of mild erotica from Surinam.

For the technically minded she was built by C. Connell & Co. Ltd of Glasgow and launched on the Clyde on 5 July 1921. She was single screwed with three DR turbines, steam being provided by two DE and SE boilers, giving a service speed of between twelve and thirteen knots.

But Dolly was not technically minded.

She took one look at SS *Drayman* as the boat lay alongside the quay at Cardiff Docks and said to Celia: 'I think they should paint the funnel a different colour, don't you?'

For the technically minded the funnel was painted black with two bands of white enclosing a band of red.

This was known to jocular persons of a nautical nature as 'two of fat and one of lean'.

Dolly and Celia were greeted at the head of the gangwalk by Mr Dugdale, who had established himself on board four hours previously.

He seemed agitated. He rubbed his hands together nervously and hopped from foot to foot.

'Natasha,' he said. 'I'm worried about Natasha. She hasn't arrived yet. I hope nothing untoward's happened to her.'

'It might have,' said Dolly. 'Linda's been murdered.'

'Really?' said Mr Dugdale vaguely, and he pressed himself against the rail scanning the dockside for signs of the object of his concern.

Half an hour later in their cabin Dolly turned to Celia and said: 'You don't think old fart face fancies Natasha, do you?'

Celia stamped her foot angrily and said: 'I wish you wouldn't use language like that. I know you only do it to make an impression on the pupils, but it doesn't go down well with me. I'm far too impressionable.'

Dolly smiled to herself, lay back on her bed, lit a cigarette and watched the steward begin to unpack the first of her trunks.

He was a thin black man with snow-white hair and slimy bloodshot eyes.

'What do I call you?' said Dolly. 'Will Sambo be all right?'

'No problem, missus,' said the steward.

He shook his shoulders in a display of silent mirth. But when he turned his back to her, the soft and amiable contours of his face were riven by a scowl of lashing venom.

Much later that night in his bunk in the cramped and verminous forecastle mess he whispered to his lover: 'Dat woman. She goin' to die pretty damn soon. Oh yes, Thomas, I tell you – she die pretty damn soon and 'orrible. No problem.'

6

Meanwhile all morning Mr Dugdale maintained his position at the top of the gangwalk.

He greeted Mamselle when she arrived at the quayside in a stiff-jointed taxicab shortly after nine thirty with the words: 'Natasha! Any news of Natasha?'

Mamselle looked at him scornfully and silently for a moment. Then she flicked the tail of her fox fur wrap over her right shoulder, sniffed from the flared nostrils of her fine-angled nose and click-clicked her way to her cabin.

When Margot arrived swathed in leather, sleeking with black satin and glinting with slim gold and silver bangles on wrist and ankle, he said: 'Natasha! Any news of Natasha?'

'Oh, shove off,' she said.

He asked the same question of Mrs Otto when she arrived shortly afterwards clutching her *Speisewagen* to her snuff-stained bosom and trailing a small, hairless dog on a lead made from twisted sisal.

She ignored him, pointed to the dog and said: 'He very old. When he die, I eat him.'

Lance Egerton presented himself on the quayside in a cavernous, marauding, chauffeur-driven turquoise and cobalt Hispano-Suiza. The driver wore snow-white jodhpurs and his skin was as brown as an okapi's elbow.

Imperiously Lance summoned a retinue of stewards, dock hands and dockside loungers to take aboard the monogrammed trunks, valises, portmanteaux and Gladstone bags stacked in a pantechnicon that had been awaiting his arrival all morning.

Lance dismissed the chauffeur curtly. He responded by flipping the peak of his cap with the fingertip of a yellow, wash-leather glove.

From the perfumed recesses of the back of the limousine a thin-shanked woman's voice said: 'Tarra, cocky. Look after yourself, mate.'

Lance Egerton smiled and strolled up the gangwalk, puffing unhurriedly at a fat Havana cigar and twirling a silver-topped ebony cane.

Mr Dugdale moved forwards but then thought better of enquiring about the welfare and whereabouts of Natasha.

A sly Welsh rain skulking out from the distant hills began to patter clumsily on the old cargo liner's decks and upperworks.

A faint mist wisped around the crosstrees of the masts and a Chinese donkeyman came up on deck for a last gulp of fresh air. He blew on his hands, stamped his feet, spat copiously over the side and then disappeared below.

Commercial vehicles arrived at the quayside bearing last-minute stores for SS *Drayman* – carcasses of mutton and beef, tins of dried milk and corned beef, bales of cotton waste and cartons of damp and flimsy toilet paper.

The pupils arrived in taxicabs and the cars of doting parents and limp-eyed guardians.

There were hugs and tears.

Sticky mouths were pressed to sticky bosoms.

There were stiff upper lips and blubbering lower lips. Pubescent spots and pimples mingled with night-soothed skins and thickly pomaded hair.

Polly said: 'Guess what I've just done.'

'I'm not the slightest bit interested,' said Perdita. 'Daddy took me to see Dame Myra Hess playing music on the piano so I'm quite past that sort of thing now, thank you very much.'

A slim young man in an ill-fitting, crumpled uniform stumbled up the gangwalk and said breathlessly to Mr Dugdale: 'Can you tell me where to go? It's rather important. I'm the ship's doctor, you see, and –'

Before he could finish the sentence he was violently sick on the deck. He tittered and staggered away, groaning softly.

The minutes ticked by. There was no sign of Natasha.

Where was she? What had happened to her? Suddenly it came to him. In a flash. A blinding flash that sent his senses reeling. She had been abducted by bandits. They had bound her and gagged her and secreted her, drugged and unconscious, in the bottom of a diplomatic bag bound for the Levant. And there she had been whipped and flayed and flogged and debased and humiliated and forced to perform acts of the most unspeakable depravity in front of –

He spun round and shrieked at Burnaby: 'For Christ's sake, boy, will you stop squeezing your boils like that. The noise is disgusting, you squalid lout, you verminous sourer of mother's milk.'

Burnaby shrugged his shoulders.

'I can't help it,' he said. 'It runs in the family.'

More minutes passed by. Sundry strangers mounted the gangwalk with varying degrees of bravado and trepidation. Major Pickavance arrived with Samira and Delphine. He had met them at Cardiff mainline station and on grounds of economy rather than propinquity agreed to share a taxicab.

'Remarkable journey from the station, old boy,' said Major Pickavance to Mr Dugdale. 'A glorious Aladdin's cave of wicked delights. All those coal-black faces with lascivious, sneering lips. The pock-marked skins and the relentless throbbing of drums. And once we got out of St Mary's Street there were the smells of spices and wood smoke and alien armpits.'

'Never mind the alien armpits,' snapped Mr Dugdale. 'What's become of Natasha? She hasn't arrived. For God's sake, man, pay attention while I'm talking to you. She's going to miss the boat. For God's sake, she's going to miss the bloody ship.'

Major Pickavance coolly removed Mr Dugdale's hands from the lapels of his overcoat. Very slowly he raised his eyebrows. And then very slowly he repaired to his cabin.

An elderly Goanese steward passed by tinkling his musical gong to announce the imminence of luncheon. He had flowing white moustaches and rosy tints behind his nut-brown cheeks.

But Mr Dugdale did not move his position at the rails.

'Care for pre-luncheon cocktails?' said Lance Egerton.

Mr Dugdale shook his head violently.

Movement on the quayside. Sauntering dockside workers grouping round bollards. Movement on the deck. Seamen donning leather gloves and easing mooring lines.

'Not coming to lunch, Mr Dugdale?' said Celia.

Mr Dugdale shook his head.

'You're not frightened of being seasick, are you?'

'Shove off,' said Mr Dugdale.

An officer appeared on the forecastle with a loud-hailer. The dockers stretched their limbs and yawned and scratched the nicks in their bottoms. The officer shouted in his loud-hailer.

Dear God, she was about to leave. They were about to lift away the gangwalk.

Natasha! Natasha! Oh, Natasha, what had happened to her?

And then he knew. He saw it. Instantly. Blindingly. Dazzlingly. The soft white body crushed beneath a plunging horse. The slender neck severed by the windscreen's shatter. The mortal illness gnawing. Corrupting, sucking away the lifeblood, festering the juices of youth.

Slip of wire. Rope swish and scamper across surface of water. Clank of chains on gangwalk. Crackle of loud-hailer. Throb of engines. The skrush of screw.

And then he saw her.

She was leaning out of the taxicab window waving and shouting.

'Stop!' shouted Mr Dugdale. 'Stop! Stop! Stop! Hold the ship! Bastard! Stop this ship, do you hear?'

Five minutes later Natasha clattered breathlessly up the gangwalk. Her face was flushed. Her slim young breasts heaved, her cool, clear eyes were flecked with fear and relief.

Mr Dugdale rushed up to her.

'Oh, my dear Natasha,' he said. 'I can't say how relieved I am to see you. I can't –'

Scornfully she pushed him aside.

She turned to a tiny, hovering, delicate-boned Goanese steward and said:

'You! Show me to Mr Lance Egerton's quarters immediately.'

7

They were to travel in convoy.

The ships assembled in mid-afternoon in Barry Roads.

The rain had ceased. Timid sunshine pattered over the wavelets. Pennants fluttered. Lamps flashed. Gulls yacked. Gash buckets spewed.

There were twenty-three merchant ships in the convoy. The commodore's vessel was a fat-arsed freighter with rust-streaked sides and two squat, dumpy funnels.

The escort was led by the destroyer, HMS *Plunderer*. There was a corvette, HMS *Campion*, and a deep-sea naval tug. The party was completed by a Royal Danish Navy sloop, sleek as a newly sharpened pencil, racy as a silken whippet. Even in the sheltered waters of the roads she pitched and wallowed and gulped at the sea.

The corvette, *Campion*, fussed alongside them and the officer on the bridge shouted at them through a loud-hailer, reminding them that they were to maintain single file until it was signalled for them to take up convoy position.

'And good luck,' he shouted. 'We're going to need all that's going.'

And so they set off for the Caribbean Sea and the Island of St David's.

Of what was in store for them they had not the slightest notion.

Their progress was slow and stately.

Later in the afternoon they were joined by two more ships nosing their way tentatively out of Swansea Bay.

One was a low-slung, heavy-bellied ore carrier. The other was a hangdog tanker with scruffy washing flapping from the galley door.

The ships were bullied into position by *Campion*, and slowly night fell and the whispers of Wales shimmered across to them over the moonlit waters. The magic of the rock-strewn mountains. The secrets of the shallow valleys meandered by streams and hung with oak. The gannet stacks and the cliff-top choughs.

They settled themselves into their accommodations. Dolly shared a cabin with Celia. Mamselle shared a cabin with Mrs Otto, Mr Dugdale shared a cabin with Major Pickavance.

Lance Egerton occupied a suite with bedroom, drawing room, study, dining room, and brass and marble bathroom.

Four decks below Burnaby and the Doucemain twins lolled in a cramped, perspiring cabin with the stains of long-squelched cockroaches on the tiles. Next door were Margot, Delphine and Samira. At the end of the alleyway was a dormitory, where Natasha presided over Polly, Perdita, Jassy and Louise.

'What was Dame Myra Hess like?'

'Fat.'

'Did she play well?'

'I don't know. I forgot to ask Daddy.'

Dolly poured out another glass of Bombay gin.

'This voyage is going to be absolutely ghastly,' she said. 'I can feel it in my water.'

Celia nodded vaguely.

She sipped at her vermouth thoughtfully.

Then she turned to her aunt and said: 'I'm certain of it now. Absolutely certain.'

'Certain of what?'

'That Mr Dugdale has got a crush on Natasha.'

Dolly took a long pull at her Bombay gin, eased a ruck in her cleavage and said: 'Well, thank God he hasn't got a crush on Burnaby.'

At that moment the only person who had a crush on Burnaby was Burnaby himself. He lay on his bunk hunched and tight-fisted, panting and grinding his teeth.

The Doucemain twins, Guy and Charles, looked on with curled lips and sneer-laden eyes.

'God, he's at it again,' said Guy.

'It's too disgusting,' said Charles.

'I can't help it. It runs in the family.'

Guy took off one of his shoes and hurled it at the bunk. It struck Burnaby flush on the left temple. He howled in pain.

The Doucemain twins looked at each other and grinned.

How they loved inflicting pain. It ran in the family. Slaughter, massacre, carnage, unbridled butchery – it had flourished in the family for generations.

Sly-lipped soldiers had plundered and pillaged. Fat-jowled sailors had sailed up muddy creeks and sliced through the native throngs with grapeshot and cutlasses.

Pain was etched into their souls.

Charles threw a hairbrush at Burnaby. It bounced off the crown of his head and clattered to the cabin floor.

Once more he howled in pain.

Once more his tormentors grinned.

In the cabin next door Margot stood naked in front of the mirror admiring her breasts. They were full and firm. They pranced, proud in their pomp.

'Aren't they lovely?' said Margot. 'Aren't they simply gorgeous? Lucky, lucky me.'

There was a knock on the door, Margot screeched, threw her dressing gown over her shoulders and clutched it tight to her body.

Delphine cautiously opened the door a slit's width.

'Yes?' she said.

They heard a rich, deep, burry West Country voice say: 'I'm the bosun. I just want to say if there is anything you need or require of a nautical or personal nature, please don't hesitate to make contact. I shall be only too willing to oblige and help out sort of thing. Do you follow my meaning?'

'Yes,' said Delphine. 'Thanks most awfully.'

They heard the fruity rumble of his chuckles and Delphine slammed the door hard.

'Very interesting,' said Margot, letting the dressing gown slip to her waist. 'Very interesting indeed.'

The bosun rolled jauntily along the alleyway and smiled broadly when he heard the shrill voices in the dormitory.

Inside Polly was wrestling with Louise, and Perdita was belabouring Jassy about the shoulders and head with the life jacket she had dragged from a locker beneath her bunk.

Oblivious to all this noise and disturbance Natasha sat at the small writing desk.

Her pen lilted across her springy, scented notepaper.

She wrote thus:

Oh, my darling, darling, darling, darling Lance,

How happy I am to be in the arms of the sea. But, dearest, how much happier I should be to find myself in your own, dear, precious manly arms.

24

Aren't the sea gulls noisy?

I love you, love you, love you, love you.

I do hope we won't be seasick.

Lots and lots and lots of adoring love from,

One who cares.

One deck above Major Pickavance carefully stowed his golf socks in a shallow, salt-warped drawer and said: 'It's a damn disgrace, you know.'

'Mm,' said Mr Dugdale.

'I mean, nothing personal against you, old chap, but I don't see why a man of my stature and status should be compelled to share a cabin with you.'

'Mm.'

'It's bloody insulting.'

'Mm.'

'It's embarrassing, too.'

'Mm.'

'I hate being looked at when I'm taking my trousers off. It's such an intensely personal activity, taking off one's bags.'

'Mm.'

'That's another thing I've got against the army.'

'What?'

'It makes no concessions to a chap who wants to remove his bags in private.'

'Mm,' said Mr Dugdale.

Then he stood up, rubbed the glass of the porthole furiously with the sleeve of his cardigan and sighed deeply.

'You don't think she looked peaky, do you?' he said. 'You don't think she's sickening for a fever?'

'Who?'

'Natasha, of course. Natasha.'

Major Pickavance stamped his tiny, twine-toed feet and hissed:

'Don't be such a disgusting old goat.'

8

They felt the first motion of the distant ocean when they assembled in the lounge for drinks before dinner.

The ship quivered. She raised her hackles to the wind. She sighed and rolled her hips to the rhythm of the seas.

Then all was calm.

The stewards, black men and Goanese, pottered soft-eyed and subservient.

Dolly wore a plunging-necked, flowing velvet evening gown of deepest, richest, sun-ripened mulberry. Her hair was piled on top of her head, beribboned and burnished auburn. Her noble bosoms heaved and strained like proud, arch-necked, flighty mares pulling a gilded coach.

'I need a man,' she hissed to Celia out of the side of her mouth. 'Oh my God, do I need a man.'

She swept her eyes imperiously round the room.

In a corner by the bar the first engineer coughed voluminously into his sodden hankie and pointed to his carpet slippers.

'Sorry about these,' he said to Burnaby. 'You'll be just like this when you get to my age.'

Natasha gazed in silent admiration at Lance Egerton. He sat, refined and elegant, in a bottle-green leather armchair sipping chilled crème de menthe and talking to a hairpin-chested, gaunt-toothed man, dressed in frock coat and high-winged starched collar.

'I am a minor diplomat by profession,' he said to Lance. 'I shall remain a minor diplomat for the rest of my career in the service. I believe it is my life's mission to be minor in thought and deed. I had a minor birth. And I pray I shall die a minor death in a minor country.'

Lance smiled and offered him a cigar.

'Most kind, dear sir. Most kind,' said the minor diplomat and he placed his hand on Lance's knee. 'May I give you a word of advice, young man?'

'Please do.'

He pointed to the large, pouting cigar in Lance's mouth.

'Don't smoke too many. They play havoc with the wind when you come to play footer.'

Natasha's gaze never faltered. She tried to melt him with her eyes, but his cold heart turned them to stone, and she left the room sobbing bitterly.

Mr Dugdale started to move after her, but Major Pickavance grabbed him firmly by the sleeve of his jacket.

'Don't,' he snapped. 'Don't.'

Mr Dugdale sagged in his grasp. Then he sank back weedily in his chair next to the middle-aged army Captain with the smoker's wheeze and the smoker's teaselled teeth who said: 'As I was saying. I've got my sappers stowed out of harm's way down in the bowels. God knows what would happen if they were let loose on this gang of charmers.'

He pointed to the senior girls who were clustered round the baby grand piano on which Margot was playing Poulenc.

Spangles of gold sparkled in her hair and glinted on her bare shoulders. Her legs in their sheer silk black stockings were long and lithe and lissom.

'My God,' said the army Captain. 'My God, if only I were . . .'

He rose to his feet.

Major Pickavance yanked him back to his seat by the hem of his jacket.

'Wait,' he snapped. 'Wait.'

Dolly gulped greedily at her pink gin, smacked her lips and said: 'I'm banking all my hopes on the Captain.'

'What hopes?' said Celia.

She was wearing a home-knitted blush-pink angora jumper, a Mac-Gregor tartan skirt and high-heeled, patent leather rhumba pumps. Her hair was bundled up in a paisley turban.

'What hopes?' she repeated.

'Hopes of an active nature,' said Dolly.

'Ah,' said Celia. 'Ah.'

And then she waved timidly at Mamselle, who was sitting next to a deeply slumbering Mrs Otto. Behind their backs was a small stage drooping doggedly with sickly resentful potted plants.

Mamselle pursed her lips. The lights from the crystal chandelier romped and rilled through the masses of her deep, lustrous russet hair. She was wearing a high-necked, gold lamé tunic top and white silk pantaloons.

Lurking in a dark corner and watching her carefully was a swarthy man with greasy strands of dyed, jet-black hair stretched tightly across his bald pate. He sucked at his gold tooth, licked two fingers and passed them thoughtfully across his toothbrush moustache.

And then the steward with the flowing, white moustache passed through the room rippling at his gong and slowly the passengers and officers put down their drinks and made their way into the dining room.

'I hope they won't be dishing up guinea fowl,' said Major Pickavance to Mr Dugdale.

'Why?' said Mr Dugdale.

Major Pickavance tutted irritably.

'Well, I should have thought that was obvious to a man of your so-called refinement and sophistication,' he said and put-putted his tiny legs into the dining room.

It was a large room.

It had a hoarse voice.

The tablecloths were starched and unfriendly.

The cutlery was cumbersome.

The crockery was too sure of itself by half.

Dolly sat between Lance Egerton and the minor diplomat at the Captain's table.

At the head of Natasha's table the young man in the crumpled, ill-fitting uniform said: 'May I introduce myself? I am the ship's doctor. My name is Roger Carey. If there's anything I can –'

'Pardon?' said Natasha, her eyes overflowing with Lance. 'What's that you say?'

Major Pickavance, Mr Dugdale, Celia and Mamselle sat at the first officer's table.

He was a portly man with dry hair and a fiery red face. He looked at the menu and said: 'Snorkers! Good-oh!'

There were vast expanses of empty tables.

They looked forlorn.

Dotted amongst them like thinly inhabited islets in a worried, long-neglected archipelago were tables occupied by the pupils and the sparse throng of other passengers.

The swarthy man with the greasy, plastered hair and the toothbrush moustache turned to Margot and said: 'If you are looking for entertainment of a novel kind, my cabin is number 32. Bring your own face cloth.'

Delphine, deeply concerned with her soup, looked up. She looked straight into Mr Dugdale's eyes and in an instant her heart was struck with pity.

Poor old man, she thought to herself. How awful to be as old as he. The old prince dying. The old prince lashing his daughter with his shrivelling tongue. His son wished to marry. The prince would not allow it. He sent his son away. Away to the wars he went. The grenade tore into his flesh. How awful to be so old that you send your son away to die.

She was still staring at Mr Dugdale. In his eyes she saw reflected her dumpiness and her dowdiness. Hastily she returned to her soup and sucked hard and noisily.

Dolly turned to the minor diplomat and said: 'Why aren't we being served? We're on the Captain's table. Why aren't we being served first?'

The diplomat's wife smiled icily.

'It is the custom of the sea, my dear,' she said. 'Passengers do not commence dining at his table until the Captain is present. He'll be here shortly. I expect he's having trouble with his steering wheel.'

At that moment the Captain entered the dining room.

He was small and bald and plump and pink. He had moist sensuous lips and sad eyelids.

Shyly he weaved his way through the tables. The head waiter drew back his chair and the Captain seated himself at the head of his guests.

The head waiter clicked his heels, tugged at the cuffs of his shirt and said: 'Captain Billaney is now pleased to invite his guests to dine.'

They ate their soup silently.

No one spoke as they slithered with their sole.

Suddenly the Captain threw down his fork and shouted: 'I can't stand this. It's too awful for words.'

His guests looked at each other, alarmed yet deeply curious.

The Captain continued: 'It's all very well for you lot, but I have a wife at home and two cocker spaniels. And I miss them most fearfully – particularly the dogs. So why should I talk to you? Why should I listen to your idle chatter and your inane questions? I'm lonely. I'm homesick. And I'm frightened. I'm terrified out of my wits.'

He stood up and extended his arms towards the window.

'Out there! Do you know what's out there?' he said. 'I'll tell you. U-boats. Pocket battleships. Dive bombers. And why are they there? I'll tell you. They're out to get me. Every single one of them. They're out

29

to blow me to smithereens. Roast my flesh in oil, shatter my limbs and scatter my bones to the dead-eyed fishes.

'So why should I bother my backside talking to you lot? When they blow me to perdition I intend to be talking to my wife and my dogs.'

He wiped the corners of his mouth fastidiously on his napkin, bowed and said: 'We shall see no more of each other on this voyage.'

He turned, began to move towards the door and then he stopped and turned back to his guests.

'A tip for you,' he said. 'Don't eat the parsnips. They'll give you the most fearful wind.'

'Nice little man,' said Dolly.

'Yes,' said Celia vaguely. 'Yes.'

She was certain she'd seen the ship's doctor somewhere before.

9

Next morning they had lifeboat drill.

It was relaxed and easy-humoured.

'Raise your arms high, my lovely,' said the bosun to Margot.

Margot raised her arms high.

'Cor,' said the bosun. 'Cor blimey, Charlie.'

He moved even closer to her and settled the life jacket on her shoulders.

'Now then, my lovely, you just press yourself close into me and I'll secure these tapes about your waist.'

Margot pressed herself into him.

'Cor,' he said. 'Cor blimey, Charlie.'

Margot looked up into his eyes and said: 'What do I do next?'

The bosun looked over his shoulder furtively and then he clenched hold of her buttocks and pressed her into his groin.

'How lovely,' said Margot. 'How enchanting.'

He bent down and whispered into her ear: 'Tell you what, my lovely, do you fancy a bit of rough in my cabin?'

'Yes. I rather think I should,' said Margot.

She smiled at him again and said: 'By the way, what is a "bit of rough"?'

'Cor blimey, Charlie,' said the bosun. 'Cor, stone the bleeding crows.'

The porpoises played about their bow.

A petrel pattered in their wake.

Gannets plunged and the ship curtsied briefly to the first caress of the ocean swell.

Dolly stood at the rail and gazed out to sea.

On such a morning long ago she had stood at the rails of the skittish flighty ocean liner bound for the Cape and seen the tip of Madeira's peak rise slowly above the horizon.

The old couple had made her most welcome in the dove-pink mansion high on the hills above Funchal.

Their grandson had been a most attentive and courteous pupil.

His death had upset her most grievously.

The black funeral horses, cockaded and prancing. The crack of the whip. Clump of earth on coffin lid. The murderer, head shaven, manacled at wrist and ankle, goaded through the streets to the frigate and his execution in a country stranger to him than his death.

Slivers of land jaggered the distant horizon.

Celtic skerries teeming with kittiwake. Misty coves lolling with plump grey seals. The pucks and fairies skulking in the lee of dry-stone walls. Hedges of fuchsia. The milk churn clank. Porter black as a stallion's eyes. And all creeping away from their sight.

The broad ocean stretched before them and its breath was sly and wicked on their brows.

Delphine cast a sly glance above her book as Mr Dugdale passed by.

Poor old man. Poor hopeless old man. Poor hopeless, useless old man.

Where had he abandoned his prime?

In a woodcutter's hut in a forest of birch and stunted oak? On a battlefield coursing with stricken grenadiers and tattered gunners? In the moneylender's ice-cold palm?

Natasha stood alone at the stern rail.

She seemed distracted.

How beautiful she was. How joyous. How beautiful with her humours. How sensuous. How seductive.

Natasha at the rail. Natasha in her book. The beauty of it. The symmetry. At times like this it mattered not one jot to be dowdy and dumpy.

She saw Mr Dugdale pass by Natasha. He stopped. He pressed himself behind a lifeboat stanchion and from that hidey-hole he fixed his gaze on the beautiful young woman standing alone and distracted at the stern rail and his shoulders drooped.

Poor hopeless, useless, lonely old man.

IO

In the afternoon Lance Egerton rapped firmly on the door of the sickbay and without waiting for an answer entered and threw his cane on the operating table from which the attendant, Josh, was eating his tea of polony sandwiches, iced buns and a bottle of medical comforts.

'Where's the doctor?' he said.

'Search me,' said Josh. 'Who wants him?'

'I do.'

'Then find him yourself, arsehole.'

Lance Egerton found Roger Carey in the cubbyhole, toying with a jigsaw.

'Ah, doctor,' he said. 'Just the man. I was wondering if you had anything suitable for nausea.'

'Nausea?' said Roger Carey and a fluster came to his eyes and his hands.

'That's right, old man,' said Lance. 'Nausea.'

Roger Carey rose slowly from his chair and joined Lance in the surgery. He licked his lips drily and rubbed the side of his chin rapidly.

'Er . . . er . . . is it any particular type of nausea?' he said.

'Yes. Nausea of life,' said Lance. 'Surely you have a suitable draught I can take?'

'Yes,' said Roger Carey, and there was a desperate tone to his voice and a desperate flicker to his eyes as he looked round the room.

Lance lit an Egyptian cigarette and watched through narrowed eyes as Roger Carey approached the medicine cabinet on the wall with fearful, diffident tread.

At length he opened the doors of the cabinet to reveal a mass of bottles, flasks, phials, cartons, tubes, tins, flat boxes, fat boxes, sachets, packets, pipkins, skippets, brass cases, ebony cases, cedarwood cases and glass jars of every size, shape and hue.

'There we are,' he said. 'Take your pick.'

Lance smiled softly to himself.

'I should like you to join me in my staterooms,' he said.

33

'Me?' said Roger Carey.

'Yes. You,' said Lance, and taking him by the arm led him in the warmest, friendliest manner to his quarters on the boat deck.

On the low-slung, marble-topped coffee table in the drawing room was a fat, lime-green scented, bulging envelope.

Without opening it Lance Egerton ripped it into shreds and tossed the debris to the floor.

'Whisky?' he said.

Roger Carey nodded. He glanced shiftily round the room, licked his lips drily once more and perched himself awkwardly on the edge of a black leather chesterfield. Lance Egerton handed him a tumbler filled to the brim with single malt Skye whisky from a bottle monogrammed with his initials.

He perched himself on a high stool, crossed his legs fastidiously, smiled and said: 'Now then, my friend. What's this all about?'

Roger Carey flushed. He took a long gulp at his whisky. He coughed and spluttered and tears spurted from his eyes and nostrils.

Lance Egerton stared at him unblinkingly.

'You're in disgrace, aren't you?'

'Yes.'

'How splendid,' said Lance, clapping his hands with delight. 'Mixed up in a backstreet abortion racket, were you?'

'No.'

'I know. You had an affair with one of your patients, did you? Yes? Married woman. Yes? Rather drab. Rather wan. Fearful working-class accent. But there's still passion in those narrow loins. Yes? She throws herself at you. She strips herself naked and –'

'No. No. No. It was nothing like that.'

'Well, what is it then?' said Lance crossly.

Roger Carey took a slow sip at his whisky.

'God damn you, man,' cried Lance. 'You sit here knocking back my whisky. You smell abominably of disinfectant and polony. Your fingernails are filthy. You've got bags beneath your eyes like airships, yet when I ask you a perfectly civil question, you refuse to answer me. Well, I won't stand for it, do you hear? Now come on, old man. Spit it out. What was your disgrace? Why are you here?'

Before Roger Carey could answer there was a loud wail of the ship siren and then the alarm bells began to clang and clatter.

'Good grief, what's all that racket in aid of?' said Lance.

34

'How should I know?' said Roger Carey. 'I'm only the ship's doctor.'

They dashed out of the stateroom and found the boat deck filling up with crew and passengers strutting like penguins in their life jackets and casting nervous glances at each other.

'Oi, little Lord Fauntleroy!' shouted the first officer to Lance Egerton from the bridge. 'Get that bleeding life jacket on. Pronto! Now! Move!'

Lance flounced back to his suite, and summoned his steward, who attired him in his life jacket.

When he returned to the boat deck, all the passengers and crew were assembled at their allotted stations.

The first officer stared down at them silently for a moment. Then he said: 'Bloody awful. Bloody diabolical. It won't do. It won't do at all.'

There was silence.

Then Major Pickavance called up nervously, 'Would you like us to try again, old man?'

'Shut up, short arse!' screamed the first officer. 'Shut up! Shut up!'

Silence again.

Then the first officer spoke once more. 'I've called you to your stations because of that,' he said. He pointed with his thumb over his left shoulder. 'See it?' he said.

Oh yes, they saw it.

Far off, away to the starboard of SS *Drayman* they saw an aircraft. It was a large aircraft. It had four engines and it droned and circled the convoy beyond the range of the escort's guns, taunting, smug and hunched in menace.

'That's a reconnaissance plane. A Jerry. And do you know what he's doing? I'll tell you right now, ladies and gentlemen. He is radioing our position, our course and our speed back to base. And base will then transmit those details to . . .' he paused and looked around the scared, frightened faces, '. . . to the seven U-boats hunting us at this very moment.'

Once more he paused to quaff deeply from the gasp of fear and the pallor of terror that invested the faces of his audience.

He smirked.

'Oh yes, my friends,' he said. 'This morning the commodore had a message from the Admiralty. Seven U-boats in the vicinity.'

The aircraft banked steeply, showing its belly to the convoy, snarling its engines at the helpless faces turned towards it.

The first officer smirked again.

35

'Yes indeed, ladies and gentlemen,' he said. 'Tonight after sundown we shall be attacked by the full might of Jerry's U-boats.'

'Bugger!' said Margot to Delphine. 'There goes my bit of rough.'

But it was not U-boats that attacked them that night.

It was the full fury and frenzy of an Atlantic storm.

II

There was fear in all their hearts as they prepared themselves for dinner that evening.

Dolly did not speak as she dressed.

Celia said: 'I think I'll wear a frock for a change.'

Dolly stood behind her and rested her hands on her niece's bare shoulders.

'I can look quite nice at times in a frock,' said Celia.

Dolly squeezed her hand.

'I must find one that doesn't clash with my life jacket,' said Celia.

And Dolly burst into tears.

'Dearest, darling precious Lance,' wrote Natasha on her springy, lime-green, scented notepaper,

> As the poet said: 'If I should die, think only this of me. That in some corner of a foreign field blah blah blah' – I've forgotten the rest.
>
> Oh Lance, tell me that you love me. Give me some sign that you care as much for me as I for you, and I shall die happy beneath the briny deep in Davy Jones's locker.
>
> If, however, we should survive the conflict and come through this together, then we shall know that fate has ordained we shall, we two, be for ever conjoined in . . .

She stopped writing.

She spun round.

Four pairs of eyes were staring at her. Four pairs of terrified eyes were boring their way into her conscience.

'Oh, my poor precious darlings,' she cried out.

They bolted towards her and she scooped them up in her arms and sobbed and sobbed.

'Guess what I've done,' said Polly.

*   *   *

'It makes a hell of a difference being military at times like this,' said the sapper Captain to Major Pickavance.

'Does it?' said Major Pickavance. 'In what way?'

'The experience of blood and gore.'

'How do you mean?'

'Bellies ripped open and guts spilling and coiling all over the place. Shattered limbs. Bits of brain spattered and splattered. The odd decapitation – you know the sort of thing.'

'Excuse me. I think I've left my propelling pencil in my cabin.'

Mrs Otto snored thunderously on her bunk, clutching her *Speisewagen* tightly to her tummy.

Mamselle sat before the dressing-table mirror applying rouge to her cheeks.

The high-padded shoulders of her cocktail gown. The slink of her hips. The lilt of her calf. The saucy rake of her ankle.

'Clara, you'll never get nowhere, love, if you don't join in with the others,' her mother had said.

'Such a shy child,' the headmistress had said. 'She's so nervous. She's so timid.'

'Such a plain child,' the doctor had said. 'So gawky. So sickly. So desperately insignificant.'

'By Christ, Clara, you've got a smashing arse on you,' her boss at the bacon counter had said.

Half an hour or so later he had said:

'And your other parts aren't too shabby neither.'

Roger Carey sat in the sickbay with Josh, drinking medical comforts from the neck.

Lance Egerton sat alone in his suite drinking kümmel from a silver flask.

Mr Dugdale sat in the lounge drinking sherry with the minor diplomat.

'I hope it won't be a major U-boat attack,' said the diplomat.

'Mm,' said Mr Dugdale.

God, what would happen to her if they were attacked? The slender neck frizzled with burning oil. The slim, yielding body nuzzled by dead-eyed fish and chomped at by squid and cuttlefish.

The screams echoed in the vaults of his mind.

'Another sherry?' said the minor diplomat.

'Yes, please,' said Mr Dugdale. 'Make it a major one, will you?'

It was a tipsy congregation that sat down for dinner that night.

And yet there was a sober shadow to their mien and their voices were hushed.

Louise had a fit of the giggles, but Polly pinched her plump thigh hard and she squeaked and began to sob softly to herself.

Roger Carey tried desperately to focus on Natasha.

Oh, what beauty.

Oh, what radiance.

The rich, red fullness of her lips.

The fine, delicate strut of her noses.

The slender swaying contours of her three necks.

The nine heads sighing and coiling and curling with long blonde hair, flecked with tawny and tipped with ash.

He was in love with the girl.

No doubt about it. Not the slightest possible conceivable doubt. Roger, my dear old thing, you are in love with that gorgeous, wondrous, magnificent, devastating, stunning, stupendous girl.

He hiccupped.

Natasha glared at him with disgust and hatred, and returned her long, lustrous, yearning gaze to Lance.

12

Shortly before eight o'clock the storm attacked them.

For some time there had been a growing motion in the ship. The dining room would heave and shudder like the flanks of an old dog dreaming deeply.

Suddenly there was a loud crash and the smash of shattered crockery. It was as though the ship had been kicked hard in the guts. On the Captain's table the wine glasses toppled in unison and rolled over while the diners clutched desperately at the table to keep themselves upright.

Another thud. Another crash.

The roar of the ocean and the judder of the old ship's spine.

The gale unheard, unseen and unfelt had been mounting for the past hour, waiting for them to stumble into its lair, waiting to pounce on them and engulf them in its fury.

It fell in full force on the ship's bows.

Another crash. Another thump. Another teeth-rattling judder.

A high, nervous babble of laughter. Waiters laid napkins on the pools of spilt wine. Diners tried to talk, but no one listened. Everyone was waiting for the next attack.

It came heavier than the last.

A waiter tottered wildly, carrying a tureen on a tray high above his head. His feet scrabbled madly on the tilting floor. It was like an act in a circus. Faster and faster went his feet as he tried to keep his balance. And then he could no longer fight the motion of the ship. He was hurled headlong into the wall. The tureen hurtled from the tray and crashed and clattered, bucked and heaved down the room, showering the diners with soup.

'This is where I say good night to everyone,' said the minor diplomat's wife.

Her husband led her away to their cabin, wildly clutching at chairs and tables to try to keep himself upright.

Another climb. Another vast, stomach-churning drop.

Someone screamed.

Roger Carey took hold of Natasha's hand and said: 'Don't worry. I have seen this before.'

She snatched her hand away angrily. She was about to speak when a vast coffee urn flew head-high across the room and smashed into a window.

Dolly and Celia fled.

Perdita burst into tears.

Polly shivered.

The Doucemain twins looked at each other fearfully.

Another crash.

Lance Egerton was propelled backwards out of his chair like a shell from a howitzer. Natasha watched with horror as he did a back somersault, landed crouching on his feet and received a flying soup bowl slap in his belly.

He howled, clutched at his mouth and staggered outside.

One by one the diners dispersed, clinging to each other for support or pirouetting as they succumbed to the vicious spin and corkscrew twisting of the ship.

Presently of the passengers only Roger Carey and Natasha remained in the room.

The waiters and stewards groped and clawed fearfully on hands and knees as they tried to mop up, gather in smashed crockery and batten down moving objects.

The SS *Drayman* skidded down the wave troughs and soared to their summits, straining at the leash of the wind and hurtling at the eye of the storm.

'Should we go outside?' said Roger Carey, all his drunkenness dispersed by the frenzy of the storm.

To his surprise Natasha nodded.

They left the dining room. They walked round the ship on the covered deck. The girl held his arm tightly, but there was no warmth, no intimacy in her touch. Her mind seemed somewhere far far away.

The wind howled and the spray leapt up from the darkness and smashed frothing white and murky brown against the windows.

The deck was distraught.

In the fat days and lazy evenings of its calm it had sprawled with cane chairs and wicker footstools. The smell of bouillon and stern black coffee had reeked its nostrils. The gentle throb of the engine. The matting dank with salt. The lifebelts' solemn pout. Woollen shawls and tartan rugs. The soft rise and swell. A distant whale humping the placid seas. The gentle throb of gossip.

Now it was deserted, ravaged and looted by the storm.

Another screech of frothing white and muddy brown smashed against the windows.

'That's enough,' said Natasha. 'I want to go to my cabin.'

'Let me take you there,' said Roger Carey.

Natasha shook her head, and he watched her trot lightly and nimbly along the deck.

Completely sober now he returned to his cabin and wedged himself tightly in his bunk.

The storm hurled itself at the ship like a dying wolf with its belly slit. Its savage teeth whipped the waves and sent the spume over the decks, screaming and raging and snarling.

But Roger Carey was calm.

Never in the whole of his life had he been so calm.

He was in love.

She was exquisite.

The dreads of his past skulked out of sight in the scuppers of his memory. All he saw now was that lissom young girl with the long, lithe legs and the smooth, slender neck.

He would marry her.

They would live in a *castello*. He knew the very spot.

A tiny bay. Houses rising steeply from the quay. The old domed church standing out from the ochre and white walls and the rust-red pantiles.

And rising above that the hillside, terraced and vined, and then higher still bouldered and briared.

And there perched on its summit was the *castello*, its garden glowing with mimosa.

He had seen it before.

He had been taken there as a youth.

For the first time in his life he had tasted wine. It was brown and heady.

He vowed that one day he would return and claim that *castello* for himself.

He smiled.

Yes, he would claim that *castello*.

And he would claim Natasha, too.

Perfection!

He closed his eyes and let the rhythms of his body move to the rhythms of the storm and sank instantly into a deep and peaceful sleep.

When he awoke next morning, the wind had dropped a little, but there was still a very heavy swell running.

The sky was lumbering and fat-bellied. The sea fizzed and spat. The wind yowled.

'Bloody marvellous,' said Josh. 'Perfect weather. Couldn't be better. We won't get no U-boats sticking their beaks in now. If this holds out for the rest of the voyage, we'll be in clover, doc.'

Roger Carey grunted.

Josh had brought him breakfast to his cubbyhole in the sickbay. He tucked in heartily to the kedgeree and the Bradenham ham.

'I wouldn't take too long on the nosh, doc,' said Josh. 'You got your dispositions to make, ain't you?'

'Dispositions?'

'Yes. Dishing out the seasick potions.'

'Seasick potions?'

Roger Carey fought hard to keep the panic from his voice. Josh chuckled and shook his head.

'I don't suppose you ever treated seasickness before, eh?'

'Well, I . . .'

'No worry, doc, me old wingsy bash. Leave it to me. I know what to do.'

The old cockney with the wet lips and the brown-blotched hands whistled happily through his teeth as he took powders and liquids from the medicine cabinet and swirled and shook them until he had produced five bottles of a liquid the colour of a baboon's backside and the consistency of sump oil.

'Here we are, doc,' he said proudly. 'Leave it all to me, mate. I'll dish out the old gut rot. You piss off and see Mr Egerton. He's been squealing for you all morning something chronic.'

Roger Carey finished his breakfast unhurriedly and then made his way to Lance's staterooms.

He found him lying in bed propped up by three fat pillows. By his side stood a stewardess he had not seen before. She was a pillar of starched rectitude and servile composure.

Lance turned his head on the pillows and smiled wanly at Roger Carey.

43

'How sweet people are to me,' he said.

'Do you need anything?' said Roger Carey.

'Oh no, doctor,' he said. 'Mrs Banks here is being so terribly sweet. I only called you because I wanted you to tell me what's happening on board.'

Before Roger Carey could speak the stewardess placed herself sternly between him and Lance, to whom she turned and said: 'Now, now, sir. The less we are disturbed today the better.'

'See what I mean, doctor? People are so terribly, terribly sweet,' said Lance. 'Come again quite soon and give me all the news.'

And then the wind veered to the beam and as the ship rolled to starboard, shuddering and straining at every rivet, heeling steeper and steeper, heavier and heavier, Lance vomited sweet as a nut down the front of Mrs Banks's starched linen pinny.

In the thrashing chaos of her cabin Dolly screamed at the top of her voice: 'I want to die.'

'So do I,' shouted Celia. 'Wait for me.'

13

There was no abatement to the storm that day.

The convoy was scattered far and wide across the ocean. The tanker from Swansea was hove to. The destroyer, *Plunderer*, fretted and fumed as she tried to bring order to her charges. The corvette, *Campion*, was thrashed and throttled as the storm tossed and shook her by the scruff of her neck.

On SS *Drayman* the passengers cowered in terror or groaned piteously in the grip of their sickness.

Only Mrs Otto snored on, impervious to fear or sickness, as she lay whale-stranded on her back, cradling her head on her *Speisewagen*.

'Ooh, ooh, ooh,' howled Margot.

'Arrgh, arrgh, arrgh,' wailed Mamselle.

Mr Dugdale whispered: 'Natasha. Natasha. Natasha.'

Suddenly Major Pickavance rose from his bunk and bellowed at the top of his voice, 'Stop it! Will you please stop this obscenity! How dare you lust so carnally. How dare you . . .'

He moaned, lurched to the hand basin and splattered it with tomato-stained vomit.

Mr Dugdale clenched his jaw and stuffed his knuckles hard against his nostrils.

'Natasha,' he moaned. 'Natasha.'

'Oooh, ooh, ooh,' howled Margot.

'Arrgh, arrgh, arrgh,' wailed Mamselle.

'Please, Margot, please,' sobbed Delphine.

'Hello,' said Roger Carey.

'Hello,' said Natasha.

They stood at the entrance to the dining room.

'Do you feel up to it?' he said.

'Yes,' she said.

They entered the dining room.

Only one person was sitting there. He waved to them and said: 'A very minor storm. Thank goodness for that.'

They ate in silence.

When they finished their meal, Roger Carey said: 'Would you care to take a stroll?'

'All right.'

They walked once round the covered promenade deck. Roger Carey held the rail. Natasha took his arm. When the ship rolled heavily he swung her round so she could hold the rail with her other hand.

The voice inside him whispered: you have seen this all before, my friend. But where? Where, where?

On the enclosed deck the howl of the wind was subdued. But the whole ship creaked with strain and the sky was purple and grey and the sea was bleak and black.

'Would you care for a drink?'

'All right.'

They paused outside the lounge arm in arm.

The doors had been torn away from their hooks and were swinging free with the roll of the ship regularly and relentlessly. First one, then the other opened and shut. They paused at the completion of each half-circle, began to move slowly and finished fast with a resounding crash.

Where? Where have you seen this before?

Roger Carey said to Natasha: 'Ready to try it?'

'All right.'

They walked through the doors without flinching. Roger Carey rejoiced to feel Natasha's hand steady on his arm.

'Bravo!' said the minor diplomat who was sitting in a nearby chair. 'I don't mind telling you I was rather looking forward to seeing one of you, or even both of you come to that, seriously maimed or injured. Nothing personal, of course.'

They sat down opposite each other separated by a squat table. The steward loped up to them, his sure step unaffected by the motion of the ship. He bowed his woolly head.

'Sir? Miss? What is your pleasure?'

Roger Carey smiled at Natasha.

'You choose,' she said.

'Certainly. Two large brandies.'

The steward bowed again and padded away softly, content and aloof from the storm. When he returned with the drinks, he dampened the tablecloth with water and placed the glasses upon it.

'Sir will keep his eyes on them,' he said.

'I shall,' said Roger Carey.

Those high cheekbones. The scent of her hair. The glisten of soft down on her arms.

He wanted to nuzzle her. That's all. He wanted to nuzzle her soft and secret parts.

'Mind if I join you?'

The minor diplomat came lurching towards them and sat down heavily.

'Nothing like a bit of rough weather for bringing people together, eh?' he said.

'Very true,' said Roger Carey.

The minor diplomat looked from Roger Carey to Natasha and smiled. Then he leant forward and said confidentially: 'I, too, have had some romantic experiences at sea in my turn.'

'Really?'

'I should say so. If the young lady will allow me, I should like to tell you about a little encounter I had on the Bismarck Sea when I was much younger than I am now.'

He told them in minute detail of his adventure and when he had finished, Natasha stood up and said: 'I'm tired. Please excuse me.'

'Let me escort you to your cabin,' said Roger Carey.

'All right.'

She took his arm and once more they passed through the doors without flinching.

The sea was as high as ever. Inky clouds swirled in the thunderous skies and the glass still streamed with water.

Outside her cabin door he said: 'Shall I see you at dinner?'

'No.'

'Shall I see you tomorrow?'

'If you wish.'

'Where?'

'I don't know.'

'Will you come to my place? I'll have Josh bring us breakfast.'

'All right.'

'I'll call for you at nine.'

She nodded and slipped into her cabin.

The little girls lay sprawled and stricken on their bunks.

'Oh Lance,' she said softly. 'Oh, Lance, Lance, Lance.'

47

14

Next morning at nine o'clock precisely Roger Carey tapped on the cabin door.

It was opened instantly and Natasha slipped out softly.

She took his arm and he led her to the sickbay. Her footsteps were secure and steady. They were both at one with the storm.

'I took the liberty of bringing champagne to you and the young lady, doc,' said Josh.

'Thank you.'

'We got to think ourselves lucky the kitchen's still open, eh? Some poor fucker could easy . . . oh, beg pardon, miss. What I meant to say was some stupid old bleeder could easy get hisself scalded in a motion like this.'

'Very true.'

'Right then, doc, I'll leave you two to it. Don't worry, I'll knock hard on the door before I come back to fetch the tray.'

They ate their breakfast in silence.

The marmalade was thick and bitter.

'Do you think it's rather daring drinking champagne at breakfast?'

Natasha shrugged.

She had a speck of cinnamon glistening on her upper lip. He wanted to lick it off. He wanted to lick her all over.

Josh banged loudly on the door before entering to collect the tray.

'Your cabin's all in order, doc,' he said. 'I've given you fresh sheets. Very soft. Very conducive. Know what I mean?'

He winked, leered and left.

A few minutes later the phone rang. Roger Carey picked up the receiver and listened.

'Right,' he said. 'I'll be along straight away.'

He turned to Natasha who was sitting straight-backed and expressionless.

'I have some business to attend to,' he said. 'I shan't be long. Will you wait here till I return?'

'All right.'

At the door Roger Carey turned and said: 'Shall I give your good wishes to Mr Egerton?'

Immediately Natasha sprang from her seat and rushed towards him.

'Lance? You're going to see Lance?' she said.

'Yes.'

'Oh, please may I come with you? Please, please, please take me with you.'

'All right.'

She took his arm, but now there was warmth and passion in her touch. Her step was jaunty and her eyes sparkled. She waved happily to the minor diplomat and she put her hand to her mouth and giggled when Roger Carey caught his elbow on a fire bucket and cursed.

As soon as they entered his bedroom Natasha broke free from Roger Carey's arm. She dashed across the room and threw herself onto Lance's bed.

'Oh, Lance, Lance, how are you, my darling?' she cried. 'You look so pale. You look so thin and wasted.'

Lance turned his head weakly towards Roger Carey.

Natasha buried her head in his chest.

'Oh really!' said Lance.

She looked up at him. She stared longingly into his eyes and began to smooth back his hair.

'Lance,' she moaned softly. 'Darling Lance.'

Lance Egerton winced and screwed up his eyes.

'I rather think I'd like to be left alone, doctor,' he said. 'Perhaps you'd be sweet enough to return later in the day.'

'Of course,' said Roger Carey.

'And alone, if you please.'

Roger Carey nodded. He took Natasha gently by the wrist and led her out of the room.

She took his arm, but this time there was no comfort in her touch.

They were joined at luncheon by the minor diplomat.

'Are you sure you don't mind?' he said.

'Not at all,' said Roger Carey.

The minor diplomat told them stories of his service in the Solomon Islands.

'An exceedingly minor blot on the atlas of the world,' he said. 'Quite delightful. Enchanting.'

After luncheon, Roger Carey and Natasha made their way to the lounge. There had been a brief lull in the weather, but now it was blowing harder than ever and the ship was pitching, tossing, rolling and writhing.

The doors of the lounge had been fixed by large wooden wedges. A pity, he thought. He had been looking forward to the firmness and calmness of her grasp. He had wanted to reel once more on the lilt of their triumph.

They hardly spoke as they drank their brandy. Once Natasha said: 'He looked so ill. He looked so helpless.'

They took dinner with the minor diplomat. He regaled them with stories of his service in St Helena, the Dutch West Indies and the Gilbert and Ellice group.

'You seem to have quite an affinity with islands,' said Roger Carey.

'Most certainly,' said the minor diplomat. 'But only minor ones, of course.'

They walked on the promenade deck. Her touch was still cold and distant. They paused and looked out into the blackness.

'What are you thinking of?' he said.

Natasha said nothing.

'Ghosts of the old corsairs bringing treasure from the Spanish Main maybe?'

Natasha shrugged her shoulders.

'Turkish galleys?'

'I want to go to my cabin,' she said.

When they got to the cabin door, he put his arms round her waist and drew her to him.

Very slowly she drew back her head and looked deep into his eyes.

'No,' she said. 'No.'

There was no expression on her face when slowly she slid into her cabin.

'Ooh, ooh, ooh.'

'Oh, Dugdale. I think I've made a mess in my pyjamas.'

'I want to die. I want to die.'

'Shut up, Dolly! For God's sake, shut up!'

'So sweet, Mrs Banks. So terribly sweet of you.'

'Natasha. Natasha. Oh, Natasha.'

'How much longer? Oh Lord. How much longer hast Thou destined for our turmoil and strife?'

'Shut up.'

'Arrgh, arrgh, arrgh.'

The storm showed them no mercy.

Next morning the wind howled and wailed and shrieked, and the seas pelted and plundered, and the ship was tossed and turned, heaving at its belly and shuddering in its spine.

Roger Carey breakfasted alone in his cubbyhole.

He visited Lance Egerton.

'How sweet of you, doctor. Do give me all the latest news. How many people have been washed overboard? Have there been many cases of madness? Has Dolly been clapped in irons and thrown naked into the brig?'

As he was leaving the bedroom Lance called out to him, 'And as for Natasha.'

'Yes?'

'Mad, old chap. Stark raving bonkers.'

Roger Carey prowled the decks in search of her. He prowled the public rooms. He prowled the alleyways. He visited the bridge.

The steward brought up food to the first officer.

'Snorkers! Good-oh,' he said.

Roger Carey retired to his cubbyhole and commenced to sup slowly at a bottle of medical comforts.

At ten minutes past three there was a knock on the door of the sickbay.

'Come in.'

Natasha entered.

Soft as down she walked to him and sat down.

'Why didn't you call to collect me?'

'Well, I . . .'

'I waited for you.'

She was wearing a long fawn gaberdine raincoat and a thick purple woollen muffler. Her hair hung free and wild.

'I love you,' he said.

'I know,' she said. 'What do you want me to do?'

He led her to his cabin.

He undressed her rapidly.

She was ready for him.

51

He entered her swiftly.

She looked at him open-mouthed.

She made no movement.

Then after a while she closed her eyes.

She made no noise as he worked.

But deep inside her she began to moan softly and then when he had done, she cried out still deep inside her.

'Lance! Lance! Laaaaaaaance!'

Next day the seas were flat calm and the sky was stinging blue.

Oh, how the passengers rejoiced.

The guzzling. The quaffing. The joking. The larking. The pranks and the jolly japes.

The night sky crackled with stars. The moon-washed sea crooned softly.

And shortly before midnight the torpedo struck.

15

But it did not strike SS *Drayman*.

It struck HMS *Campion*.

It hit her smack amidships and almost blew her out of the water.

This is how it happened.

When dawn broke the storm had vanished, the seas were calm and the skies genial and good-tempered and SS *Drayman* found herself completely alone.

The lookouts scoured the horizon with their binoculars. They saw nothing. A deckhand clambered to the crow's nest and looked out. Nothing.

'That's it then,' said Josh. 'We're on our own. Talk about being in the shit.'

They streamed on steadily following their preordained course.

The passengers were still giddy from their release from sickness and fear, but the sailors on watch strained every nerve end and sinew.

The Captain did not budge from the bridge.

'God rot the lot of them,' he growled to himself.

And he thought of his home nestling in the lee of the Malvern Hills and the smell of fresh-baked pastry and the whine of dogs begging for their morning walk. He thought of the graveyard of the yew-strewn church and wondered whether his body would ever feel the bounties of its welcoming, sodden clay.

HMS *Campion* appeared on the horizon in mid-afternoon. Signal lamps flashed. The passengers crowded the rails as the corvette plunged at and bounded the waves in her helter and skelter to join them.

Her bow wave grinned. Her wake waved a long and loving greeting of welcome.

The passengers cheered. The matelots waved their caps.

'Not so bloody hasty,' said Josh to Roger Carey as he sat dreary-eyed and flushed with love in his cubbyhole. 'They won't be cheering and waving when they're in the drink and the oil's burning at their lungs and flaying back their skin.'

'Mm,' said Roger Carey, and his brain tossed and bucked in memories of the slither and slip, the scream and the frenzy, and the scalding gush.

The corvette soon settled into her escort position, occasionally veering off to make a wide sweep fore and aft of SS *Drayman*, fussing and fretting, huffing and puffing.

Most of the passengers had dispersed for afternoon tea, but Mr Dugdale remained at the rail. After a while he was joined by Major Pickavance.

'I have something to say to you, old boy,' he said.

'Have you?'

'Yes.'

'What's it about?'

'Natasha.'

Mr Dugdale waited for his companion to speak. But the minute Major merely shuffled his feet on the deck and coughed nervously once or twice.

'Care for a snorter?' said Mr Dugdale after a while.

'Rather,' said Major Pickavance eagerly.

They repaired to the lounge and drank whisky and soda.

'Natasha! Oh, Natasha, Natasha, what have you done to me?'

'I'm going to see the bosun,' said Margot.

'What does he want?' said Delphine.

'I don't know,' said Margot. 'He told me to come prepared.'

'Prepared for what?'

'I don't know.'

Samira smiled.

She knew.

But she wouldn't tell.

Let them find out for themselves. Silly children. Now, if only they had been brought up with a father like hers.

'You can do it again,' said Natasha.

'Thank you,' said Roger Carey.

'Any time you like.'

'Thank you.'

'But you know I don't love you.'

'Yes.'

'You know I love someone else.'

'Yes.'

'And it makes no difference?'

'None whatsoever.'

'Good, I'm glad.'

'Shall we get cracking then?'

'All right.'

Mrs Otto snored.

Dolly plucked a hair from her nipple with a wicked-thonged tweezer.

Celia let her thoughts stray to Roger Carey. Such a handsome young man. So polite. So gentle. So gallant. She was sure she had seen him somewhere before. But where? Where? Where? Where?

SS *Drayman* sailed on blithely and blissfully and Mamselle received a billet-doux from the swarthy gentleman with the gold tooth and the sticky, stretched-down strands.

16

And still HMS *Campion* ploughed on through the ocean unaware of her ghastly fate.

The passengers decided to throw a party that evening. It was to be fancy dress. They tackled the enterprise with gusto.

'I think I shall go as Bellepheron,' said Lance Egerton.

'Very nice, my dear,' said Mrs Banks. 'And who's she when she's at home?'

The minor diplomat was dressed in formal court attire. His black silk stockings shimmered. The buckles on his patent-leather pumps glinted. The powder on his wig sparkled frosty white.

'How very splendid,' said Dolly. 'And who are you supposed to be?'

'Oh, just a minor diplomat from the court of Czar Alexander,' he said.

'It makes me sick,' said his wife. 'It never occurs to him to give himself promotion on these occasions.'

Dolly's cleavage sucked in the eyes of all those present in the lounge that evening.

The first officer stared at it with undisguised lust.

'Bangers! Good-oh,' he said.

'What a very remarkable sight,' said the sapper Captain. 'I'll ask if she wouldn't mind showing them to the men tomorrow. It would do no end of good to morale.'

'Dolly, you look ravishing,' said Lance. 'I expect you to save them solely for me, if we should be forced to swim for it.'

'If she goes on deck flashing her tits like that, we'll have every U-boat captain within a thousand miles turning up to gawp,' said Josh. 'You won't be able to move for periscopes.'

And then he turned to Natasha as she sat with Roger Carey in his cubbyhole.

'At least I hope they're bleeding telescopes,' he said.

He leered, winked and shuffled off towards the door.

'Don't worry,' he said. 'I'll knock like buggery before I come in.'

The door slammed shut.

'Did you enjoy it this afternoon?' said Roger Carey.

Natasha shrugged her shoulders.

'Weren't you roused?' he said. 'Weren't you excited?'

'Were you?'

'Yes. Yes, of course I was.'

Natasha smiled.

She wore a simple white shift slit to the waist. Her arms were bare. Her coltish breasts swung free.

Mr Dugdale and Major Pickavance stood side by side on the boat deck.

Major Pickavance was dressed as Snow White. Mr Dugdale, in acknowledgement of the festive occasion, wore a knotted handkerchief on his head.

'I have something to tell you, old boy,' said Major Pickavance.

'Have you?'

'Yes.'

It was a clear, moonlit night. HMS *Campion* veered away from them to commence another of her sweeps.

'It's about Natasha.'

'What about her?'

Major Pickavance cleared his throat and adjusted his pigtails. Then he said: 'I don't mind.'

'What don't you mind?'

'Your lusting. Your carnal slavering.'

'Ah.'

'You see, old boy, I sympathise. I understand.'

'Do you really?'

'Of course, old boy. You see, I've been through it all before.'

'Have you indeed?'

'Oh yes. I should say so. There was a chap in the regiment once. He had extremely large lobes to his ears and he developed this intense craving for the affections of the regimental mascot.'

'What was it?'

'A goat.'

Mr Dugdale smiled to himself. Poor little twerp. Poor tiny truncated twat. Harmless really. What was his deceit? What lies had he weaved about himself? What terrors awoke him at night? What fears snuffled and slobbered in his footsteps?

57

That was the only reason he tolerated his company – in the anticipation that he would ultimately and inevitably expose his fraudulence.
Once he had done that he would discard him. He had doled out the
same treatment to every single person he had encountered during his
long life – colleagues, superiors, pupils, wives, mistresses, harlots, silly
girls with downy gapes.

'. . . and then finally he had himself transferred to the Green
Howards.'

'Very wise.'

'On reflection, old boy, I have the feeling that Dolly would not entirely
disapprove of your lusting and unseemly lasciviousness. I don't know if
you've noticed, but our revered headmistress does tend to go in for
somewhat advanced thinking on that subject. I think that on occasions
she herself goes out of her way to attract the attention of members of
the opposite gender. I mean, did you by any chance happen to notice
her attire this evening? Now I'm no prude, old boy. Far from it. I
remember once at the garrison theatre there was this lady contortionist
who got up to the most extraordinary antics with a trombone and . . .'

Poor little bugger. How he had flushed and squirmed when Dolly
had thrust those towering bosoms into his nose. How he'd rolled his
eyes and tugged his moustache and . . .

Natasha! How lovely she looked this evening. The simplicity of that
white dress. The slimness. The slenderness. The tilt and the sway. The
smoothness and the supple flow of her limbs. He knew at once that she
had been taken in love. Who had taken her? It did not matter now.
She could never be his. This craving was useless. The first timid wavelets
of old age were nuzzling at his feet. Fruitless to resist them. Futile to
rage against them and rant. The dead sea wrack would garland his neck
soon enough. Better to lie down and succumb gracefully to the surge
of the relentless tide. In any case there were other fish in that sea. Older
fish, maybe. But just as appealing, just as opulent, just as inviting when
laid out on the slab of his desires. Only this afternoon Mrs Banks had
proved most satisfactory on that score.

He was just about to invite Major Pickavance below to share in a
celebratory bottle of champagne, when the night was torn asunder.

A violent explosion some two or three miles to starboard.

A brilliant orange flash split the darkness, died down, flared up again
and then guttered away to nothing.

'The corvette,' whispered Mr Dugdale hoarsely.

Before Major Pickavance could reply, SS *Drayman* heeled violently to starboard and headed at full speed towards the source of the explosion. She rattled. She juddered. Her engines raced and rumbled. The passengers thronged the decks, their gaiety shattered in an instant by the gut-wrench of terror.

'What is it?'

'Where is it?'

'Oh, Louise, do stop treading on my toes.'

'I'm not.'

'You are.'

And then a mile away they saw them.

The Carley rafts.

Two of them. Oily, naked bodies washing about amongst *Campion*'s wreckage. The cries. The waving arms.

They lowered a boat. The bosun still fizzing with the juices of Margot's ecstasy, got his crew rowing strongly.

'For Christ's sake, shift yourselves,' shouted the first officer. 'We're a sitting duck stuck here like this.'

They did what they could rowing about in the darkness. Some men slithered from their grasp before they could be hauled aboard. Others choked and writhed before they could be reached. Others disappeared soft as a hangman's whisper into the blackness of the night.

The boat's crew did their best to rescue and succour.

They collected fourteen men. One was dead. One was dying. Eight were wounded. The others cowered and shivered.

The cries of the first officer grew more urgent.

They struck out hard for the ship.

They brought the survivors aboard.

The passengers looked on in silence as the first survivors were hauled on board – black-faced men, trembling and quivering, one with his scalp streaming with blood, another with his arm flayed from wrist to shoulder by scalding steam.

Then came the wounded lifted on deck by slings and stretchers. Some were silent. Some were moaning and coughing up the fuel oil which was burning deep within their guts.

'The doctor!' shouted the first officer. 'Where's the fucking doctor?'

'I know,' said Polly. 'But I'm not telling who he's with.'

Dolly clipped her behind the ear and she screamed and scampered off.

59

The wounded men groaned.

One shrieked at the top of his voice: 'Mother! Mother!'

And then he fell silent.

Roger Carey appeared buttoning up his trousers and tripping over his flapping shoelaces. His hair was awry and his face was flushed.

'About bloody time,' snarled the first officer.

Roger Carey looked at the wounded men laid out on the deck, and he began to tremble.

'Well, come on,' bellowed the first officer. 'Get doctoring. That's what you're paid for.'

'But I'm not a doctor,' said Roger Carey.

'What?'

He fell to the deck sobbing.

'I'm not a doctor. I'm not a doctor.'

Lance Egerton clapped his hands with delight.

'So that's his grubby secret,' he said. 'How marvellous. How adorable.'

17

'Right then. I'll take charge.'

Dolly's noble bosoms glowed like planets.

'Move,' she cried. 'Shift yourselves.'

Tenderly and a little diffidently Mr Dugdale turned to the unwounded men who were huddled in the lee of a lifeboat stanchion.

'Anyone care for a snorter?' he said.

There was no response. They stared blankly into the darkness, which was the grave of their ship and the charnel pit of their mates.

'Follow me,' said Mr Dugdale softly. 'Keep in line and follow me.'

Delphine and Samira darted out of the shadows. Their faces were drawn and pinched by shock. Never before had they seen naked men. Never before had they seen open wounds. Never before had they seen death.

They took hold of the arms of the men and with infinite care and compassion led them below to the lounge.

Dolly organised stretchers for the wounded.

The Doucemain twins took one stretcher. Burnaby and the steward with flowing white whiskers took another. Celia fussed and flustered. Mamselle simpered. The sapper Captain and the minor diplomat took another stretcher.

'Mind those stockings,' snapped his wife. 'I don't want them laddered.'

The bearers laid down their charges carefully in the sickbay.

'What do we do now?' said Celia.

Josh stepped forward.

'May I suggest medical comforts, ma'am?'

The groaning. The sobbing. The screaming. The silence. Then the choking. The pleading. The writhing. The stench of oil and vomit.

The Doucemain twins looked on with wonder.

Here at last was their inheritance – carnage, massacre, death in all its glorious squalor and diversity. At long last they had been blooded.

Somehow during that long night the volunteers managed to tend to the wounded and the dying.

They cleaned their bodies from the cloying oil. Josh forced down their throats potions of venomous hue and quagmired texture.

Mamselle wiped fevered brows. She remembered the fevered brows she had created in the past. The panting, slop-bellied lodger straining for the final thrust. The damp-chested clerk groaning with sated lusts. The sagging teacher of arithmetic pleading, pleading: 'Don't tell my wife. Don't tell the head. Don't tell the governors . . . Don't tell your mam.'

And still the men pleaded with her. Here in the foul-stenched sickbay they pleaded with her piteously. And so she clasped hands shaking with pain and terror and squeezed them. And so she fluttered her eyelids at them and pursed her lips.

And Celia hovered.

Was she doomed for the rest of her life to hover in the background? Was she the sun-kissed bee too timid to probe into the heart of the flower and surrender to its heady scents? Would she always cower away from the thrusting mast of desire and hide her eyes from the rut of her secret passions? Yes, that was her fate in life. She was one of Mother Earth's classic hoverers, too timid by far to rock the golden cradle. There was no escape for her.

And Dolly never shirked for a moment.

She dressed wounds. She peeled back charring flesh. She jammed her fists into the mouths of men screaming with pain. She cracked the cheeks of men thrashing with panic. Her breasts streamed with blood. Her flowing raven hair was caked with it. She did not pause for rest or refreshment.

And Celia hovered on.

'What are you dressed as, ma'am, if I might be so bold as to ask?' said Josh, swigging deeply at his bottle of medical comforts.

'Abbot and Costello,' said Celia.

Dolly stood by a bed and watched a tall man with ice-blue eyes and steely grey hair vomiting into a bucket held by a wide-eyed, white-faced Burnaby.

'Are you the skipper of the ship?' she asked gently.

The man nodded.

'You poor man,' said Dolly. 'We shall talk about it later. Meanwhile . . .'

The bucket splattered.

At three thirty the sailor with the flayed arm died. He gave no warning. He just upped and died.

'Blast!' said Josh to Mamselle. 'I thought we had a budding amputation on our hands there.'

In the lounge Mr Dugdale padded softly between the chairs and the sofas in which he had installed the unwounded survivors.

He offered them brandy. He offered them cocoa.

He sent Delphine in search of warm clothing.

'Aargh, aargh, aargh,' cried Margot in her cabin.

'Oooh, oooh, oooh,' cried Major Pickavance in his.

Mr Dugdale knelt on the floor beside a young tow-headed sailor.

'Are you are all right, my boy?' he said. 'Is there anything I can do for you?'

'Yes,' said the sailor very softly. 'I want to go home.'

Delphine and Samira returned with Mrs Banks and bundles of clean, warm clothing. They soaped the men. They bathed them. And then they dried them.

The little girls stood in the shadows, open-mouthed and silent, and looked on.

'Just lift your leg. I won't look,' said Delphine.

'Turn over. Can you turn over? There's no need to be shy,' said Samira.

Mrs Banks turned to Mr Dugdale and said: 'Shall I fix up cabins for them, sir?'

Mr Dugdale looked at the men. There was horror in their eyes.

'Not just now,' he said. 'We'll settle them in here for the time being.'

Relief flooded the eyes of the men. The tow-haired boy began to cry. Delphine put her arms round his shoulders and pulled him into her. Mr Dugdale saw her and smiled, and she blushed deeply.

They brought pillows and blankets.

They sat and they waited. One by one the men fell asleep.

When they looked round they saw the little girls huddled together beneath the counter of the bar. They, too, were sleeping.

Natasha had joined them. But she was not asleep.

She sat crossed-legged on the floor and stared straight ahead.

She had left Roger Carey in his cabin.

He had been sobbing.

'Where? Where have I seen this before? Where? Where?' he had cried.

18

Next morning they buried the dead. Then they swabbed the decks clean of oil and gore.

They were joined by the Danish sloop. She was to escort them back to the convoy. She showed no sadness at the events of the night. She flirted with the waves.

And then Lance Egerton summoned Roger Carey to his staterooms.

He sat in a large bamboo, winged armchair, smoking a fat cigar and rustling the wide sleeves of his brocade dressing gown.

'Well then, my dear,' he said. 'Now is the time to tell all.'

Roger Carey said nothing.

During the night he had crept out of his cabin, skulked his way to the deck and hidden himself in the dark, dripping salty shadows. He had heard the screams of the wounded. He had heard the gentle, soothing voices of the volunteer nurses and stretcher bearers. The night air chilled him to the marrow and congealed his limbs with cold. He was soaked to the skin. Presently he had scrambled painfully into a lifeboat, curled himself into a tight ball and fallen asleep.

When he awoke, he did not know what to do.

Carefully he peered above the side of the lifeboat.

Out to sea he saw the Danish sloop. Ahead on the horizon he saw the smudges of smoke from the distant convoy. He was just about to lower his head and search the lifeboat for rations, when a voice said:

'Gotcha.'

He almost jumped out of his skin. He spun round and there was Polly grinning at him.

'You've been doing it with Natasha, haven't you?'

'What?'

'Margot's been doing it with the bosun. Mamselle's had mucky letters from the Mafia man with the gold tooth. Dolly got blood on her tits and the Head Shit's a fairy.'

'What?'

Polly giggled. 'He wants to see you.'

'Who?'

'The Head Shit. He's in his state thingies. I was summoned to fetch you. I've never been summoned before.'

Roger Carey sighed and sank back into the well of the lifeboat.

'It's no use trying to hide,' said Polly. 'You're well and truly in it, so you best go and face the music, hadn't you?'

He eased himself gingerly out of the lifeboat and lowered himself carefully to the deck.

Polly gambled and frolicked by his side as he made his way reluctantly to meet Lance Egerton.

'I saw a dead man last night. He'd got this huge blue tongue. I didn't go to bed till two o'clock.'

Then she stuck out her tongue and scampered away chanting: 'I know what you did with Natasha. I know what you did with Natasha.'

He entered the staterooms. He walked slowly into the drawing room and Lance rose from the depths of his bamboo, winged armchair and said: 'Well then, my dear. Now is the time to tell all.'

After a while Roger Carey collected his thoughts and said: 'I am not a doctor.'

'I know you're not a doctor,' screamed Lance, beating his fists on his chest in anger. 'I want to know what you really are.'

'I am on the run.'

'Golly! Are you a mass murderer?'

'No.'

'I know. You're a white-slaver, aren't you?'

'No.'

'You're a German spy. That's it. You're a German spy and you're on board to spy on the convoy and signal to the U-boats and call up the spotter planes and –'

'I am not a spy.'

'Then what are you, for God's sake?' screamed Lance Egerton, beside himself with rage and frustration.

Roger Carey spoke softly.

'I was in this pub in Cardiff. I was on the run. I was rather drunk. No, I was exceedingly drunk. The beer had attacked my skull and I was reeling. And then the Captain came in. He was exceedingly drunk, too. He swayed over to my table and he sat down. He just stared at me. I stood up to leave and he shot out his hand and gripped me by the wrist.

' "I've seen you before," he said. "I know who you are." '

'Oh Christ, I thought to myself. Oh sweet Christ.

'I didn't know what to do. I didn't want to run. I didn't want to cause a disturbance so I sat down and he squinted at me and tittered.

'Then he said: "I need a doctor for my ship. I've got to have a doctor. We sail tomorrow. What do you say, doc?"

'I didn't know what to say. I was on the run. I wanted to hide. I wanted to disappear. This was the perfect chance. It just dropped in my lap. He bought me more rum. I don't remember much after that. I remember being sick. And I remember falling over in the back yard. And then next thing I was in a tailor's shop being fitted out for a uniform. Then I had a curry. And I was sick again. And . . . and . . .'

'Yes?' said Lance eagerly. 'Yes?'

But Roger Carey had fallen asleep. His head hung slackly on his chest and his arms hung limply by his side.

Lance Egerton hurled his cigar across the room. He rang the bell to summon his steward. He pointed to the supine body lying on the sofa and snapped: 'Get rid. Take him to the Captain.'

The Captain was eating pilchards on toast in his cabin when the first officer brought Roger Carey in.

'Who's this?' he said.

'The bastard who pretended to be a doctor,' said the first officer.

The Captain stared at him silently.

Then he said: 'I'm rather constipated at the moment. I wonder if you . . .'

The first officer dragged Roger Carey out of the cabin and frog-marched him to the sickbay.

'I'll deal with you when we get back,' he snarled. 'Meanwhile you can make yourself useful.'

He hurled him into the sickbay and said: 'Right then, Josh, he's all yours.'

Josh put down his bottle of medical comforts and said: 'Right then, twat. Get swabbing.'

19

They joined the convoy after lunch.

HMS *Plunderer* greeted them with a fierce slew of her bow wave and tossed back cascades of foaming spray over her bridge.

There were signals. Voices crackled over loud-hailers.

The convoy was now intact save for the hangdog Swansea tanker. There was no sign of her. They would have to leave her to her own devices.

SS *Drayman* was to take her usual station.

The Admiralty had signalled to the Commodore that there were eleven U-boats in the vicinity.

But of this information Dolly's army knew nothing.

She had dispatched her assistants to their respective cabins for sleep and refurbishment. Some had gone gladly. Some had resisted.

Josh, fortified by medical comforts and the sight of his former superior scouring bedpans, volunteered to keep watch.

Dolly had taken off her dress and washed herself from head to foot. Josh looked on.

'That's a great pair of do-dahs you got on you there, missus,' he said.

'Thank you.'

'Are they heavy to cart around?'

'No.'

'Good. Well, if you ever need a hand . . .'

The minor diplomat returned from his cabin to report for duty.

'Crumbs,' he said when he saw Dolly's naked body. 'Very definitely not minor.'

Dolly was not embarrassed by their presence. She chattered on as she dressed herself in a grubby surgeon's gown and tied up her hair in a ribbon of gauze bandage.

'Right,' she said. 'Let's get cracking.'

They did their rounds.

The skipper of the corvette HMS *Campion* was sleeping. But it was a

67

troubled sleep, and the bandage over the wound in his side was sodden with blood.

'What do we do, Josh?' said Dolly.

Josh clucked his tongue and scratched his chin.

'Medical comforts?' he said.

'I think we should wake him up and change his dressing,' said the minor diplomat.

'I agree,' said Dolly. 'I'll do it myself. You see to the others.'

She placed her hand gently on the skipper's shoulder and shook him slowly and softly. He awoke with a start and tried to raise himself up.

'Shush,' said Dolly. 'Shush.'

She peeled away the dressing. The skipper screwed up his eyes and clenched his fists, but he could not hold in the cry of pain.

'Don't worry, my love,' said Dolly. 'Don't worry.'

The sight of the wound repulsed her. Its smell nauseated her. She felt faint. Perspiration streamed down her forehead and squittered sourly into her eyes.

What to do? Never in the whole of her life had she . . .

'Allow me, ma'am,' said Josh.

He moved her to one side. Not roughly. Not angrily. He just moved her aside so he could deal with the wound. He worked quickly and deftly, whistling through his teeth and ignoring the skipper's cries of torment.

Dolly could bear it no longer and she moved over to help the minor diplomat, who was pressing his ear to the chest of a broad-beamed stoker.

He looked up and said: 'I think he's dead.'

'So do I,' said Dolly, and she burst into tears.

Mr Dugdale did not sleep a wink all night.

Neither did Delphine. She stayed by his side as he watched over his stricken charges, festooning the armchairs and sofas, swathed in blankets and decked out in ill-fitting clothing purloined and borrowed from the crew.

He was not really an old man, she said to herself.

His movements were sprightly. The tired eyes seemed fresh and vibrant even in the deepest fastness of the night. What a beautiful smile he had. There was a lot to be said for grey hair when it grew long at the nape and luxurious at the temples. It was smooth and silky.

68

He dispatched her to his cabin to see if Major Pickavance would volunteer his assistance.

'No,' said Major Pickavance. 'Certainly not.'

What a nauseous little shit, she thought to herself.

She had never liked him. He was a fraud, if ever she'd seen one. He did not know his subjects. She knew for a fact that Lima was not the capital of Ecuador and that sisal was not grown in Rangoon. And how she hated the way he looked at her. How he looked at all the girls, in fact. Sly and shifty. Unclean and unhealthy. Dolly did not disapprove of teachers associating with pupils. Indeed, she actually encouraged it. Imagine associating with him! He only came up to her shoulders. She would poke him in the eyes with her nipples and blind him.

'So what am I to tell Mr Dugdale?' she said.

'You are to tell him, young lady, that I have no intention whatsoever of involving myself in his absurd undertaking. I am a passenger. This ship has a crew fully trained to treat with such emergencies. Our interference in these matters is thus totally redundant. I bid you good night. Please do not disturb me any further.'

She withdrew from the cabin. She felt his eyes sliming through the cleavage in her buttocks.

As she passed Lance Egerton's staterooms on her way back to the lounge she saw a slim, coal-black youth with sinuous hips slip silently and swiftly through the door.

He left behind him the scent of patchouli.

Dolly sat by the side of HMS *Campion*'s skipper.

Josh had given him a draught of morphine, but his sleep was still fitful and disturbed.

The minor diplomat was exhausted. He lay huddled on the floor in a corner of the cubbyhole. Mamselle and Celia had failed to return from their cabins. Roger Carey was scrubbing down the alleyway outside. Dolly was alone with Josh and the noxious stench of his breath.

'Talk to me,' she said.

'Right,' said Josh.

He opened another bottle of medical comforts and said: 'The name? Josh Denham. The age? That'd be telling. The birthplace. Deptford. The street? Unknown.'

He took another loud smack at the bottle.

'Marital status? Bachelor of this parish. Not that I ain't had my moments. Old Josh! Moments galore he's had. Niggers, chinks, wops, spicks, gippos, nips, taffies, micks, jocks, large, small, fat, thin, Muslims, Hindus, yids, coggers, cannibals, blonde, brunette, bald – you name 'em and old Josh has had 'em. He ain't prejudiced, I tell yer.'

The drone of his voice was a comfort to her as she looked down on the skipper. He had a strong face. A rugged face. A handsome face. A face that had seen great tenderness. A face that had seen great hardship and danger. A face that had seen passion and pain. A face that had been kissed by wistful women and cruel women and deceitful women. A face that had been worshipped and adored.

'. . . and she'd got legs like a pelican. Know what I mean? Her legs were identical to the legs what are the property of the genus pelican pelicanus. Know what I mean?'

His eyes were closed. What horrors had they seen? How many deaths? How much agony? How much fear and panic? And what joys and pleasures had they seen? Children building sandcastles? A loving wife knitting socks by the fireside? A mistress in foreign, tropic climes unwrapping her sarong?

'. . . and she'd got teeth like a picket fence what ain't in very good nick. Know what I mean? Follow my meaning?'

Suddenly the skipper stretched out his right hand. He groped with it, floundering feebly. Dolly took hold of it. He smiled. She squeezed his hand. He opened his eyes, and for an instant they were unclouded, and his smile lit up the whole of his face.

And at that moment Dolly fell in love.

And shortly after this Delphine fell in love.

She had rejoined Mr Dugdale in his vigil in the lounge. She had watched him as he fetched water for a thin, hag-necked seaman dressed in chef's trousers and a bottle-green roll-collar sweater with holes in the elbows. She had watched him rearrange the blankets round a bald, pock-cheeked sailor who was thrashing in his sleep. She saw him smile at Mrs Banks when she came in to check that all was well.

'Everything fine, my dear?' she said.

She pressed her thigh briefly against Mr Dugdale.

'Yes,' he said. 'Everything is fine.'

She saw the look of intimacy and conspiracy that passed between them.

And at that moment Delphine fell madly in love.

70

20

The ore carrier from Swansea was torpedoed at eleven twenty-three that morning.

They saw it clearly. The weather was calm.

Her death throes did not last long. A mighty explosion midships: instantly the vessel broke in two. Instantly each half slipped beneath the gentle waves scarcely disturbing the surface. It took two minutes. There were no survivors.

'Crumbs,' said Polly.

Campion's skipper was awake now. Josh had dressed his wound. The skipper had clenched his jaw and bitten his lip. He did not cry out. Throughout his ordeal Dolly held tightly to his hand.

When Josh had finished, the skipper smiled weakly.

He wanted to talk.

'No, no, my love,' said Dolly. 'Best to save your strength.'

He shook his head. He wanted to talk. He had to talk. And so he did talk.

He was a lieutenant commander in the Royal Naval Reserve. His name was Agnew. He was a widower. His wife had died during the blitz on Liverpool. The circumstances were thus:

HMS *Campion* had returned to her home port after a long and perilous convoy. They had lost seventeen out of twenty-three ships. They were relieved to be back. And then as they crossed the Mersey Bar they saw the wrecked and pillaged skyline of the city. And as they streamed up the river they saw Birkenhead, riven and shattered, the straight, narrow streets tumbling their tight-terraced houses to the water's edge, rubbled and sacked by the German bombs.

The skipper had grieved. He had grieved for the city and grieved for his men who had wives and sweethearts there. But he had not worried for himself. His wife lived in a rented cottage in a small village deep in the Wirral.

And then he found out.

A stray bomb unloaded by a wounded bomber limping home. It hit the cottage. His wife was killed. So was his Persian cat.

'How awful. How dreadful. Oh, my love. My poor love.'

The survivors in the lounge were too frightened to go below to the cabins prepared for them under the supervision of Mrs Banks.

That noble lady of the slim ankles, the snow-white arms and wine-dark eyes in all her long years of service at sea had prepared many cabins for many men. Never once had she disappointed them. From Frisco to Sydney. From Murmansk to the Spanish Main she had dedicated herself to her duties. She had always been ready to oblige. She had always been anxious to please.

But now all her blandishments were in vain. The men refused point-blank to go below. No words could persuade them.

And so they were allowed to camp like Bedouin tribesmen in a corner of the lounge next to the stage of straggled potted plants.

'Do you think they're happy?' said Delphine.

Mr Dugdale smiled.

'Who can say?' he said. 'I suppose it's possible they're marginally happier being here than being huddled in an open boat.'

How wise he was. What experience he had of the ways of men. Had he experience of the ways of women? Oh yes. Oh yes. She had seen that look in Mrs Banks's eyes. She had seen his response.

But still she loved him.

Oh, how she loved him.

Polly came up to them breathlessly and said: 'Guess what. I've just been in the kitchens and I've seen a Chinaman spit into a vat of celery soup.'

The convoy steamed on through untroubled seas and placid skies.

HMS *Plunderer* pestered and chided the stragglers. The Danish sloop swanked and the stocky naval tug squared its jaws and tossed at the sea with its snub, angry nose.

Samira leant on the rails and gazed around her.

Where were the U-boats lurking now? Was she being watched by blue Germanic eyes? Were you fried alive in oil or did you implode? How long did it take to drown? What was it like drowning? Was it like getting bath water up your nose or was it worse? Did it hurt when you got hit by a torpedo?

She smiled to herself as the Danish sloop lifted her skirts and pranced towards a distant wheezing tramp.

I wonder what it's like being a tramp, she thought to herself.

The afternoon drifted into evening.

'I'll always love Lance.'

'Mm.'

'I know he doesn't give a jot about me. But I love him. I love him, love him, love him.'

'I know.'

'I don't mind being with you. In fact I like being with you. I like it lots and lots and lots. But I'd rather be with Lance. Do you understand?'

'Not really.'

'Neither do I.'

The ship shuddered as she changed course. The toothbrush glass in the bathroom rattled. The cabin was lit up stark and shocking by a snowflake shell. They heard the sound of distant gunfire.

'I don't mind if we do it.'

'Mm.'

'Do you want to do it?'

'No.'

The ship juddered and changed course again. She rolled heavily to port and the locker clunked and rattled.

The soft whisper.

'Why did you say you were a doctor? Why, why, why?'

The ship lolloped now to starboard and the toothbrush glass rattled once more.

During the night they lost a Polish freighter and a tanker in ballast bound for Galveston.

The billet-doux shoved under the cabin door.

The fluttering of the eyelashes, the pursing of the lips.

Another day.

The scents of patchouli on the deck outside the stateroom door.

Slim hips caressed.

Another day.

'Do you want to know something?'

'Yes. Tell us.'

'I'm now the official bosun's mate.'

73

Screech of laughter. Sobs of laughter.

I wonder what it's like being bitten by a bosun.

Another day.

Flying fish. The hump of a crusted whale. Signals from the Commodore.

'Do you want to do it now?'

'No.'

Another day.

Hugging the rim of the reef now. The lighthouses skeletal and gaunt. The wide sky. The sea calm. Scents of swamp. Distant manatees. Keys slumbering in lazy wood smoke. Another freighter gone. The wheezing tramp blown asunder at the stern.

Oil. Cordite. Vomit.

Screams. Sobs.

Deaths.

Another day.

21

And so love flourished as the convoy greeted the warm waters of the tropics with a long, slow sigh and the U-boats picked off the stragglers one by one.

Dolly's love for the skipper bloomed riotous and rampant. She made no secret of it. Everyone knew. Some snickered. Some scowled. The skipper listened to her entranced.

Delphine's love for Mr Dugdale flourished timidly like tight-lipped buds. She could not disguise it. Mr Dugdale was intrigued and moved by it. The yearning eyes following his every move. The blushes. Dumpy and dowdy. Poor child. He was going to tell Mrs Banks about it. He thought it would amuse her. But then he took a long, deep reflective pull at his whisky and decided to keep it to himself.

Natasha's love lay dormant.

Lance Egerton was not to be seen. Not once did he leave his state-rooms. He had other matters in hand.

Dolly's steward, painfully slim with slimy bloodshot eyes, took his lover by the throat, snarled and rasped: 'Where you bin, boy? Where you bin, mother fucker? Goddam you, you tell me where you bin or I slit your goddam throat from ear to ear.'

The terrified eyes. The wail of terror. The scent of patchouli.

And Roger Carey's love?

He had no time for love. Ceaselessly night and day with no time for proper rest he worked in the sickbay.

'Fetch me them bandages,' said Josh.

Roger Carey fetched him the bandages.

'Where's that coffee got to, you idle bastard? Shift yourself and get to that bleeding pantry pronto.'

Roger Carey shifted himself.

'I wonder why he said he was a doctor,' said Celia to Mamselle as they watched him scuttle off to fetch them coffee.

'He's a romantic,' said Mamselle.

'How do you know?' said Celia.

'Because, *ma chérie*, it takes a romantic to tell another romantic.'

She fluttered her eyelashes, pursed her lips and with elegance and aplomb emptied a bed bottle into the sink.

Dolly was totally unaware of all this. She had eyes only for the skipper. She soothed the insides of his arms with lightly fluttering fingertips. She stroked his cheeks. She mopped his brow.

'Aren't you at all frightened?' said the skipper.

'Frightened, my darling?' said Dolly. 'Frightened of what?'

'Of being torpedoed.'

'Oh no. I don't allow fear in my school. I frown upon it most mightily. The shits are terrified of being frightened.'

She mopped his brow once more.

'Mind you,' she said. 'Everyone else on this boat is in a complete blue funk.'

'Is that so?'

'Oh yes. Mamselle's gangster sits on deck all day and night in his life jacket with a loaded revolver in his hand. And as for the diplomat and his wife! Completely gone. They lie all day in their cabin absolutely blotto. And as for that miserable Captain of the Engineers, well, he's commandeered the laundry and –'

She did not finish.

There was a tremendous explosion which clanged all through the ship, screeched in their ears and then roared and rumbled in their guts.

'Lawd. Bloody hell. Medical comforts again,' said Josh, reaching out for another bottle.

Celia and Mamselle grabbed their life jackets and raced on deck.

They found the rails lined. There was no chatter. No one spoke. Mr Dugdale held his arm tightly round Delphine's shoulders. The small girls huddled together, gaunt-eyed and motionless.

It was a fearful sight.

Earlier in the day the Danish sloop had returned triumphantly to the convoy fussing round the hangdog tanker from Swansea they had lost days earlier in the storm.

SS *Drayman* and the tanker had taken up position alongside each other. At first the tanker had looked shifty and guilty. But then she had cheered up and when night fell had come to look positively jaunty and cheerful.

Now she was ablaze from end to end. Great pillars of smoke and flame came billowing from her hull.

The ships around her had fanned away, but SS *Drayman* held her course, fascinated, appalled and completely helpless.

The explosion had hurled hundreds of gallons of oil high into the sky and now it came splattering down, setting the water alight and lathering the tanker with fiercer, more frenzied flames.

There were men in the water.

They were swimming towards SS *Drayman*.

They raised their arms and cried out for help.

Useless. SS *Drayman* could not move towards them for the raft of burning oil was coiling and swirling nearer and nearer to the men.

And then it caught up with them.

One by one they were engulfed by the flames.

The last man tried to hurl himself out of the water.

He screamed at the top of his voice.

And then he was gone.

Silence.

'Where? Where did I see it before?' whispered Roger Carey to himself. 'Where? For Christ's sake, where?'

That night the dining room was sparse with passengers.

The minor diplomat and his wife sat glassy-eyed at the Captain's table, shovelling food down the front of their clothes and spilling wine on their laps.

In the lounge Mr Dugdale and Delphine served food to the seamen in their encampment by the stage. They dished out tinned tomato soup and bully beef hash, and bread and butter pudding and mugs of iron-strong tea.

'Haven't you got no baked beans?' said the tow-haired seaman.

'I'm afraid not, old chap,' said Mr Dugdale.

'Typical! Bloody typical!'

Mr Dugdale smiled at Delphine and patted her loftily on the cheek.

She blushed and felt a sudden surging upheaval deep inside her as the wind got up and the seas commenced to heave.

There were no U-boat attacks that night. The gale howled through the rigging and snatched white-knuckled at the waves.

Mrs Otto snored.

'Ooh, ooh, ooh,' went Mamselle.

'Arrgh, arrgh, arrgh,' howled Margot.

Major Pickavance wedged himself upright on the lavatory, pyjama trousers round his ankles, his head hanging over the wash basin.

Natasha held Roger Carey tightly in her arms. Dolly whispered endearments to the skipper. Samira thought of giant squid and man-eating eels. Delphine thought of the gentle love she would give to the gentle old man with his gentle desires. Mr Dugdale thrust and Mrs Banks howled and squirmed.

Next morning they found Lance in his bedroom with his throat slit from ear to ear.

22

'Who found him?' said Dolly.

'His steward.'

'Get him.'

'Right.'

The first officer instructed the bosun to bring the steward to his cabin immediately.

'Who else knows about this?'

'Just you and me and the steward,' said the first officer.

'No one else must know.'

'Too bloody true, mate.'

The bosun brought Lance's steward to the first officer's cabin. He was a plump Goanese with gentle hands. The first officer talked rapidly in a language totally unintelligible to Dolly. The Goanese smiled and nodded. There was no hint of distress or fear in his manner.

'If Sir Graham should find out about this, it would be calamitous. Total, utter disaster,' said Dolly.

The first officer ignored her. He continued to jabber at the Goanese. Presently he turned to Dolly and said: 'Right. That's him squared off. Let's find the other one.'

They found him in the bilges, his mouth foaming, his thin body racked with convulsive shivers, his slimy bloodshot eyes rolling uncontrollably, his white tunic shirt smeared and dashed with blood.

The first officer pinned his arms behind his back and frog-marched him back to his cabin.

'Leave this to me,' said Dolly.

'Certainly,' said the first officer gratefully.

Dolly rubbed her chin thoughtfully. She looked the old steward up and down. She had never liked him. He had a deceitful look in his eyes. He was too anxious to please. He had a strange smell about him. She suspected him of trying on her clothes when she was taking meals.

She stood up from her chair, moved slowly towards him, paused in front of him and then suddenly punched him flush on the chin.

He staggered back into the wall.

Dolly pounced after him, took hold of his collar and butted him sharply between the eyes.

'You shit!' she snarled. 'You did it, didn't you? You murdered him.'

'Yes,' said the steward.

Dolly kicked the steward hard in the groin. He cried out in pain. He cowered on his knees, sobbing.

'So what do we next?' said the first officer.

'Simple,' said Dolly.

She summoned Roger Carey to the cabin.

He was nervous. He glanced at the old steward covered in gore. He glanced at the first officer sweating and biting his fingernails. He glanced at Dolly, smug and triumphant.

Briefly she told him what had happened. He felt faint. His throat rasped. His lips crackled drily.

'So this is what we do now,' said Dolly. 'Listen to me.'

Roger Carey listened.

What Dolly had to say was simplicity itself. She had a proposition to put to him. He could resume his status as ship's doctor. They would ignore his deception. They would not report it to the authorities. But there was one condition – in his capacity as ship's doctor he would sign a death certificate for Lance, stating that he had died of natural causes. It was as simple as that.

He did not hesitate.

'I'll sign anything you like,' he said.

'What about the nigger?' said the first officer.

'Simple,' said Dolly.

She strode to the steward and kicked him once more violently in the ribs.

'You hear me?' she said.

'Yes, ma'am. I hears you.'

Another kick in the ribs.

'You understand my meaning?'

'Yes, ma'am. I sure do.'

'One word from you about what has happened, here, there, anywhere, today, tomorrow or for the rest of time and I shall send the black owl with the blood-red eyes and the gore dropping from its beak to peck at your vitals and drag out your brains through the sockets of your eyes. You understand my meaning?'

'Oh, ma'am, ma'am, I sure does,' said the steward, rolling his eyes wildly and rattling his teeth like castanets.

Dolly turned to the first officer.

'Simple, eh? she said.

'What next?' said the first officer.

'We get cracking,' said Dolly.

They got cracking.

Roger Carey made out a death certificate and signed it.

They sewed the body of Lance Egerton into a canvas sack and weighted it with ingots of pig iron from the ballast. They assembled the passengers and crew on the boat deck and placed the Captain in front of them, standing on a up-turned beer crate.

Then they laid the body on a smooth plank, shaved and planed specially by the chippy, who came from Carlisle. They covered the cadaver with a Red Ensign.

The Captain mumbled.

Dolly gave the signal.

The body of Lance Egerton was tipped into the sea.

It made a gracious, elegant splash.

The first officer signalled the unfortunate death to the Commodore. He signalled back.

'Hard cheddar. Do not – repeat do not – dispose of his togs.'

Thousands of miles away in a small, discreet basement restaurant in London Sir Graham Egerton dined alone with Mrs Simister.

'Pity about fairy drawers, eh?' she said.

'Yes,' said Sir Graham, and he summoned the waiter to change his napkin.

The convoy sailed on.

Later in the afternoon HMS *Plunderer* dropped a clutch of depth charges, and the sea hubbled and bubbled and thrashed and threshed and its surface was strewn with the blank, bewildered eyes of dead fish.

23

Their last full day at sea.

'Most likely our last full day on earth,' said Josh in the sickbay.

'What on earth do you mean by that?' said Celia.

'Luck, mate, luck,' said Josh. 'Our luck can't last this long. I'll bet you half a bar to a tanner we're torpedoed before the night is out. Dead cert, mate. Dead cert.'

Dolly heard nothing of this. All her attention was focused on the skipper. His wound had just been dressed. He was getting better. He was sitting up in bed. His face was pale and strained. But his ice-blue eyes flashed and feasted ravenously on Dolly.

'Go on,' he said. 'Tell me more. Tell me about your Polish count.'

Dolly told him about the Polish count.

'Did you enjoy Madeira?'

'Oh yes.'

'Tell me about Madeira.'

Dolly told him about Madeira.

'A lucky escape,' said the skipper.

He breakfasted amply. He had kippers, fried eggs, hash-brown potatoes, fried onion, cheese, toast and thick, bitter orange marmalade.

'I like the way you eat,' said Dolly.

'Thank you.'

'You look as though you mean it.'

The ship lurched.

Celia dropped her mug. The Doucemain twins, nursing the dying stoker, looked quickly at each other and dartlets of fear zinged across their eyes. Josh, sitting on the floor under the medicine cabinet, looked up from whitening Roger Carey's tropical shoes, and clucked his tongue with disappointment when the ship resumed her placid, untroubled motion.

Dolly and the skipper ignored this disturbance. Indeed they were not aware of it. If the ship had been torpedoed, set on fire, overwhelmed by sparking, gushing, flaming oil like the hangdog tanker from Swansea, they would have continued talking, never unlinking their hands nor averting their eyes from each other's gaze.

'Where did you meet Mr Bradman?'

'In Lewes.'

'Ah.'

'It's in Sussex.'

'I know.'

She told him of her first meeting with Mr Bradman. She had answered an advertisement in *The Times*: *Attractive and innovative mature lady in the full prime of her sexuality urgently required to pursue 'progressive' ideas in a practical setting. Must be prepared to participate herself.*

'We met in a tearoom. I had Welsh rarebit. Mr Bradman had beans on toast. He was an extremely tall man. He was very conscious of it. He had large hands, too, and rather red wrists. There was always a sticky band of phlegm between his lips when he talked. He was very conscious of that, too.

'We visited the Anne of Cleves museum. I've never been all that partial to Anne of Cleves. I haven't much time for museums, come to that. This one looked as if it should have been in a museum itself.

'After the museum we visited the castle and then Mr Bradman said: "I have a room booked in the best hotel in town. Would you care to inspect its amenities?" "Yes," I said. I inspected the amenities. They were excellent. So were Mr Bradman's. He proposed marriage and I accepted. We went to Lowestoft for our honeymoon. It was lovely. Then we moved out to Lygon House and opened up the school. It was lovely. Blissful. It was such a shame Mr Bradman had to go and die.'

'How did he die?' said the skipper.

'Oh, we don't talk about that, my darling.'

Celia was relieved by Mamselle. Margot was relieved by Samira. The Doucemain twins stayed put, as Burnaby returned to his cabin and his spots.

Dolly and the skipper did not notice this movement in personnel. They were intoxicated by the magic of each other's presence.

'Tell me about your life. Tell me something about the essential You,' said Dolly.

'Right,' said the skipper.

In the First World War he had served in a destroyer at Jutland. He had skippered a gunboat in the South China Seas. When the Royal Navy dispensed with his services he joined the Mercantile Marine.

'Mercantile Marine!' said Dolly. 'Isn't that a lovely expression?'

'Yes,' said the skipper.

He had joined a company whose vessels served the ports of the River Plate. The ships were ancient and doddery. So, too, were their officers. The skipper did not prosper.

The ships stank of old men's chests. They stank of old men's legs. They creaked like old men. And they shuffled like old men in even the slightest swell. He was first officer on a vessel that foundered on a surly reef. He changed company.

There he did prosper. He was given command. Out of Liverpool he sailed. Slow, murky creeks. The screech of jungle. Black boys begging and diving for coins. Colonials with blistered knees and porpoise-skin boots. Slavered nights. Sticky bars with fly-blown naked bulbs. Askaris. Berbers. Armenians.

The war broke out. He was recalled to the navy. He was given command of HMS *Campion*. How proud he was when he first paced the bridge. How devastated when she rolled over beneath the waves.

Distant gunfire.

Depth charges.

The rasp and rattle of the dying stoker.

'Tell me about your wife,' said Dolly.

24

The skipper told Dolly about his wife.

'She was very ordinary. So-so, you'd call her,' he said. 'I knew her father. I suppose that's why I married her.'

'What did she look like? Describe her.'

'She was short and stout.'

'I knew it! Tell me more. What colour was her hair?'

'Mousy.'

'I knew it! I knew it! Was she bad-tempered?'

'No. She was very placid. Unruffled.'

'Why did you marry her?'

'She was a very nice person. She had a nice smile. She had a nice smell. I hadn't had much experience with women. Nice women, I mean.'

'And do you like nice women?'

'I find them disturbing. They mess things up. They play havoc with your routine.'

'I know.'

He told her of the dogs he had owned. He told her of his son. He told her of the house on the Wirral. He told her of his wife sitting by the fire knitting socks when he came home on leave.

'What was her name?'

'Evelyn.'

'Was she a passionate woman?'

'Oh no. Not at all.'

'Are you a passionate man?'

'I don't know.'

The luncheon gong sounded.

'I'm just going on deck for a breather,' said Josh. 'Well, I prefer being uptops when the torpedo hits us.'

'I love you,' said Dolly.

'And I love you, too,' said the skipper.

They kissed.

'I have to warn you about my owl,' said Dolly.

'Your owl?'

'The black owl with the blood-red eyes. It sits on my shoulders. It always comes to me when I'm happy. And it sits there and broods and spits and hisses when anyone gets too near. It screeches at people. It attacks them. And it drives them away. And I can't do anything to stop it. I shout and scream at it to leave me alone. But it won't. It just sits there day after day till I'm left on my own and I'm miserable once more.'

The skipper took hold of her hand.

'I don't see any owl,' he said.

'Maybe he won't come this time,' said Dolly, and tears began to well in her eyes and cascade down her cheeks.

The skipper did not move. He stared at her without expression as she sobbed. When she had finished he said: 'We used to go on bicycling holidays, my son and I.'

'How lovely,' said Dolly. 'And where did you go to?'

'The Cheshire hills. The Welsh Marches. Once we went to Holland.'

'I love you.'

'And I love you.'

Josh returned from his spell on deck.

'I've just heard,' he said. 'We leave the convoy at midnight. A quick dash on our own to St David's. Lawd help us, if it don't blow up a bleeding gale. Sitting ducks we'll be. Sitting bleeding ducks.'

All through the afternoon the convoy sailed through calm waters.

Dolly and the skipper ate dinner off a tray.

'Where shall we live when we get married?' said the skipper.

'Anywhere you like,' said Dolly.

'You choose.'

'Right.'

Dolly chose a stone cottage by a beck. Then she changed her mind and chose a houseboat with bent stove chimney and striped awnings and a pug dog yawning in the sun.

The lights flickered dimly. One of the wounded men called out for water. Mamselle brought it to him in a beaker and fluttered her eyelids.

The Doucemain twins never left the side of the dying stoker.

'I wouldn't like to live abroad,' said Dolly.

'Why not?'

'Because I've spent too much of my time abroad,' she said. 'I've been all over the place, you know.'

'Ah.'

'I was a nanny, you see.'

'Ah.'

'Then I was a companion.'

'Ah.'

'To rich old ladies mainly.'

'Ah.'

'I was companion to a rich old lady in Boston. She died and left me her house. Then I went to Winnipeg. I married an Estonian gentleman. When he died, he left me his house.'

'Just like Mr Bradman.'

'That's right.'

She smiled and squeezed his hand tightly.

'Oh boy,' she said. 'Have I got a story to tell you.'

At midnight the ship changed course and they felt the surge as she increased her speed to make her lone dash to St David's.

The skipper reached out to her and took her in his arms. He held her there.

'Ooh!' said Dolly. 'Ooh! Yes, you are indeed a passionate man.'

'Come with me,' said the skipper.

'What?'

'Don't get off the ship at St David's. Come home with me.'

He felt the tension in her body. He felt the swift surge and rise and fall of her breasts. Her lips nuzzled at his ears.

The rise and fall of her breasts. The rise and fall of the ship charging at the grudging seas, scattering the moon on her wake.

'What about my school?' said Dolly. 'What about the shits?'

'Leave them.'

Josh poked his head out of the cubbyhole.

'Any minute now,' he said. 'Torpedo slap into our guts. You wait, mateys. A dead cert.'

The stoker faded away. The Doucemain twins covered his face with a sheet.

Celia tiptoed to Dolly and said: 'Go to bed. Get some sleep. Mamselle and I will look after things.'

The skipper held tightly to Dolly. She pressed herself tightly into his chest.

'Well?' he said. 'Will you? Will you come home with me?'

Slowly Dolly pulled away from him. She placed her hands on his naked chest. Then she licked his nipples slowly.

'Well?' he said. 'Will you?'

'Yes,' said Dolly.

25

And then the black owl landed on Dolly's shoulders.

She did not feel it when she awoke next morning. She was happy. Her guard was down. The black owl preened itself and waited.

Dolly went on deck and breathed in deeply the heady scents of the land unseen beyond the distant horizon. Seabirds soared and swirled in the ship's wake and swooped screaming and squabbling for the gash from the buckets.

She went down below to the sickbay. The skipper slept deeply and peacefully. She bent over him and kissed him softly on the mouth. He grunted in his sleep and smiled.

Josh smiled, too.

'Still time,' he said. 'Bags of time for us to cop a packet.'

Natasha knocked on the door of Roger Carey's cabin.

'Come in.'

She entered. Her eyes were heavy. Her limbs were heavy. Her shoulders drooped. Her fresh young skin was blotched and pallid.

'I've come to say goodbye,' she said.

'Goodbye,' said Roger Carey.

'I have to tell you that you cheered up my voyage no end,' said Mr Dugdale to Mrs Banks.

'You're most welcome, my dear. Most welcome, I'm sure.'

'You have perked me up.'

'So I noticed.'

'I was getting in a rut.'

'Don't we all, my dear.'

'But now I have made the momentous stride across the Rubicon and abandoned the nubile in favour of the mature.'

'That's right, my dear.'

'You have a most splendid bottom, Mrs Banks.'

'Thank you, I'm sure.'

'Not at all. Would you perhaps care to . . . ?'

'Why not? One last time won't do no harm, will it?'

Half an hour later Mr Dugdale said: 'Goodbye, Mrs Banks. It has been a real pleasure knowing you.'

'Likewise I'm sure, my dear.'

She left the cabin.

As she walked along the alleyway she bumped into Delphine. She pointed with her thumb towards Mr Dugdale's cabin.

'You make sure you take care of him,' she said.

'Oh yes, of course I will,' said Delphine. 'I'm in love with him, you see.'

Oh, to be at a ball with him, she said to herself. Her gown would be of black velvet. It would be low cut. She would wear pearls. Young men would ask her to dance the mazurka and quadrille. But she would have eyes only for him.

Oh, how she adored him.

Dolly banged with her fist on the cabin door of the minor diplomat and his wife.

There was no answer. But she heard the sound of clinking glasses and hiccups and slurred giggles.

'Bye bye,' she shouted. 'Farewell, you joyous, lovely, rampant drunken minor shits.'

On the boat deck Major Pickavance, cravatted and blazered, extended his hand to the sapper Captain.

'I wish you every success in your campaigns to come,' he said. 'May they be blessed by slaughter and carnage, pillage and destruction, investment and capitulation and the most perfect weather throughout.'

'Thank you,' said the Captain. 'I suppose as an old military man yourself you wish you were coming with us.'

'Good God, no,' said Major Pickavance and he flushed his nostrils to the breezes from the land. 'I smell wealthy widows out there.'

Dolly returned to the sickbay.

Josh was sitting in the cubbyhole drinking medical comforts.

'I can see it all,' he said. 'Oh yes, it's all vividly clear, mate. St David's hoves into view. Jubilation on deck. Fond farewells. Tears. Embraces.

Exchange of addresses. Promises to keep in touch till eternity runs dry. And then without warning – wallop! The torpedo rips out our guts. All hands lost. Not a sinner saved.'

He smacked his lips gleefully.

'You're a goner, mate,' he said to Dolly. 'Just you wait and see.'

The skipper was awake. He smiled at her broadly and said: 'I love you.'

'I love you, too.'

'You haven't changed your mind?'

'No. Of course I haven't changed my mind.'

The black owl jerked its head from beneath its wing. It clenched and flexed its claws. It chuntered. But Dolly did not hear it. She did not feel it.

She leant over the skipper and her breasts pattered across his chest. She smothered his neck with kisses. She nibbled at his ear. She licked his eyelids softly. She sucked his tongue deep inside her mouth and licked off its moisture.

'I'm so happy,' she said.

'So am I,' said the skipper.

The swarthy man appeared on deck just before St David's nudged its twin peaks above the horizon.

The greenish, yellow pallor of seasickness and fear had left his face. He was pomaded and perfumed. He wore a navy-blue silk shirt and canary-yellow tie. His ducks were spotless white, and his blue and white co-respondent shoes glowed with polish. His gold tooth flashed.

He bowed to Mamselle.

'I hope you got my notes,' he said.

'Yes, I did,' said Mamselle.

'Well?'

'Your handwriting was quite nice, but your grammar was atrocious.'

And then Burnaby shouted out: 'Land ho! Land ho!'

He pointed to the starboard quarter, and there it was – the distant smudge of St David's. The twin peaks with the wispy haze of cloud around their summits. The faint smell of cinnamon and ginger.

They all clung to the rails. They chattered with excitement. They strained their eyes. They hopped from foot to foot. The little girls pinched each other and giggled. Then they raced away dodging among the legs of the passengers and crew.

Major Pickavance idly clipped Louise behind the ear as she wriggled past him. She sank to her knees and howled.

He smiled, sniffed the breeze again and said to the yawning, scratching, sleep-sodden Mrs Otto: 'Yes, I certainly pick up the scent of wealthy widows.'

Natasha stood apart from the others.

The Red Ensign. The plank. The sack guzzling beneath the waves. The rot. The corruption. Blind fish. Worms.

Her hair flayed at the breeze. But it had lost its lustre and its sheen. The full mouth was pinched. The lissom limbs were sluggish and listless.

Yet still the beauty shines through, thought Mr Dugdale. Still the radiance refuses to die. But he was not moved. He felt sorrow. He felt no desire.

He looked down at Delphine, who was crouching at his feet tying an errant shoelace. Plain and dumpy Delphine. Podgy Delphine with the bottom ready to drag and the breasts preparing to droop. He was deeply moved.

'Pumps,' he said.

'Pumps?' said Delphine. 'Why did you say pumps?'

'I really don't know,' he said. 'How odd. How very curious.'

Samira looked on. She smiled and wondered what it would be like to be impaled on a bamboo stake.

'One more. One last time,' said Margot.

'Okey-dokey,' said the bosun. 'Here we go.'

'Ooh, ooh, ooh.'

'Yi yi yi yi yi.'

In the sickbay the skipper said: 'Have you told them you're coming with me?'

'Not yet. I want to make the most of it. I want to spring it on them out of the blue. I want to see the horror on their faces. I want to see Celia's fear. I want to see Dugdale's dismay and Pickavance's panic. I want to see Mamselle shake and shiver and Mrs Otto drop her *Speisewagen*. Above all I want to see the shits grovelling and screaming and wailing and sobbing. I hate them. I hate them all.'

The black owl clicked its beak and ruffled its feathers and slowly extended its wings.

26

The island drew nearer and nearer.

They could make out the white houses and the plantations loping up the hills. They could see the masts of shipping and the harbour crane clawing its lazy finger at the sky.

They were all packed and ready to disembark.

'Will you say goodbye properly?' said Natasha to Roger Carey.

He did not take in the sight of her sitting naked at the foot of his bed. He did not hear her voice. All he saw were the stricken seamen, scalded and burnt, stinking of oil and vomit. All he heard were the screams of pain and his own voice howling: 'But I'm not a doctor. I am not a doctor.'

Natasha slid forward up the bed towards him. He flinched away from her touch.

'I can't say I love you,' she said. 'I'd like to. But I can't.'

Roger Carey said nothing. He huddled back into his pillow. The scents of her body didn't rouse him. The feel of her breath on his cheeks did not excite him. Her lips nuzzling at his mouth and her tongue flickering on the tip of his nose didn't stir him.

She dressed quickly.

'Goodbye then,' she said.

After she had left, Roger Carey said very softly: 'Goodbye, Natasha.'

Celia saw Natasha leaving the cabin.

She moved to speak to her, but Natasha pushed past her. There was no expression on her face.

The sadness of the fond farewell, thought Celia. Such a pleasant young man. So handsome. Such lovely manners. Why had he pretended to be a doctor? Where had she seen him before? Where? When? She would like to bid him farewell herself. She would like that very much. She had wanted to bid him a fond and passionate farewell from the moment she first set eyes upon him.

She set off to the lounge for a farewell gin and tonic. She bumped into Mamselle.

'Have you seen Dolly on your travels?' Celia said. 'She's left me to do all the packing.'

'She'll be downstairs exposing herself to her jolly jack tar,' said Mamselle. Then she lowered her eyelids and tutted her tongue. '*Ma chérie*, such a distinguished man.'

Dolly was indeed down below with her skipper.

They were silent. He had his arm round her waist. She rested her head on his shoulder. They would live in a stave house in a forest clearing, she said to herself. There would be geese strutting in the garden. Badgers would come to drink from the brook. Fallow deer would crop timidly at the forest's edges. In the dark they would hear the churr of nightjar and the roding of woodcock. And they would cuddle together. And dormice would whisper and he would make love to her. Oh, how wild he would be. How fierce. How passionate. And when they had done with each other, how gentle he would be. And their happiness would clamber and writhe like wood smoke from a charcoal burner's fire.

And then without warning the black owl struck.

She heard its shriek. She felt its plunge. She screamed as its talons ripped into the flesh of her shoulders. She screamed as she looked deep into the blood-red of its eyes and cowered from the wicked jabbing of its beak.

She wrenched herself free of the skipper's grasp.

'What's the matter?' he cried.

'I can't do it,' she howled. 'I can't. I can't.'

And she fled from the sickbay, blundering away down alley and companionway and only the black owl heard her wails and her sobs and the piercing screams of her rank and total misery.

An hour later they disembarked.

'Cheerio,' said the first officer winking at Dolly. 'Your secret's safe with me.'

And he pinched her bottom.

The Captain said: 'Goodbye, ma'am. Such fun, our trip, don't you think? Such fun.'

Dolly did not speak. Head bowed, shoulders sunken, she did not look back as she hurried down the gangwalk.

'If only we'd been torpedoed,' said Josh to the skipper as he lay rigid in his bed in the sickbay. 'It would have made all the difference, mate. Solved all your problems, eh?'

Roger Carey sat rigid and silent in his cabin.

The arm flayed from shoulder to wrist. The raft of flames. Wide-open eyes. So still. So silent. Long blonde hair flecked with tawny. Why had the flames spared them? They didn't deserve that luck.

In her cabin Mrs Banks entertained the bosun.

'Nice to be back,' he said. 'I've missed you.'

'Course you have,' she said. 'A bit of old tail does wonders for a bloke like you, don't it?'

The sappers scratched and perspired deep in the bowels of the ship.

The minor diplomat and his wife supped long and hard in their cabin.

The Captain of the sappers leant on the rails and stuck up his thumb at Major Pickavance.

The swarthy man slipped ashore unseen. His jacket clanked metallically, and his gold tooth flashed.

Deep in the jungle in the house called Marchmain's Rest the bright green parrot screeched.

Three-quarters of an hour after SS *Drayman* slipped her berth she was hit by a torpedo. It was in full view of the watchers on the shore. The torpedo struck the precise spot on the ship where the sappers had stored their explosives. A huge orange ball of fire flew high into the air from deep within her guts. Then a great pulsating, rolling, rumbling pillar of black smoke. Then another explosion. Deafening. Shattering. Metal splashing red-hot into the sea. Metal foaming in the sea.

Then nothing.

There was only one survivor.

He said nothing to his rescuers.

He stared at them sightlessly through his slimy bloodshot eyes.

PART TWO

27

The Island of St David's was not discovered by Christopher Columbus.

He was far too busy.

In 1941 its principal export was salt.

The Northern two-thirds of the island were British. The remaining third was French.

In 1903 the smaller of its twin peaks exploded. It tried again in 1929, but failed.

Bananas were grown throughout the island.

In the past it was settled successively and sometimes concurrently by French pirates, Dutch prisoners of war, Spanish mutineers and English planters of uncertain means and temper.

Then as now the Stollmeyer's flightless rail was indigenous to the island.

The total area of the island was 56 square miles.

The British capital was Johnstown and the French capital was Port Cedric.

When Dolly and her party arrived on the island, the British section was garrisoned by units of Home Counties infantry and native levies. The French section was under the care of a detachment of Vichy French marines and Foreign Legion light cavalry.

The British Governor and his family were absent from the island.

'Haven't got the foggiest where they are,' said the military commander, Colonel Ryder. 'I expect they'll potter back soon. They usually do.'

They were quartered in the Governor's residence.

Owing to 'difficulties in the interior' Marchmain's Rest was not deemed ready to receive them.

Dolly locked herself in her bedroom and would see no one but Celia, and then only under considerable duress.

'Go away. Go away. I don't want to speak to anyone,' she said.

'But we've got to talk about things,' said Celia. 'There are plans to be made.'

'What plans?'

'Plans for the future.'

'What future?'

'Our future.'

'Go away. Bugger off.'

Very soon a mood of lethargy and despondency overtook them all.

The little girls were taken ill with fever. They were removed to the military hospital.

After three days Perdita died. Her funeral was sad and listless. Dolly refused to attend. She said she had urgent business to attend to.

'What business?' said Celia.

'My black owl.'

'What black owl?'

Dolly screamed and slammed the bedroom door in her face.

Sometimes they were visited by Colonel Ryder.

'I'm not very good company, I fear,' he said. 'Truth to tell I'm an exceedingly boring person. I used to collect matchboxes, you know.'

There were no lessons. The weather was sickly and humid.

There was a giant cedar tree in the garden. All day long Natasha sat beneath it and thought of Roger Carey. If only she had told him she loved him. It would have been a lie, but it would have made him happy. He would have died a contented man. How blissful to be happy. Curious. It was not Lance's death that made her unhappy. She was unhappy because she could not fall in love with Roger Carey. Mr Dugdale loved her. She could see that in his eyes. He tried to pretend that it was not so. But she knew better. Delphine loved Mr Dugdale. She could not disguise it. There was so much love around. Yet love for her was as black as the cedar tree which soared its pungent darkness above her.

Samira fell foul of the fever that had taken the life of Perdita. She was taken to the same hospital. She lay in bed perspiring and shivering. She wondered if they would bury her at sea.

All day long Mr Dugdale sat in his bedroom with the shutters closed. Sometimes Delphine bathed his feet. Sometimes she mopped his brow. Sometimes she sat on the floor at his side saying nothing.

Mr Dugdale brooded deep in thought. Poor Mrs Banks. Such a vulgar woman. But so inventive. So carnal. So convivial. At first he had been shocked. Then he had been excited. The ship exploding. The roar. The rumble. The towering pillar of smoke. The huge, violent orange flash. Just like that first night with poor Mrs Banks.

Mrs Otto slept and snored. Her threadbare dog had disappeared down a burrow at the bottom of the garden. Her *Speisewagen* was clamped to her bosom by her purple podgy arms.

Mamselle, pale and pensive, lips unpainted, nails unvarnished, skin unlotioned, thought of the swarthy man with the gold tooth.

He was a gangster. No doubt about it. She had seen gangsters in the cinema. They carried sub-machine-guns and talked out of the corners of their mouths. She felt a close affinity with gangsters.

At her interview Dolly had asked: 'Do you speak French?'

'*Mais certainement.*'

'Are you prepared to indulge in and promote activities of a progressive nature?'

'*Ah oui. Naturellement.*'

On both counts she had lied.

She was a gangster herself.

She looked out of the window into the garden. The Sikh major-domo was talking to Margot.

'We could dine together tonight, if you wish,' he said.

Margot flinched her shoulders apathetically.

'I have rather a penchant for entertaining young ladies. You will not be disappointed. *Au contraire*, I am certain you will be enthralled, enchanted and –'

'Excuse me,' said Margot.

And she was violently sick in the shrubbery.

An hour later she was rushed to the hospital to join Samira and the Doucemain twins, who had been admitted by stretcher that morning.

Back at the Governor's residence Burnaby observed glumly that his spots were disappearing and he was beginning to grow a faint fuzz of whiskers.

Celia hammered on the bedroom door and bellowed: 'You've got to do something. You've got to take command.'

Dolly lay rigid in bed, staring unblinkingly at the ceiling as the gecko gulped.

28

Only Major Pickavance was sprightly.

Every evening he would call on Mr Dugdale with a bottle of rum and two glasses.

'I'm so happy,' he would say. 'I'm so wonderfully happy.'

'Mm.'

'Are you happy, old boy? Are you blissfully contented?'

'Mm.'

One night he brought a bottle of cherry brandy and two tumblers. He filled the tumblers to the brim and drank each one in a single gulp.

'Everything's fitting into place, old boy,' he said. 'I smell wealthy widows. They are out there waiting for my grasp. Yearning for it. Oh, lucky, lucky me.'

He tittered and scratched his arid ankles rapidly.

'Mm.'

Delphine stood by Mr Dugdale's side fanning him with a large palm leaf she had gathered in the garden earlier in the morning.

Major Pickavance drank another tumbler of cherry brandy. He coughed, straightened the cuffs of his jacket, fastidiously brushed a speck of invisible dust from his trousers, coughed again and said: 'I have a confession to make.'

'Mm.'

'I am not a major in His Majesty's army.'

'Mm.'

Memories of a handsome grey-haired old man with a dumpy and dowdy girl fanning his brow.

The girl had said: I would like you to see Abruzzi and visit my family at Capracotta. She was his pupil in Milan. She had plump pink cheeks. She lay by his side, her plump pink hand stroking the fever of his thighs. I would love you to go to the Abruzzi, she said. There is good hunting. You would like the people and though it is cold in winter, it is clear and dry. You could stay with my family. My father is a famous hunter.

'I have never been a major in His Majesty's army. Quite the reverse, in fact. I was a temporary second lieutenant in a regiment of East African yeomanry.'

'Mm.'

'That's where the deception started. Under the bright stars of the Veldt on annual manoeuvres. The crackle of the campfire, old boy! The askaris chuntering softly. The cries of wild animals. And I said to myself: What are you making of your life, Skomer? What future have you? None, old boy, I said to myself. Absolutely nothing. That's when I hit on the idea of the wealthy widow.'

'Mm.'

'I don't know if you've noticed, old boy. But I am an extremely small person.'

'Mm.'

'I am but five feet one inch in my stocking feet. Or in anyone else's stocking feet come to that. It's always been something of a handicap when it comes to treating with women of the opposite gender. They seem to have an in-built aversion to exiguity.'

'Mm.'

More memories of a handsome old man.

The girl had said: I should like us to go fishing in Burguete. She was his pupil in Bilbao. Olive skin with flat, meagre breasts and sharp plum-red nipples. They travelled by bus and drank wine from the skin. They drank *aguardiente* in a *posada*. The room was low and dark. It was cluttered with saddles and harnesses, and hay forks made of white wood and clusters of canvas, rope-oiled shoes and hams and slabs of bacon and white garlics and long sausages hanging from the roof. Their room was on the north side of the inn. They drank to keep warm. Deep down in the depths of his fur-lined sleeping bag she let her lips soar and glide and he arched his back. Once in the night he woke and heard the wind blowing against the shutters. It felt good.

'Once I thought of embarking on a relationship with a midget. But, alas, white midgets of "a certain age" are an extremely rare commodity in the distant outposts of Uganda.'

'Nipples,' said Mr Dugdale.

'I beg your pardon?' said Major Pickavance.

Mr Dugdale grunted. How odd. How very curious. Why had he said nipples? He had not intended to. His brain had given him no warning. Two hours ago quite involuntarily he had said palindrome. How odd. How very curious.

101

Major Pickavance poured out two more glasses of cherry brandy and drank them both.

He continued: 'So I took the plunge and shipped myself to Blighty. I took up a position as a commercial traveller specialising in the sale of school exercise books and blotting paper. They were lean pickings, old boy, lean pickings. But still I lived in hope of finding my wealthy widow. On the road I was. Continually. A knight of the long acre. And nothing did I find. Not a dicky bird. And then one afternoon in a small tearoom in Oswestry I saw it. An advertisement in *The Times*. *Attractive and innovative mature lady in the full prime of her sexuality urgently required to pursue "progressive" ideals in a practical setting. Must be prepared to participate herself.*

'I applied for the job, but was pipped at the post by Dolly. However, after her appointment as headmistress she most graciously consented to give me a position on her staff. I don't mind confessing, old boy, that for a time I nursed hopes that Dolly herself might be the wealthy widow for whom I was yearning.'

'Mm.'

More memories of an old man listening to the squeak of bat and the swish of leaf. I should like to take you to Venice in winter, he said. I would like that, she said. She was his pupil in Budapest. High cheekbones and soft-fanned bush. They kissed for a long time, standing straight and true in the cold of the open windows that looked on to the Grand Canal. She kissed him so hard he could feel the sweet salt of the blood inside his lips. And he liked it. Now I will comb my hair and make my mouth new and you can watch me, she said. Do you want me to shut the windows? he said. No, she said, we will do it all in the cold.

Major Pickavance drained his glass of cherry brandy and continued: 'One night Dolly came into my bedroom. I was awake, but I pretended to be asleep. I screwed up my eyes and I curled up tightly. She leant over me. I felt her breath on the back of my neck. And she said: "It's a shame to disturb you, poor little twat." And she didn't disturb me. She just padded out of the room chuckling softly to herself. I cried out, but no words came. I tried to jump out of bed, but my legs didn't seem to be working. I think they must have remembered all those years back to the first and only time I kissed a woman. She knocked out my front teeth with her spectacles. Did you know I wore dentures, by the way?'

'Mm.'

Delphine put down the palm leaf. She loosened Mr Dugdale's shirt collar and lightly dabbed his neck with cologne. He grunted with pleasure and took hold of her wrist lightly.

Lovely, lovely handsome old man. Oh, if only she were his new bride and he took her home to his estate in the country. And he would show her the new-born red-mottled calf and he would cry out, 'In two years' time I shall have two Dutch cows in my herd.' And night after night they would sit in the little drawing room drinking tea, and he would read and she would gaze out of the window at the snow, happy and secure. And she would say to the priest: 'Mr Dugdale reared this black and white Dutch calf like a baby.' And the priest would say: 'How can you be interested in these things?' And she would say: 'All that interests my husband interests me.'

Major Pickavance drank two more tumblers of cherry brandy. Then he rose to his feet, swaying and stumbling towards the door. Once there he paused and breathed in deeply and rapidly. Then he turned to them and said: 'Yes, old boy. I feel it in my bones. There's a rich widow woman just waiting to fall into Skomer's grasp. Oh yes. Yes indeed.'

He was right.

And he did not have too long to wait to meet the object of his dreams and desires.

She was the owner of the most fashionable brothel in Port Cedric.

29

The circumstances of the encounter were thus:

After Major Pickavance's confession to Mr Dugdale the days dragged on even more sluggishly.

Dolly would not budge from her room. Celia was beside herself. She pleaded. She cursed. She shouted.

Dolly would not open the door to her bedroom. She would not speak. The black owl with the blood-red eyes clung tightly to her shoulder and gloated.

'Still difficulties in the interior,' said Colonel Ryder. 'Sorry to be such a harbinger of gloom. That seems to be my mission in life. That and boring the pants off people. I think lampshades can be a faintly fascinating topic of conversation, don't you?'

Next morning Celia fell ill with fever and was rushed to hospital.

'Piano stools,' said Mr Dugdale when he heard the news.

When Major Pickavance heard the news, he merely sighed and said: 'Who cares? I have far more important matters to attend to.'

But in truth the confidence that had engulfed him when he first set foot on the island was being steadily eroded. Tiny cracks appeared in the dyke. The binding grasses shifted and withered. Small, malignant rodents burrowed and the water began to seep and hope grew sodden.

Every morning he would borrow the Sikh major-domo's bicycle and ride down the long, lazy road into town. It was a mean little town of shanties and shacks and fly-blown stray dogs. It had been completely destroyed in the eruption of 1903. It had been rebuilt in a style of sullen indifference.

The Negroes lived in clustered hovels. There was a corrugated iron Anglican cathedral and a huge low-slung, lopsided abattoir where ricket-boned cattle snorted into the dust of their panic. There were grog bars and splintered kiosks and the shops were clapboarded with the balconies jutting out over the warped duckboards of the sidewalk.

There was an English Club in a straggled garden where the commercial element drank pink gin and played cards in the evening and the planters down from the interior caroused mordantly. On the dock front there was a white stone custom house with rakish windows. There were three taverns reeking of rum and stale phlegm. Bugles sounded in the barracks and the native levies squatted outside its walls, chewing aromatic leaves and picking thorns out of their bare feet.

Major Pickavance had his routine.

He would prop his bicycle outside the Congleton Coffee Shop and inside its dark and snickering interior would drink two small cups of strong Turkish coffee with its proprietor, a stout Palestinian who had spent most of his formative years in Bogotá.

'The things I could tell you about that,' he would say. 'Oh, the things I could tell you.'

But he never did.

Next Major Pickavance would buy a packet of cheroots from the kiosk outside The Surinam Steam Laundry Company before cycling to the officers' mess in the barracks to partake of whisky and sesame buns with the duty officer.

That mission accomplished he would ride his bicycle to the English Club where he would lunch, gossip, read the newspapers and magazines and listen to the wireless.

Each morning he would set out full of hope that he would meet the object of his concupiscence. Once he saw a stout matron walking an arthritic Pekinese down the duckboarded sidewalk of the main street. His heart had turned over and missed a beat. She radiated widowhood. She was on heat with wealth. But on enquiries at the club he discovered that the lady was the wife of the director of the Methodist Mission for Sick Pack Animals and an enthusiastic ballroom dancer to boot.

Devastation. Wretchedness.

For days there was not a hint of the quarry of his lusts.

And then one afternoon he pushed his bicycle wearily up the hill to the Governor's residence. He was tired. He was feeling low. The news on the wireless had not been encouraging. The boiled mutton at the club had tasted of raw inner tubes. The kiosk had run out of his special cheroots and he had been compelled to purchase snipey-lunged Bulgarian cigarettes in their stead.

He was exhausted and dripping with perspiration when at last he returned the bicycle to the Sikh.

'Thank you so much, old thing,' said the Sikh. 'I trust you had an absolutely spiffing time.'

Major Pickavance shook his head.

'Oh dear,' said the Sikh. 'Do tell.'

Major Pickavance told him of his misfortunes of the day. When he had finished, the major-domo clucked his tongue sympathetically and patted him on his arm.

'I have the very palliative for your woes,' he said. 'A night out in Port Cedric.'

'What?' said Major Pickavance.

'Highly illegal, of course. But there are always ways and means.'

The Sikh smiled and patted Major Pickavance on the arm once more.

'A night of wild and wicked pleasures in the land of Rimbaud and Verlaine. How does that tickle your fancy?'

'Will they be there?' said Major Pickavance.

'Who?'

'Those two frogs, Rimbaud and whatshisname?'

The Sikh rocked with laughter.

'Good one, old chap. Absolutely top-hole,' he said. Then he frowned, looked over his shoulder three times and said: 'I'll pick you up at eight. Be ready.'

Major Pickavance hesitated. He licked his lips nervously. Then he said: 'May I bring a chum?'

'Is he one of us?'

'Yes.'

'You may bring him.'

Major Pickavance went straight to Burnaby's room and said: 'Now then, Burnaby, how do you fancy a night of wild and wicked dissipation?'

'No thanks,' said Burnaby. 'I'm having an early night with my psoriasis.'

'God blast you, sir,' roared Major Pickavance. 'I'm your Geography master. You'll do as you're bloody well told.'

'Beat it,' said Burnaby, and Major Pickavance closed the door hurriedly and scurried to prepare himself for the evening ahead.

30

They met at eight.

They drove through the throbbing, fire-flickered night along the island's only metalled road. They twisted and teetered through plantations. They rattled through chomping fords. They were waved through roadblocks by sprawling native troops dressed in navy-blue jerseys and baggy khaki shorts. Night birds screeched. Once far far away they heard bagpipes.

When they reached the frontier, they were greeted by a British army officer who saluted the Sikh and directed the car to be parked under cover in a layby crackling with crickets.

There was soft talk and muffled laughter and the clink of bottles and then the Sikh beckoned Major Pickavance and they walked quickly across the dark patch of no-man's-land to the French frontier post. Three legionnaires were sitting in the concrete guard room drinking wine and playing cards with a flop-gutted unshaven man of Middle Eastern appearance. They did not look up.

There was a large, sleek-flanked black Citroën waiting for them. The chauffeur settled them in the back seat. His cheeks were perfumed and he wore a necklace of shark's teeth and amber. He drove off with a roar and the tyres squealed as he swung the car round the dizzy hairpins that led down to Port Cedric.

The whole town was ablaze with light. Fairy light. Torchlight. Floodlight. The hiss of hurricane lamp. The flare of brazier. The twirling, spitting flames of rush torch. The music. The laughter. The colours. Gold. Scarlet. Light blue. Lime green. Terracotta. The pantiles. The bell towers. Soldiers arm in arm with black girls swaying their hips and swinging their bottoms. Swifts screeching. The raffish destroyer in the harbour with the snarl-bowed gunboats. Pompoms of sailors. Kepis of legionnaires. The slop and slap of sandals. Wood smoke. Cigar smoke. Rough-throated cigarette smoke. Sizzling meat. Spitting skewers. The drunk splayed in the gutter. The limping cat with the broken tail.

'*La belle France!*' said the Sikh. 'Pretty spiffing, eh?'

They drank absinthe and sharp, cold Alsatian beer in a dockside bar. They drank vermouth and cassis in a pavement café in the cathedral square. They ate curried goat and drank vintage claret in a backstreet restaurant served by an octoroon girl with one brown eye and one green eye.

They spent an hour in a Turkish bath where they drank more absinthe whilst being shaved and massaged by an Armenian albino.

They ate plump prawns in a Chinese bar and drank rice wine.

Then the Sikh took out his monocle, wiped it carefully on a lilac-and-carmine-coloured silk handkerchief, and said: 'Now then, my dear old thing, time for the *pièce de résistance*.'

'And what is that?' said Major Pickavance.

'A visit to Monsieur Willy's.'

'And what precisely is that?'

'My dear fellow,' said the Sikh. 'It is a house of pleasure, of course.'

'I see,' said Major Pickavance. 'Do you think I should change my socks?'

The Sikh laughed. He took Major Pickavance firmly by the arm and led him down a cool, twisting alley. They came to a high stone wall. Set in it was a low brass-studded wooden door. Over it hung a flickering lantern. The Sikh pushed open the door and led Major Pickavance inside.

There were lawns vivid green and strutted with peacocks. Small, gaudy parakeets flashed through the well-groomed bushes. The gravel paths were cool. There was a fronded pond croaking with frogs. At tables sitting under parasols were women dressed in flimsy white shifts. Some were deep in earnest conversation with men. Some were laughing with men. Some were sitting on men's knees, stroking their chins or fondling their hair. Some sat alone as the Sikh and Major Pickavance passed.

'I have a fancy for Baluchis this evening,' said the Sikh. 'What about you?'

Major Pickavance coughed nervously and licked his dry lips.

'We'll see,' he said. 'We'll see.'

They entered the house through french doors open wide to the balm of the tropic night.

A footman in white breeches and powdered wig bowed low to them and led them into an anteroom. He motioned for them to be seated, bowed again and shut the door softly.

'Madame will be here shortly,' said the Sikh. 'We shall let her choose for you this first time.'

Major Pickavance tugged at the cuffs of his jacket. He coughed. He licked his lips. He crossed his legs. Then he uncrossed them and drummed his fingertips on his kneecaps.

The Sikh smiled warmly.

The room was quite bare save for two armchairs and a small writing desk and its grim, harsh-backed chair.

'Madame believes in providing the sumptuousness elsewhere,' said the Sikh.

'Ah,' said Major Pickavance, 'Splendid.'

He crossed his legs once more, tugged at his collar and dabbed rapidly at his brow with his handkerchief.

The Sikh smiled slowly.

And then Madame entered and of an instant Major Pickavance knew that his quest was at an end.

He had found her.

At long long last he had found her.

31

That night a wild-eyed man in ragged stinking clothing climbed over the wall into the Governor's residence.

He was shivering with fever. His legs were covered in festering sores. His hair was lank and matted. His ribs stuck out through the rents and tatters of his rotting shirt.

He looked around him desperately.

He was terrified.

He wanted to run away.

He could not. He had to find her. Only she could save him.

He steeled himself and crept cautiously through the shrubbery. The house was in darkness save for a light in an attic window. He looked around him and bounded up the stone steps that led to the terrace. The effort exhausted him, drained him and forced him to slump to the ground. He gasped for air and then he began to cough. It was a dry rasping cough and he spluttered and choked as he tried to suppress it. After a while he hauled himself to his feet.

Where was she?

Which room was hers?

Had he the strength to climb up the clinging sprawling creeper to slip through that open window?

Had he the courage?

His body was racked by coughs once more. This time he could not suppress them. His whole body was convulsed.

Someone opened a window and shouted: 'Who's there?'

He recognised the voice.

He cringed into the shadows.

The window was slammed shut.

His coughing stopped.

He tried to stand up. He couldn't. He sobbed. He moaned. He groaned. He strained. He heaved. But he could not stand up.

When she found him on the terrace next morning, Natasha fainted on the spot.

It was Roger Carey.

'She's the most delightful woman, Mr Dugdale. Wonderful. Stunning. Stupendous. Good-looking? My word, yes. Sumptuous? I should say so. Fine-boned. Statuesque. Well-endowed in the upstairs department. Striking nose. Curved like a scimitar.

'What a woman, old boy. Urbane, witty, cultivated. A lover of fine wine and classical music. A gourmet and a connoisseur of the very highest taste and refinement.

'And, my dear fellow, she's a widow. And she is exceedingly wealthy. And we are in love. My dear Dugdale, we are in love.

'We are in love, in love, in love.'

She had managed to get him into her bedroom unseen.

She had cut off his fetid clothes. She had bathed him. She had cleaned the sores on his legs and soothed the bruises on his cheeks. She had massaged his limbs and cut and tidied the tangle of his hair.

He lay on her bed sleeping.

Once he opened his eyes wildly and struggled to raise himself.

Gently she pressed him back onto the bed. She rested her head on his shoulder and whispered: 'I love you. Now at last I love you.'

Delphine could not declare her love for Mr Dugdale. She was too timid. She did not wish to be repulsed. She did not wish to be mocked.

Oh, the heat.

If only it were cold, she would wrap him in a sheepskin coat and they would ride side by side in the back of the carpet-lined sledge with traces jangling and the tasselled, plaited horses prancing and the one-eyed coachman curling and snapping his whip.

Oh, the heat.

It was like lying in the mouth of a panting dog.

He told her his story.

He had jumped from SS *Drayman* as she was casting off.

The policeman had chased him along the quay. He had lost him in the skitter-skat of dockside alleys.

He had no money. He had only the clothes he stood up in. He had begged for food and water. He had been beaten and locked in a shed. He had heard Major Pickavance in an adjoining room talking softly with the flop-gutted Palestinian. He had been beaten again and manacled to the wall. At first he would not talk, but they had brandished pliers at his teeth and fingernails, and he gave in instantly. He told them his identity. He told them of SS *Drayman* and the voyage from Cardiff. He told them of his deceptions and his misdemeanours. He told them of Dolly and the school and Mamselle and the gangster and Lance Egerton with his throat split from ear to ear.

He heard Major Pickavance talking to the Palestinian once more. Ransom. Share of spoils. No police. No deal. In that case he dies. Not to worry, old boy, I shan't let on. I shan't tell a soul. Good, my friend. Very good, my little major.

They came to his shed. He was petrified. They unlocked his manacles. They dragged him out of the shed. A van was waiting at the end of the alley. A large Negro stood watching him, legs apart, swaying softly on the balls of his feet and grinning.

There was only one thing to do.

He bit the Palestinian hard on the flab of his neck. His teeth sank into the flesh and blood fountained and spurted.

The obese Levantine screamed and writhed and threw himself on the ground, rolling and convulsing his body and shrieking at the top of his voice.

The giant black man bent down to help his master. Instantly he wriggled free of his tormentor. He ran down the alley. He ran and he ran and he ran. He ran up the hill until he reached the Governor's residence.

'I love you, Roger,' said Natasha. 'I love you.'

'I should very much like you to meet the object of my affections, Dugdale.'

'Mm.'

'You see, Dugdale, I look on you as an old and cherished chum. And I think it only right that you should share in my joy and happiness.'

'Mm.'

'I shall discuss the matter with Claudette next time we meet. I am pretty certain she will be gracious enough to grant you an audience. She might even offer you one or two small favours if you like that sort of thing. Oh, Dugdale, what a woman. A paragon of all the virtues. Such elegance. Such gentility. Such voluptuous beauty.'

'Pumice stones.'

'I beg your pardon?'

'Sorry,' said Mr Dugdale. 'I didn't mean to say that.'

*   *   *

On the morning of her return from hospital, Celia beat her fists on the bedroom door. She hammered with her shoes.

'Open up! For Christ's sake, open this bloody door.'

Dolly lay rigid in her bed.

Her eyes were wide open. So was her mouth. She did not move. She could not move.

The orange ball. The crashing metal scalding the water. The ice-blue eyes. The houseboat with the bent stove chimney. The pug dog yawning in the sunshine.

The black owl preened itself contentedly.

'I feel poorly again.'

'So do I.'

'I feel dreadful.'

'So do I.'

'I can't stop shitting.'

Polly, Louise and Jassy were readmitted to hospital.

The following day Margot died and they had a funeral.

'A pleasant girl,' said Mamselle. 'She would have made someone a marvellous drudge.'

'At times like this it is fearfully difficult to know what to say,' said Colonel Ryder. 'If anyone's in need of a spare coat hanger do get in touch. Isn't it curious the way canaries can stand on one leg?'

Samira smiled to herself and wondered what it would be like to be Margot now.

'Right then. That's it,' said Celia to Mamselle. 'Something has to be done.'

She summoned the Sikh major-domo. She ordered him to equip himself with sledgehammer and marlin spike and accompany her to Dolly's bedroom.

'Are you coming out, you old hag?' she cried.

No response.

She nodded to the Sikh. He beamed with delight and smashed down the door with his hammer.

Celia marched into the bedroom.

'Right,' she said. 'Just you listen to me, you old faggot.'

But Dolly was not there.

The room was empty.

32

They organised search parties.

Armed infantrymen combed the back streets and alleys of Johnstown. The native levies scoured the countryside and the deserted beaches and the secret coves.

There was no trace of Dolly.

'Somehow I find it difficult to work up any enthusiasm for the task,' said Colonel Ryder. 'I seem to be trapped in a chronic torpor of mind and body.'

It was a mood recognised by all the other inmates of the Governor's residence.

'Do something,' screamed Celia. 'Get off your backsides and do something positive.'

She was amazed at her daring. She was amazed at her boldness. Never before in the whole of her life had she asserted herself. She wanted to be sick. She felt faint. Red veils of mist swirled in front of her eyes.

'Well?' she bellowed. 'Have you nothing to say?'

Mr Dugdale smiled.

He took hold of Delphine's hand and stroked it.

Delphine smiled.

Celia howled and beat her fists on the table.

Darkness fell and still there was no sign of Dolly.

As they lay entwined together in bed Roger Carey said to Natasha: 'I think I know where she might be.'

'Do you, my darling?'

'Yes.'

He told her. She told Celia. An hour later the corporal and his three private soldiers found her. She was bedraggled. She was silent. Not so the Palestinian. He screamed with pain when the corporal hammered him in the belly with the butt of his rifle. He sank to the floor writhing and convulsing his limbs. Idly the private soldiers kicked him in the ribs from time to time.

They brought Dolly back to the Governor's residence.

'Ah, Mrs Bradman,' said Colonel Ryder. 'I was just telling your niece here about the many and varied uses of alum.'

The Sikh major-domo was not at home to welcome Dolly.

He was on his way to Port Cedric in the company of Major Pickavance and Mr Dugdale.

For the first time since he had arrived on the island Mr Dugdale felt free of languor and lethargy.

'Erections,' he said.

'What?' said Major Pickavance. 'What's that you say?'

Mr Dugdale smiled. Curious how unworried he was by his growing propensity for involuntary speech. How odd that he didn't care.

Was it a sign of old age? Was it a sign of madness?

Old age no longer frightened him. It had when he was a youth. It had when he was in his prime. It had when he started on the voyage to St David's. But now? All those bucking girls. All those wilful girls. The scrapes. The disgraces. The crises and the disasters. So? So what?

A lovely child. So dumpy. So dowdy. So easy to please. So loving. But so young. So tirelessly, relentlessly young.

He fingered the old Nansen passport he always carried in the inside pocket of his jacket. How proud his mother had been when he showed it to her for the first time. He had left the city that very night in the rusty whaler.

'Shortarse,' he said as the Sikh opened the low brass-studded door in the high stone wall.

'What's that?' snapped Major Pickavance. 'What's that you say?'

The footman bowed low. He conducted them to the anteroom. He bowed once more and closed the door softly.

Major Pickavance could not sit still. He paced the room. He hopped from foot to foot. He scratched his ankles.

'Wait till you see her,' he said. 'Oh, Dugdale, Dugdale, just you wait.'

And at that moment Madame entered the room.

There were smudges of talcum powder on her moustache.

Dolly lay on her bed.

'Right then,' said Celia. 'Tell me what happened.'

For a while Dolly did not answer. She stared into space and slucked together the palms of her hands.

Then she said in a soft voice, 'I was looking for him.'

'Who?'

Dolly said nothing. She rolled a coil of her damp hair between her fingers. She chewed at her lower lip.

Then she turned to Celia and said: 'You know – Him.'

She burst into tears. They spattered down her cheeks. The sobs plundered her body. They soared.

'Right,' said Celia. 'Right, you old bitch. It's time for some good solid home truths.'

'Well, Dugdale, what do you think?' said Major Pickavance, hugging himself and cackling with delight.

Mr Dugdale turned his eyes away from his minute colleague and allowed them to rest on Madame.

She was a large woman. Everything about her was large. Her feet. Her nose. The lobes of her ears. Her molars.

She was a portly woman. Her bosoms sagged down to her waist and rested like slumbering walruses on the folds of her belly. The buttresses of her thighs bulged in the straining silk of her pantaloons. The black velvet choker grappled with the flubbers of her chins.

The mottled podge of her fingers sparkled with diamond and ruby, emerald and Elastoplast.

She wore a ginger wig. She had a black beauty spot painted on her left cheek. Her false eyelashes were clogged with grease. Her lips were gashed vivid and gaping with purple lipstick. She had a smoker's cough.

'Quite a find, my dear Major,' said Mr Dugdale.

'Isn't she?' said Major Pickavance.

They drank white rum and nibbled at Bath Oliver biscuits. Major Pickavance sat on Madame's knee and she tickled his ear.

He was beside himself with glee. He could not stop giggling. He could not stop grinning and winking at Mr Dugdale.

The Sikh returned from his assignation with a girl from Martinique. Her name was Antoinette and he expressed his satisfaction with the liberality of her favours.

'Absolutely top-notch,' he said.

Then he turned to Madame and said: 'Well, my dear good lady. 'Tis time for us to depart, I fear.'

Major Pickavance slipped off Madame's knee.

'A real joy, my dear,' he said. 'Total delight. Sheer ecstasy. Perfection in every quarter. See you next week.'

'Oh no,' said Madame. 'Oh no.'

She rang a small silver bell attached to her waist by a leather thong. Instantly the door burst open and two footmen appeared. Madame spoke to them rapidly in a language that seemed to owe more to faulty digestive processes than etymology. They nodded, took hold of Major Pickavance and threw him to the floor.

Madame stood over him.

'You no go. You no never go. You stay here. You my slave. You my slave for ever.'

And with that she stamped her foot on the back of his neck.

'Oh, I say, Dugdale, I say,' cried Major Pickavance. 'Aren't I the luckiest chap in the whole wide world?'

33

'You will listen to me,' shouted Celia. 'You will. You will. Do you understand me? Do I make myself clear?'

Dolly groaned.

'There's no use groaning like that. There's no use sighing and going all weepy. There's no use storming into a tantrum and throwing things and slamming doors. I'm immune to your threats. I'm immune to your bullying. Has that sunk in? Has it? Has it?'

She was amazed. What had come over her? Shy, timid, nervous Celia. Who was this person raising her voice and stamping her feet and taking command? She felt dizzy with her elation.

Dolly turned away from her. Immediately Celia sprang forward and yanked her round roughly to face her.

'You will look at me while I'm talking to you,' she said. 'Is that understood? Is it? Is it?'

Dolly nodded.

'We're in a mess. We're in a total shambles. Perdita's dead. Margot's dead. Samira and the little girls are delirious. The Doucemain twins are hanging on by the skin of their teeth and Burnaby's shirt fronts are as stiff as draining boards. And what do you do? Nothing. You do sweet bugger all.

'And what about the fit ones here? We're all sunk in gloom and despair and total lethargy. Everyone's sitting round doing nothing and moping. There's no energy. There's no guts and gumption. And it's all your fault. You dragged us into this shambles and now you throw up your hands and say you can't cope. Well, you've bloody well got to cope. Don't leave it to me. Shift yourself. Do something positive.'

The blood pumped through her veins. Her cheeks were flushed. Oh, if only he could see her now. That poor doctor. Such a handsome young man. Such a dreadful waste of life. Such a –

She bellowed at the top of her voice: 'Do something positive.'

Dolly groaned again.

'I can't help it,' she said. 'It's the black owl.'

'Bollocks to the owl,' Celia cried. 'That's just an excuse. It always has been. "Don't blame me," you say. "It's the world. I can't help it being against me all the time." Bollocks! You're not the only person who gets wet feet when you walk on damp grass. You're not the only person who gets pestered by wasps when you eat out of doors. The world hasn't singled you out as a target for all its spite. There's no great conspiracy against you. So your great one true lover has just been killed. I'm sorry. I really am. But other people lose their loved ones, you know. Other people have happiness dashed from their grasp. I know that. Boy oh boy, do I know.'

The great ball of orange. The explosion. Its roar. Its shatter. The salt-sea sting of death.

Dolly turned away again. Once more Celia pulled her back to face her.

'You make me sick. You make me throw up. One minute you're all for something. Next minute you're against it. No half-measures with you. No warning. One minute happiness. Next minute desolation. One second warm and loving. Next second cruel and vicious. "It's my black owl," you whinge. "I can't help it. Blame it on my black owl." Bollocks! I blame everything on you. Absolutely everything. And above all, I blame Me on You.'

Dolly said nothing.

The gecko gulped.

A spindly shouldered spider strutted slowly across the floor.

Then Dolly rose slowly from her bed.

She smiled at Celia.

She nodded slowly.

She smiled again.

And then suddenly without warning she flew at her and grabbed her by the throat.

She shook her till her teeth rattled and her face turned scarlet. She rammed her against the wall and beat her head and shoulders with her fists. Celia slumped to the floor.

Dolly looked down at her.

'How dare you talk to me like that,' she roared. 'You ungrateful bitch. You pathetic snivelly little coward. Do something, you say. Do something. Right then I shall do something. Beware! Oh beware!'

She kicked Celia in the ribs.

And somehow her niece felt deeply comforted.

She felt comforted and secure.
Dolly was going to do something.
How lovely.

34

And Dolly did indeed do something.

She threw Celia headlong out of her bedroom and slammed the door so violently that great darts of plaster fell from the landing ceiling and skittered down the stairs, clunking and clanking and terrifying the Sikh's wall-eyed Boston terrier.

Half an hour later she appeared at the top of the stairs in all her finery. The flowing jet-black velvet gown. The rippling feather boa. The cascading earrings. The spuming fountains of her hair. The peaks and canyons of her bosoms.

She summoned a staff meeting.

'Right,' she said. 'I have been accused by a certain member of staff of neglecting my duties. I have been accused of letting matters get out of hand. I have been accused, by this pap-gutted, spatter-tongued creature of . . .'

Celia stood up and attempted to leave.

'Silence! Stay where you are, Judas!' thundered Dolly.

Wonderful woman, thought Mr Dugdale. A Kanchenjunga of a woman. A Great Rift of a woman. How he would have adored to roam her teeming savannahs and scale the buttresses of her summits and curl up in her base camp crooned by the burr of sated bee and the swoosh and sweep of lammergeyer. But that was long long ago in the days of his prime.

'Tits,' he said.

'I beg your pardon?' said Dolly.

Mr Dugdale put his hand in front of his mouth and snickered softly.

Dolly glared at him silently for a moment. Then she glared at each member of staff in turn.

Mrs Otto slumbered peacefully, chin lolling on her *Speisewagen*, her legs wide apart, woollen stockings wrinkled at the ankles and thigh tops.

Dolly directed her gaze to her neighbour.

'Mamselle!' she snapped.

'*Oui?*'

'You have let yourself go. Wash your hair. Paint your face. Perfume your orifices.'

She turned to Celia.

'And as for you.'

Celia lowered her head and her lips began to tremble.

Dolly smoothed the jet-black velvet over the curve of her belly and the flood of her thighs and placed her hands on her hips.

'There is far too much slackness in the camp,' she said. 'Things have gone to the dogs. But no longer, my friends. No longer. It is time for action.'

She was as good as her word. She swept out of the meeting, summoned the Governor's Lagonda, drove out of town and stormed into the hospital.

'Right,' she bellowed. 'Where do I find the shits?'

An orderly directed her to the ward which contained Samira, the Doucemain twins and the little girls.

'Right, you lot. On your feet,' she commanded.

'Madame, I beg you. Please not to disturb them,' said the doctor, clutching at her sleeve. 'They are very sick children. They are in danger of their lives.'

'Nonsense,' said Dolly. 'Are you a wop?'

The doctor drew himself up and said: 'Madame, I am from Malta.'

'Same thing,' said Dolly. 'A dago.'

She ushered her pupils out of the hospital and into the Lagonda. Once back in the residence she inspected the little girls. They cowered in their dormitory, pinch-cheeked and faint with fear and fatigue.

'Poor little shits,' said Dolly. 'On your feet. On your feet this instant. There's work to be done.'

The girls scampered out of their beds and when Dolly had gone, Polly said to Louise: 'You know, I'm feeling much better.'

'So am I. Frightfully better.'

Dolly ordered Natasha and Delphine into her presence. She stared at them through narrowed eyes.

She said to Natasha: 'You've been at it, haven't you?'

And to Delphine she said: 'And you'd like to be at it.'

Both girls nodded.

Dolly beamed broadly.

'Good,' she said. 'Keep it up.'

They smiled.

'I have invited you here because I wish to disclose to you the plans I have for our school,' she said. 'And why you? Because unlike most of our acquaintances in this establishment you are not old and enfeebled.'

Delphine was about to protest, but Natasha kicked her on the ankle and she thought better of it.

Dolly continued: 'The two of you are young, sound of health, keen of kind, willing of spirit and loyal of temperament. You will assist me in my enterprises.

'Number one on the agenda: When we reach Marchmain's Rest I intend to form netball and lacrosse teams for the girls and construct a real tennis court for the boys.

'Number two, we shall organise a *bal masqué*.

'Number three, we shall have a festival of one-act drama with prizes for the best original work written by a person under the age of thirty-three.

'We shall hold eisteddfods and exhibitions of watercolours.

'We shall hold night classes for the natives on the subjects of stamp-collecting, chutney-making and planned parenthood.

'That is all. You may ponder on these matters and give me the results of your deliberations when we are established in our new quarters.'

The girls padded softly out of the room.

'Gosh,' said Natasha.

'Crumbs,' said Delphine.

Samira smiled to herself when Delphine told her of the meeting. The jungle. Now that would be a most fulfilling place in which to die. The love song of the gibbon. The crucified goat. The wild figs. The toucan's rattle. How lovely to be ripped to shreds by a tiger's claws.

They heard Dolly bustling along the corridor.

They heard her throw open the door of Burnaby's room.

They heard her shout: 'If you don't stop doing that, it'll turn into a parsnip.'

'I think it already has,' said Burnaby glumly.

Half an hour later Colonel Ryder arrived to make his daily courtesy visit. Dolly told him of her plans. They were to set off for Marchmain's Rest at the end of the week. She would need pack mules, field kitchens, armed outriders, mechanised tracked transport, guides, scouts and auxiliary nurses.

'But, my dear lady, it is quite impossible,' said the Colonel.

'Why?'

'Difficulties in the interior.'

'What difficulties?'

'Pestilence. Famine. Drought. Insurgents. Bandits. Revolutionaries. Religious fanatics. Anarcho-syndicalists. Rape, arson, pillage. Things like that.'

'That is no problem, Colonel,' said Dolly. 'I have on my establishment a military man specially trained to deal with matters of that sort. Major Pickavance is his name. He's a bit of a shortarse, but then so was Napoleon, was he not?'

Colonel Ryder sighed.

How boring life was. All the things he could have been doing, if war had not intervened and he had been posted to this godforsaken island. He could have been opening an agricultural show. He could have been addressing his dining club on the subject of keyrings. He could have entertained an admiral's widow to tea at his cousin's in Torquay.

He sighed again.

'Very well then, Colonel,' said Dolly. 'It is all settled. I shall expect you and your men here on Friday morning at six hundred hours sharp. And now I shall not detain you any longer. I am sure you have heaps of people to bore the living daylights out of.'

'Rather,' said Colonel Ryder brightly.

Later that night Dolly plodded wearily to her bedroom. Celia helped her undress. She bathed her feet. She tied the ribbons of her nightgown. She brushed her hair. She poured out whisky.

'Well?' said Dolly.

'Wonderful,' said Celia. 'You were wonderful.'

Dolly smiled and sank back into the pillow.

'By God,' she said, 'I could do with a man.'

35

The mule driver said to his mate: 'I once saw a snail as big as a man's head.'

'Did you?'

'Yes.'

It was hot.

The mules scowled. They twitched at the oozing flies. They gnawed at their halters.

'We ate it.'

'Ate what?'

'The snail.'

'Ah.'

It was Friday morning.

They were preparing to set off for Marchmain's Rest.

Roger Carey stood on a chair and looked out of the attic window. He saw two ancient armoured cars and a Bren gun carrier. There were four trucks with canvas tops and a single-decker Bedford bus in the blotched and faded livery of the North Western Road Car Company. Its destination board read: *Macclesfield via Pott Shrigley.*

There were flat lorries, handcarts, dogcarts and native levies with their women and children. There was a horse-drawn cart especially fitted out for the camp followers.

There were mules and motorcycles. A chain of shirt-sleeved, perspiring, swearing soldiers was loading boxes, cartons, trunks, chests, canvas bags, desks, chairs, lavatory seats, kitchen utensils, hat stands, blackboards, easels, rolled-up wall maps, fire buckets, stirrup pumps and hurricane lamps (among other things) onto the lorries.

'They're bound to have forgotten summat,' said one of the soldiers.

'Certain,' said his mate. 'Bastards!'

Colonel Ryder sat in the front seat of the open-topped staff car smoking a bulldog pipe and wishing he were in Paignton.

In the midst of the confusion stood Dolly.

She was wearing riding boots, voluminous white canvas culottes, a Harris tweed hacking jacket and a wide-brimmed hat festooned with a bee-keeper's protective veil.

She was checking off items from a large list held by Celia.

She whacked woolly heads with her riding whip and humped pink Caucasian backsides with the toe of her boot.

She shouted. She barked.

Roger Carey turned away from the window. He jumped down from the chair.

'I know what you're going to do,' he said.

'What?' said Natasha.

'You're going to leave me.'

'Don't be silly, Roger.'

'I'm not being silly. You're going to leave me. And they'll find me and throw me into jail and I'll get diseased and I'll starve and they'll beat me and thrash me and . . .'

Natasha took hold of him round the waist and kissed him under his chin.

'Don't be so silly,' she said. 'It's all been arranged.'

She took hold of his hand and led him carefully down the back stairs of the servants' quarters. They stepped out into a yard frisking with sunlight and clucking with beady-beaked chickens. Standing in the centre was a large snouty lorry, its vast load covered by tarpaulins, its chassis squatting forlornly under the great weight.

'Dolly's wardrobe,' said Natasha. 'I've had a word with the driver. Everything's fixed.'

The driver, an extremely minute Hindu with timid teeth, smiled at them and pulled back a length of tarpaulin.

'In you go,' said Natasha. 'There's plenty of whisky and water for you. I'll come and see you at the first stop.'

She kissed him again.

'I love you,' she said.

'I love you, too,' he said, and he climbed aboard the lorry.

It coughed, spluttered, golloped and grated, and then in slow and grudging fashion lumbered out of the yard to join its fellows in the convoy now finally settled in front of the Governor's residence.

'All set then?' said Dolly.

'Yes, Dolly,' said Celia.

'The shits are safely aboard?'

'Yes, Dolly.'

'What about Major Pickavance? I haven't seen him all morning. Come to that, I haven't seen him all week. Where the devil's he got to?'

'I don't know, Dolly.'

Dolly strode purposefully to the Bedford single-decker which contained her staff and pupils and said: 'We're missing a body. Anyone seen Major Shortarse?'

Mr Dugdale told her in great detail all he knew about the minuscule military gent's disappearance.

'Good grief,' said Dolly. 'She'll kill him.'

'I rather think that's what he's hoping,' said Mr Dugdale.

Samira smiled to herself. What fun to die in a frenzy of lust, she thought to herself. Even nicer than being disembowelled by an infantryman's bayonet.

Dolly and Celia dismounted the bus.

'Well, that's a devil, isn't it?' said Celia. 'One teacher short. What are we going to do now?'

'This,' said Dolly. 'Follow me.'

She pounded her way to the lorry bearing her personal effects and ripped back the tarpaulin to reveal Roger Carey nuzzling a half-full bottle of whisky.

'Oh Lor'!' he said.

Dolly sneered back her upper lip. She tapped her thigh with her riding crop. She growled. Then she said: 'Young man, I have something to say to you.'

'What?' said Roger Carey nervously.

'What is the capital of Ecuador?'

'Quito.'

'Are you certain?'

'Yes.'

'In that case, my dear sir, consider yourself appointed our new Geography master.'

Dolly nodded to Celia, who replaced the tarpaulin. As she was doing so she smiled at Roger Carey and whispered, 'Jolly good. I'm glad you're coming. I rather like you. I think we might become good friends.'

On their way back to the open-topped staff car she said to Dolly, 'How did you hear he was there?'

'The driver told me, of course. He told me as soon as Natasha organised it. Charming little chappie. He's a great chum of my Palestinian at the Congleton Tea Rooms.'

They climbed into the staff car.

Colonel Ryder raised his arm wearily and the convoy set off on its journey into the interior.

For the first mile the streets were lined by natives who spat at them and threw blunt nails and dried dog turds.

It took them five hours to cover the first four miles along the island's only metalled road. The scouts running barefoot in front of the convoy insisted on stopping every few yards to consult and sniff animal droppings, to prostrate themselves in front of wayside shrines draped with headless lizards and poisonous gourds and to bathe their feet in buckets of water brought from the rear of the column by their womenfolk.

'We ought to shoot the buggers,' said Dolly.

Colonel Ryder sighed deeply. What would he be doing now if he were back home in England? Eating calf's-foot jelly and junket with the Admiral's widow in a sea-front hotel in Poole? Buying a carpet in Leamington Spa? Changing the ferrule on his walking stick?

The heat thwacked down on the single-decker bus. It laboured and it wheezed. It was far from home. Far from gritstone peaks and the ancient packhorse tracks bringing salt from the plains. Far from dry-stone walls and dove and dale and dipper. It blew hard and panted.

In the stifling heat of its interior Mr Dugdale thought of cloudberries, and ptarmigan hung by their necks outside a timbered shop by a sliver of the sea.

At one thirty the scouts stopped once more. They stood in a group waiting patiently and silently. A stout sergeant with a fiery shaving rash huffed and puffed with them. He opened his leather satchel and there was the clink of money.

And then the scouts turned and in a neat and orderly formation loped off steadily in the direction of town.

'Where are they going?' said Dolly.

'Home,' said Colonel Ryder.

'Why?'

'Because we're turning off the beaten track now. They only know their way on the main road.'

The convoy plunged into the jungle.

The track twisted and stumbled.

Squeak of breaking springs. Crack of axle. Mule scream. Branch twang and whip. Curses. Cries of pain. Roar of exhaust. Whine of gears. The insects bit and buzzed and cracked against the windscreen, their blood oozing on the glass like squashed damsons.

'We have to stop,' said Dolly.

'No,' said Colonel Ryder. 'No. We must make base before nightfall. Difficulties in the interior, you see.'

They groaned and they creaked and they heaved and they hauled.

They passed a deserted sugar mill and a great cloud of bats flew out and darkened the sky above them.

In the distance they heard the throb of drums and once or twice through a gap in the jungle they caught a glimpse of the sparkle of the sea.

Then they came to an old cobbled track. After a while it widened out. And just as dusk prepared to drop her skirts they reached Marchmain's Rest.

They staggered out of the vehicles, stiff-limbed, cramped, sticky, filthy, thirsty, totally exhausted.

No one spoke.

The gardens rustled and rasped in the evening breeze. It was a chill breeze.

A parrot shrieked.

A cock crowed and then screamed in terror.

And then there was silence.

No one moved.

Delphine clung tightly to Mr Dugdale's arm. Natasha's heart pounded as she pressed herself close to Roger Carey. Mamselle's mouth was dry.

The muleteers crouched out of sight in the undergrowth.

Then Polly spoke.

'My God, the garden,' she said.

'What about it?' said Louise.

'It smells of dead horses.'

36

The mule driver said to his mate: 'Have you ever been to grand opera?'

'I'm not sure. Have you?'

'Yes.'

The mules huddled. They laid their ears flat along their necks. They flashed the whites of their eyes. They stank of fear.

'There's a lot of singing in grand opera.'

'Is there?'

'Oh yes. They have to sing to make themselves heard above the music, you see.'

'Well, they wouldn't, wouldn't they?'

Suddenly Dolly threw back her chin, squared her shoulders, thrust out her chest and said: 'This is absurd. Cowering here like a load of coolies. Where's your gumption, Colonel Ryder? Where's your courage? Shift yourself and get your men unloading.'

Colonel Ryder flapped his glove.

It was the action of a man who fervently and profoundly wished he were at that moment staring deep into a rock pool on the shores of the Solway Firth.

None the less he gave his orders, and the men commenced to unload the vehicles.

Dolly snorted her approval.

Then she barked to her charges, 'This way. Follow me.'

She turned.

What she saw made her scream at the top of her voice.

She was staring straight into the eyes of a black woman.

She was deep deep black. She was blue black. Smouldering black. Night black. She had a razor-sharp nose with flared nostrils. Her cheek-bones were high. The whites of her eyes flashed blood red from the fiery glow of the setting sun.

Dolly screamed again.

The black woman smiled.

She wore a black dress. On her head was a vivid scarlet scarf tied at the front in two high points. She had claw marks on her shoulder.

'Sir Graham, he has warned us,' she said. 'We have tried our best.'

Dolly had never felt such fear in the whole of her life. The blood-red eyes bored deep into her. The blackness engulfed her. Her hair prickled. Her legs trembled. On her shoulder she felt a stinging chill.

'I warn you,' said the black woman. 'This house? It is a house of tragedy. Many deaths here. Oh yes indeed. Sir Graham's wife, she poisoned. His daughter, she drowned. Master Lance? He is not with you?'

Before anyone could answer she turned abruptly on her heel and commenced to walk towards the house. They followed her. They could not help themselves. They were in the grip of some powerful force beyond their control.

Colonel Ryder hesitated. He smiled weakly at his driver. Then he squared his shoulders and made to hurry after Dolly and her brood. But he could not move. Neither could the driver. The two men turned to each other. There was stark terror in their eyes.

The sun sizzled, flame-scared red, and then plunged into the sea.

The black woman led them into the house.

They climbed a flight of shallow wooden stairs and walked along a paved, roofed-in terrace that ran the whole length of the house.

The black woman stopped.

'This the glacis,' she said. 'You sleep this night here.'

And then she disappeared.

Pupils and teachers looked at each other.

They did not speak.

They simply curled up on the floor of the glacis and fell asleep.

When they awoke next morning, the sun was beating down and hummingbirds flickered and hovered and swallows swooped and butter-flies fluttered and Polly said:

'Guess what I've done.'

Colonel Ryder and his men had disappeared.

There was not a trace of them.

Dolly snorted contemptuously.

And then suddenly an extremely thin black man with slimy bloodshot eyes appeared on the glacis.

'You!' said Dolly with a gasp: 'You!'

'Right, missus, right. No problem,' said the black man.

He smiled again and said: 'Here? Damn sight better than pisspot of boat, eh? No problem.'

Dolly continued to stare at him with amazement.

He chuckled.

'Mighty fine day, eh? Mighty fine. You call me Rodney. Dat's my name. No problem.'

And with that they all smiled at him and he pattered off, nodding his head, clicking his tongue and giggling to himself.

Now they were all in good humour. They were bursting with it. The fear and exhaustion of the night before had vanished completely.

With cries of delight and shrieks of merriment they explored the house.

It was a higgle and a piggle of a mansion. Most of it was clapboard. But there was a stone-built wing stuccoed pink. The rooms were on different levels. There was a drawing room with folding doors. Three stairs led down from that to the retiring room and from these five steps led up to the study. Upstairs there were creaking, rickety corridors and a multitude of bedrooms of every shape and size.

'Nothing agrees with itself,' said Jassy, who hadn't spoken for six weeks.

Dolly was swift and efficient.

She allocated bedrooms and dormitories. She designated staff room and common room. She chose classrooms and directed the rearranging of furniture.

Then Rodney said: 'Okay den. Now I show you de kitchens. Rodney show you de kitchens. No problem.'

The kitchens were in an outbuilding twenty or so yards from the house.

Dolly wrinkled up her nose at the ancient cooking pots and calabashes and the charcoal brazier smouldering dull red and contented.

But everything was spotlessly clean. The stone flags glistened with fresh stream water. The knives and the ladles, the spoons and the spatulas sparkled.

'Pretty bloody buggering damn good, eh?' said Rodney. 'And now I show you Ernestine.'

There was a small room next to the kitchen. Rodney put his finger to his lips. Then softly and slowly he opened the door. They looked inside. There were tracts pasted on the walls and pictures of the Holy Family. On the bed was a bright, patchwork counterpane. There was a broken-shouldered clothes-press. There was a lopsided rocking chair.

And sitting on that chair staring straight into Dolly's eyes was the black woman with the razor-sharp nose.

'Dis am Ernestine,' said Rodney rolling his eyes. 'No problem.'

Ernestine said through thin, pale lips: 'Sir Graham, he warn us. We can only do our best. Nothing more.'

Rodney winked at Dolly and said: 'Do our best, missus. No problem. No problem at all.'

In the afternoon they explored the garden.

The little girls whooped with delight and scampered and scrambled. For the first time in weeks Natasha felt her whole body glowing. And it showed in her eyes and in the lilt of her step and the tilt of her head.

'It's gorgeous. It's heavenly,' she said to Roger Carey.

'Yes,' he said.

'I love you, Roger,' she said. 'Love you, love you, love you, love you.'

Mr Dugdale fanned himself with the brim of his panama. The lethargy had gone. The languor had disappeared.

He felt gloriously, fulsomely, wholesomely old. He was contented. Fulfilment was within his grasp. He was happy. Delphine had never looked dumpier and dowdier.

'Skid marks,' he said.

The garden had gone wild. The paths were overgrown. There were giant tree ferns. There were orchids everywhere. There was a tree tentacled like a gigantic octopus cascading with bell-shaped flowers of white and mauve and deep purple. The smell was sweet and strong. It made Samira reel with dizziness. How exquisite to die of dizziness, she thought.

The little girls found a bathing pool at the bottom of the garden. It was in a cool crook of a meandering stream. The water was so clear they could see the pebbles at the bottom. They were striped blue and white and red and ochre and green. The little girls whooped with delight once more, tore off their clothes and plunged into the water.

Their cries attracted the others.

The pupils stripped off their clothes and hurled themselves at the pool.

'Come on, Roger. Come on,' cried Natasha. 'Don't be shy, my darling.'

Roger jumped into the pool.

Dolly looked on beaming with pleasure.

'Magnificent,' she said. 'What beautiful bodies. How well they are all endowed.'

'Why don't you join them?' said Celia.

'Do you know, Celia, I rather think I shall.'

Very slowly she removed her clothing. Very slowly she entered the pool. Her luxurious bosoms floated on the surface of the water garlanded with blossom from the overhanging trees and hovered by hummingbirds.

Rodney gazed out from the depths of a thorn-addled thicket.

'My oh my,' he said, rolling his eyes and smacking his lips. 'Wait till dem darkies hear about dis. No problem, Rodney. No problem, man.'

37

They settled in their new quarters in no time at all.

The pupils were eager for their lessons. They listened intently and enthusiastically to their teachers.

'Now this is a diagram of the male thing,' said Dolly. 'You will be pleased to know that it is not to scale.'

'*Je suis. Tu es. Il est. Elle est. Nous sommes. Vous êtes.* And so on and so forth,' said Mamselle.

'My own feeling is that Tolstoy was not through the character of Pierre attempting to abuse the hegemony of the Masonic movement, but was through the agency of Prince Andrei's contented, fulfilled and profound self-doubt seeking to divine a pantheism which Rostov found so radically in the vigour and excitement of the hunt,' said Mr Dugdale.

'The capital of Argentina is Buenos Aires. The capital of Norway is Oslo. The capital of Costa Rica is . . . is . . . oh, bugger me, I've forgotten,' said Roger Carey.

All day long the parrot screeched and cackled and shot out its beak at anyone who approached too near.

'Skid marks,' it said one morning.

In the evenings after school the teachers would relax on the glacis. They would drink wine or spirits and discuss the business of the day while Mrs Otto snored fruitily.

'Burnaby's stopped scratching.'

'I think Guy Doucemain's got rather lovely eyes, don't you?'

'I think one of the most appealing characters in the whole world is old Kutuzov. I have feelings of distinct empathy towards him.'

The pupils bathed in the pool.

The Doucemain twins worked hard building a tree house.

The sound of Natasha's laughter was everywhere. Her smiles lit up the dusk and held the night at bay.

Delphine busied herself in Mr Dugdale's room, polishing and dusting and stacking neatly his pipes and his books.

And Burnaby had his first sexual awakening.

It was in the pool. He was alone. Samira appeared. As usual she slipped out of her clothes with scarcely a whisper. Burnaby was just about to splash water over her when he felt a curious swelling and tightening in his nether regions. He looked down into the water.

'Cripes!' he said.

And then he looked across at Samira. Her long, lustring black hair hung down her back to nestle on the smooth curves of her bottom. Her breasts were thin and curving and pouting and firm. Her tuft glistened. She looked at him, smiled and lowered her eyes.

'Cripes!' he said. 'Cripes.'

That night his dreams were disturbed. He was in the pool. He was licking the tips of Dolly's nipples and fanning Natasha's back with Mr Dugdale's panama. And then he was floating above the surface of the water and Samira was garlanding him with blossom. Then he was whizzing through space on a swelling, tightening broomstick and Natasha was laughing and Polly and the little girls were giggling and Samira beckoned to him and lowered her eyes and suddenly he was consumed in a roaring, bellowing eruption of dazzling ochre and purring deepest purple blooms and blossoms.

Along the corridor Natasha whispered into Roger Carey's ear. He was fast asleep, sated with loving, exhausted by its passions and frenzy. But still she spoke to him.

'I've always been happy, Roger. I was born to be happy. I shall always be happy. But there are times when I can't bear this happiness. It weighs on me. It haunts me. It seems to want to destroy me.

'Oh, Roger, I'm so happy.'

Next door Delphine lay wide awake. Oh, how she wished she were like Natasha. That lovely, long slim body. Those boyish breasts. The blonde hair flecked with tawny, ash grey at the tips. And her own body? So dumpy. So dowdy. She wouldn't even store potatoes in it. Oh, to be Natasha, to have her laughter and her radiance and the sparkle of her eyes and the fullness of her lips. How could Mr Dugdale spurn her then? How could he refuse to take her into his bed?

What if Dolly gave that *bal masqué*?

How breathtaking it would be. Delphine in her snow-white gown. The pitta pitta of the Polish dancing master's feet. The ballroom flanked by princelings and noblemen. The officers of Life Guards and hussars. The Klimt and Moser ballgowns. The grenadiers, the chasseurs, the cuirassiers, the dragoons, the officers of the garrison, the spotty blushing midshipmen home on leave from Pola. And all their eyes would be on Delphine. The royal personage would consult his aides: 'Who is that ravishing, radiant young woman with the lithe and lissom limbs and the blonde hair and the slender neck?' But she would have nothing to do with his attentions. Oh no. She had eyes only for one man and he took her in his arms and they whirled and twirled and spun and slid and he looked straight into her eyes and said:

'Skid marks.'

Mr Dugdale smiled in his slow, contented sleep. Felix chasing sticks. His precious stock of claret. Steep Holm and Flat Holm. The ships fussing in the Roads. Avocets on the mudflats in the bay. Sea swallows with black tips to their jagged red beaks. The *Western Mail* and whisky in the snug. He smiled again and he murmured in his sleep.

'Dowdy.'

The house slept on. Celia in her dreams saw him in his ill-fitting uniform. That slim young man with the doleful lashes. The slim young man who had cried out with fear and shame when they brought aboard the oil-soaked seamen from the doomed corvette. She sighed and she stretched out her legs. Oh, how lovely it would be if he were to stroke these limbs.

Mamselle thought of Coq d'Or chocolate biscuits and Atalanta dry cleaners and the wheels of creamy, white crumbling cheese and whirls of polony and butter bubbling on salt-sizzling potato cakes.

Mrs Otto, wide awake and grunting like a coypu, prowled the passages and the rooms and the corridors and snickets searching for refills to her *Speisewagen*.

And outside in the thickets and the undergrowth the Negroes silently watched and waited and Ernestine smiled at the blood-bubbling severed head on the spattered stone flap of the kitchen.

38

The days passed joyously.

The sun never ceased to offer its bounties.

The rainbirds and the flickers, the todies and the twopenny chicks sang in the gardens and swooped and chattered and squabbled.

'I like Rodney.'

'So do I.'

'Why do you like Rodney?'

'He smells of eggshells.'

'Does he?'

'Yes.'

In the evenings and in the darkness Burnaby and Samira bathed together in the pool.

'Hey, man. Wowee!' said Rodney as he looked on from deep inside the tangled thorn.

The Doucemain twins completed their tree house. They slept there at night with the parrot and taught it new words and phrases.

'Wanker. Wanker,' it screamed at the top of its voice whenever Burnaby passed by.

'I love it here,' said Dolly. 'I adore it.'

'So do I,' said Celia.

'There's only one thing wrong with it.'

'What's that, Dolly?'

'The niggers.'

'What?'

'I dislike niggers. I can't stand them. They get on my nerves. They irritate me. They anger me. They disturb me.'

'Why?'

'It's the way they look.'

'What?'

'Those thick lips. Those squashy noses. Those pink palms and soles and fingernails. I find it offensive. I don't like their swagger. They have nothing sensuous in their souls. Their nature is feckless. They know things we don't.'

'I know why you talk this way, Dolly.'

'Oh yes! Well, perhaps you would be good enough to tell me why.'

'Certainly. It's because of Ernestine.'

Dolly flared her nostrils. She snorted and curled her lip.

'I shall treat that remark with the boundless contempt it deserves,' she said.

But when she thought Celia was not looking, she placed her hand swiftly on her shoulder, and when she felt nothing untoward, the constriction in her throat disappeared and the dampness left the palms of her hands.

Meanwhile every evening the little girls, Polly, Louise and Jassy, gathered in Ernestine's rumpled room next to the kitchen.

She smiled at them as they sat cross-legged and wide-eyed and motionless at her feet.

'This is a house of tragedy, my young misses. This is a house of death,' she said as she pulled on her clay pipe and the smoke squirted into her narrowed eyes. 'Gory deaths? Oh yes. Oh yes. Oh yes. The zombie, he come and he do waft out life like the light of a sickly candle.'

She smiled again.

'You people disgusting. You know that? Us niggers, we hate you. You know what we call you? I tell you. We call you white niggers.'

The slow laughter. The clunk, clunk, clunk of plunging hearts. The wide eyes. The motionless limbs. The frieze of terror. The tide-tow of compulsion, fascination and awe.

'You drink this,' she said, and she handed them mugs of steamy, fierce black coffee. She had long-fingered hands, thin and supple.

'Drink,' she said. 'Not horse piss like what your madame drink.'

They sipped at the coffee. It made their eyes water.

Slow laughter once more.

'Your madame,' said Ernestine. 'She will go. Very soon, young misses. She will go. No problem.'

'Gosh,' said Polly as they loped back to their beds across the moon-soaked garden.

'Golly,' said Louise.

One evening the whole school was sitting on the glacis.

It had been a perfect day. Lessons had gone well. They felt at ease.

All was peaceful with the world. The garden crooned with the smell of cloves, cinnamon and orange blossom. The trade winds parted the palms softly and hissed and whispered. The fireflies flickered.

Dolly poured out strong liquor for the teachers and claret for the pupils.

'Will it make us drunk?' said Polly.

'Of course it will,' said Dolly.

'Gosh.'

'Golly.'

They pondered the events of the day.

'Burnaby, it's ages and ages since I last saw you scratching.'

'It's two weeks, three days, seventeen and a half hours, Dolly.'

'Splendid. Do you want something stronger than that claret?'

Moths and beetles flew into the candles and thumped to the floor, frazzled.

Natasha put her mouth close to Roger Carey's ears and whispered: 'Why do we never quarrel, Roger?'

'Because we're so happy.'

'Are we? Are we really so happy?'

'Yes.'

'Still, it would be nice to quarrel, wouldn't it? It would be nice to say wicked, wounding things to each other. It would be nice to be miserable.'

In the far, far distance they heard naval guns.

An owl whooer-whooered.

And then Rodney padded softly into the room and said: 'De Colonel. De Colonel, he have arrived. I ask him in. Yes? Yes, I ask him in. No problem.'

The Colonel entered.

He was tall. He was slender. His sword jangled at his slim waist. His hair was roan-soft and wavy. His fine-drawn jaws. His arching cheekbones. He was young. He had fecund eyes.

He clicked his heels and bowed.

'Colonel Joubert,' he said. 'At your service.'

He was French.

'Gosh,' said Dolly.

'Golly,' said Celia.

39

'I have come to renew my connection with Sir Graham,' said Colonel Joubert.

'Sir Graham?' said Dolly.

'Correct, madame. Sir Graham Egerton. I believe I have the pleasure of being in the presence of his son,' said Colonel Joubert, looking across the room to Roger Carey and smiling and bowing his head.

Dolly glanced across at Celia. She was staring at the Frenchman, transfixed and fruity-lipped. So was Mamselle. So were Samira and Natasha. The little girls had left their stools and had arranged themselves, cross-legged, motionless and adoring at his feet. Mr Dugdale beamed. Delphine thought to herself she might grant him a dance at the ball if her beloved, perish the thought, ran out of puff.

Dolly coughed and said: 'I'm afraid Sir Graham's son met with a misfortune on the voyage.'

'A misfortune?'

'Yes. He died. Natural causes. Very natural causes indeed. The most natural causes you could possibly find.'

'Ah.'

Colonel Joubert took out a slim gold case from inside his tunic jacket and offered cigarettes.

'French?' said Dolly.

'But, of course, madame.'

Dolly took a cigarette, accepted a light and inhaled deeply.

A glow of radiant ecstasy came to her face.

The Colonel smiled to himself and offered his case to the rest of the company.

'*Merci beaucoup*,' said Mamselle.

'Ah. You speak French, Mamselle?'

'*Un petit pois*,' said Mamselle.

The Colonel was relaxed. He sat back in his chair, his legs crossed elegantly, the candlelight flirting with the smoothness of his cheeks. He smiled at them.

'You will no doubt realise that my visit to you is highly irregular,' he said.

'Is it?' said Celia, and as soon as she had spoken she blushed bright, vivid scarlet.

'Ah yes,' said Colonel Joubert. 'We are supposed to be enemies, the English and we Vichy Frenchmen. The border is supposed to be sacrosanct, inviolate. But we take little regard of such niceties, such refinements. It is not Sir Graham's style.'

'Isn't it?' said Dolly.

Colonel Joubert smiled.

'But of course not, my dear madame. You must know that.'

'Must I?'

'But, of course. I assume you are here to promote and consolidate Sir Graham's business.'

'Are we? And what business would that be?'

'Now come come, madame. Come come.'

Dolly stared at him bewildered. She looked to Celia for support, but her niece was still transfixed by the vision of French military beauty and panache. Colonel Joubert sank back into his chair, never removing his gaze from Dolly. He rubbed his chin thoughtfully.

Then he nodded his head very slowly and said: 'I think you and I, madame, should exchange private words. May I suggest we withdraw to the study?'

'Yes, if you like.'

'I do like.'

Colonel Joubert stood up. He bowed. He extended his right arm and he escorted Dolly out of the glacis through the folding doors into the drawing room.

There was silence for a moment, and then the little girls began to jabber.

'*Très chic,*' said Mamselle. '*Très très chic.*'

Natasha, Delphine and Samira were plunging and spinning in silence. Mr Dugdale was preening himself in silence.

'That backside!' growled Mrs Otto. 'Tight as a drum.'

And then she returned to her slumbers.

40

'I don't believe you,' cried Dolly. 'I simply do not believe you.'

'It is true, madame,' said Colonel Joubert, pressing his hand to his heart. 'Upon my honour it is true.'

They were sitting in the study. The Colonel had revealed the secret panel in which Sir Graham kept his store of malt whisky. They were drinking the smooth, smoke-whispered liquid from thin, fluted tumblers.

'I am astounded, Colonel, that you could imagine that I should get myself involved in such an appallingly sordid business.'

The Colonel spread out the palms of his hands and shrugged.

'It is money. Big, big money,' he said. 'And, madame, very shortly you will be in need of money to continue to run this establishment.'

'Yes, but . . .'

Dolly broke off when she saw the threatening glint in the eyes of the Colonel. For an instant it burnt its way into her and she felt the faint screechings of talons upon her shoulder. She shuddered. Of an instant the Colonel's face was suffused by smiles.

'Besides, madame, it is pleasant to share a secret, eh?' he said. 'Just you and I know it. And, of course, I should never dream of revealing it to – who shall we say? – to Colonel Ryder perchance.'

A sharper glint this time. The talons sharper on her shoulders. But beyond the terror and the revulsion there was excitement. She felt it quicken in her loins.

Colonel Joubert stood up.

'I must be away, madame,' he said. 'I trust that my visit will not be mentioned to anyone outside your establishment.'

He bowed and kissed her hand.

His lips lingered. The pressure of his fingers on her wrist was soft yet firm in its intent.

She felt her neck suffuse with pink.

'You have the most wonderful assemblage of beautiful women in this establishment, madame,' said Colonel Joubert. 'You will see a lot more of me, I promise, before we have finished preparing our new consignment.'

'New consignment?' said Dolly.

Colonel Joubert smiled.

'*Au revoir, madame. A bientôt*,' he said.

Before leaving the study he paused and said: 'Be wary of the Blacks, madame. I beg you to be always on your guard.'

'But what is it, Dolly? What is this connection with Sir Graham?' said Celia next day.

'I am not allowed to reveal it,' said Dolly.

'Is it criminal?'

'I am not at liberty to comment, Celia.'

'It is. It's criminal,' said Celia. Then she clapped her hands and said: 'How lovely! I've always wanted to be a member of the criminal fraternity.'

When Colonel Joubert arrived later in the evening, Celia sat in a dark corner of the glacis, watching him as he flashed his white and even teeth and was attentive to every move and every statement made by the ladies, young and old.

The Colonel visited them every evening.

His tunic was always spotless. His toilet was never anything less than immaculate. His manners were charming, beguiling and bewitching. And every single member of the school fell under his spell.

'Who's he after?' said Dolly. 'Who's he got his eyes on?'

'I don't know,' said Celia. 'And I don't care either.'

Each evening she withdrew further and further into the dark corner of the glacis. She would not let the Colonel see the piteous look in her eyes. She would not allow him to see the pleading and the misery of rejection.

'Mamselle! That's it! That's who he's after,' said Dolly. 'The Frogs always stick together. It's a well-known law of nature.'

Mamselle fluttered her eyes ceaselessly at Colonel Joubert. She wore her choicest gowns and her most seductive perfumes. She puckered her lips and pouted.

'A most appalling woman,' said Colonel Joubert to Mr Dugdale. 'God knows where she learnt her French. *Nom de Dieu!*'

Mr Dugdale smiled. He was enchanted by the young Frenchman. He was completely under his sway. Each evening he would take him to one side and for a few minutes they would discuss matters dear to the old teacher's heart.

'I am on my hobbyhorse again,' he said to the Colonel one evening as they sat in the small retiring room drinking white Madeira.

'If you please, my dear sir,' said Colonel Joubert. 'I am all ears.'

'It's about war,' said Mr Dugdale.

'Ah.'

'Do you agree with taking prisoners, Colonel?'

Colonel Joubert raised his eyebrows and tapped his right forefinger lightly on the rim of his glass.

'If it was left to me, I wouldn't take prisoners,' said Mr Dugdale. 'What's the point of it? Where's the sense? Chivalry? Don't make me laugh, Colonel. The Germans are our enemies. They are criminals, every single one of them. Since they are my enemies, they cannot be my friends. So they should be put to death. What do you think, Colonel? Am I right?'

Colonel Joubert slowly poured two more glasses of white Madeira. He tapped a cigarette on the side of his gold case. He indicated with a flick of his hand that the old man should continue.

'If we didn't take prisoners, we'd transform the whole character of warfare,' said Mr Dugdale, leaning forward eagerly in his chair. 'At the moment we're just playing at making war. That's what makes it so vile, so hypocritical. Magnanimity? Sensibility? Laws of warfare, chivalry, flags of truce, humanity to the wounded? Bullshit, Colonel. Absolute bullshit.

'I saw enough between 1914 and 1918 of chivalry and flags of truce. They duped us and we duped them. We plundered, we pillaged, we raped, we looted. Both of us. Both our nations. We killed our sons, we killed our fathers. And in this war we shall kill our wives and our mothers and our daughters. And then they talk of the laws of warfare and generosity to the fallen foe. Bollocks, Colonel! Total bollocks! No prisoners, Colonel. If we didn't take prisoners, if we slaughtered on the spot anyone who surrendered, there would never be war again. People would be too terrified to start it or take part in it.'

Colonel Joubert smiled and left his aged company to finish off the bottle of Madeira.

Mr Dugdale smiled.

He was old. He was getting older day by day. He was happy.

'Communication cords,' he said quite without warning.

Later in the evening on the glacis Dolly whispered to her niece: 'Who is it, Celia? Who's he going for?'

145

Samira was lying at the Colonel's feet. He had an indulgent smile on his face and he was stroking her hair softly.

Oh, to feel those hands moving from her hair and roving over her body. Oh to bestride that horn and pump and scream. Oh, the fulfilment of dying at the highest pinnacle of ecstasy!

Burnaby looked on scarcely able to contain himself. If only he had an axe, he would smash it right into the centre of the Frenchman's skull. He would drag out the body and pin it to the earth with a bamboo spear staked through his belly button. He would gloat as the red ants stripped it of its flesh and the crows lurched down and pecked the marrow from his bones. Failing that he would drown him in a vat of wart ointment.

Colonel Joubert looked down at Samira. She opened her mouth and ran the tip of her tongue over her teeth. With just the slightest motion of her head and eyes she indicated the bedroom, below which they were sitting. Colonel Joubert smiled.

'Little girl, little girl,' he said. 'It is time for you to return to your friend. He looks most distressed. Take him upstairs, *ma chérie*, and tend to his woes.'

Samira did as she was told.

'This is the best thing I know for getting rid of spots and unsightly blemishes,' said Burnaby.

Louise and Polly and Jassy sat silent, enthralled and terrified in Ernestine's room.

'I hate him,' she said. 'I hate the Frenchman with all my heart. The dead man's hand behind my press will tear out his throat. You hear me, young misses? The Frenchman is a dead man.'

And the night wind whistled through the slats of the old water mill and scythed through the spikes of the razor grass.

'Could it be Delphine?' said Dolly. 'Could it possibly be dumpy, dowdy Delphine he's after?'

Colonel Joubert was in the garden. He had hold of Delphine's hands. They were talking rapidly and intently.

'You love him?'

'Oh yes. Oh yes.'

'Then you must tell him.'

'I can't.'

'Why not?'

Delphine lowered her eyes. Colonel Joubert gripped her hands sharply.

'Why not, I ask you, Delphine?'

'I don't know how to.'

Colonel Joubert smiled. He began to stroke her shoulders and the nape of her neck.

'I will show you what to do,' he said.

'Thank you.'

'Put your arms round my waist.'

She did so.

'Press your breasts into my body.'

She did so.

'Rub your thigh deep into my groin.'

She did so.

'Now kiss me.'

She did so.

'Not like that. Like this. Hard. Strong. Passionate.'

She followed his instructions to the letter.

Then they parted.

Colonel Joubert tugged at the cuffs of his tunic jacket and smoothed the hair at his temples.

'There, Delphine, there,' he said. 'In that way you tell him that you love him.'

'Crikey!' said Dolly. 'Who'd have believed it?'

On the following evening Natasha and Roger Carey lay side by side at the edge of the bathing pool.

'Oh man. Oh wowee!' said Rodney as he looked on from the depths of the thicket.

'Does nothing ever ruffle you, Roger?' said Natasha.

'Not any more.'

'You're so bloody smug, you bastard. I hate you, hate you, hate you.'

Roger Carey smiled.

'I like it when you act like this,' he said.

She turned and began to pummel him hard on the chest with her fists.

'I hate you,' she screamed. 'I hate you, hate you, hate you, and tomorrow I am going to do something that will make you hate me.'

Next evening she dressed herself in her flimsiest gown and planted the boldest expression on her face as she advanced on the Colonel.

'That's it. That's who he's after,' said Dolly. 'It's Natasha.'

Natasha took hold of the Colonel by the arm.

'Could I have a word with you in private, Colonel?'

'But, of course, mamselle.'

'This way.'

She led him out of the glacis through the drawing room and into the main hallway. As they climbed the stairs they passed Roger Carey.

'Good evening, Colonel,' he said. 'Splendid weather we're having.'

'Perfection,' said Colonel Joubert. 'Absolute perfection.'

Natasha led him into her bedroom. She closed the door. She locked it. She stepped out of her dress. She was naked. She held out her arms.

'Now, Colonel,' she whispered. 'Now.'

Colonel Joubert smiled.

'I think not, my dear,' he said. 'I fear I have not the slightest interest in your body.'

And he withdrew from her room with a courteous bow and repaired to the small retiring room where he took up conversation with Mr Dugdale on the subject of irrigation.

'I hate you white niggers,' said Ernestine to Polly, Louise and Jassy. 'We all hate the white niggers. You get poorer by the day. The money runs out week by week. There is no more to come. Just you wait, white niggers. Just you wait.'

Dolly sat in the drawing room with Celia. All the others had long since returned to their beds. They drank a final nightcap of hot rum.

'I'm stumped,' said Dolly. 'Who can it be he's after?'

There was a pause and then Celia said very softly:

'Why can't it be me?'

'You?'

'Yes. Me. Why not? Am I all that ugly? Am I all that offensive to men?'

'Certainly not,' said Dolly. 'I mean nobody could be that bad.'

Celia fled from the room, sobbing and wailing.

Next evening the mystery was solved when Colonel Joubert slipped

148

softly into Dolly's bedroom when she was preparing herself for the evening on the glacis.

She gasped.

He put his finger to his lips.

When he entered her, she juddered and clenched her jaws to stop the scream of ecstasy.

But later she was not successful.

And the Negroes heard it with expressionless eyes and faces as they crouched in the blackness of the garden and watched and waited.

41

They were awoken next morning by a distant rumble.

The house swayed and shook. Glasses and decanters rattled. Mrs Otto's *Speisewagen* dropped from her bosom and splattered its contents all over the floor.

'What was that?' said Dolly to Ernestine. 'What on earth was it?'

'The twins,' said Ernestine.

'The twins? They've not been manufacturing bombs in that tree house, have they?' said Dolly. 'If I discover gunpowder, I'll thrash them within an inch of their lives.'

Ernestine glared at her scornfully.

'I mean the twin peaks of the mountain,' she said. 'They rumble to warn you. Soon they will spit out fire and molten rock. They will engulf the forest with lava and consume the house with flames. And you will perish. You will all perish.'

She padded away to the kitchen, straight-backed and supple of hip.

'Did you hear the eruption this morning?' said Colonel Joubert as they lay side by side in bed later that day.

'Yes,' said Dolly. 'Is it dangerous?'

'Aren't all eruptions dangerous, my dear Dolly?'

'Oh yes. Oh yes indeed,' said Dolly. 'Shall we have another one before we go down for supper?'

Roger Carey and Natasha sat side by side on the edge of the pool, wriggling their toes in the cool, clear water.

'You make me so happy, Roger,' said Natasha. 'Yet you make me so angry.'

'I know.'

'I hate Colonel Joubert.'

'I know.'

'Stop saying "I know" all the time. It drives me mad.'

'I know.'

'For Christ's sake, Roger. Do something positive.'

Roger Carey smiled and she punched him hard in the ribs. The smile did not leave his face. She picked up a springy stick, ripped off its bark and slashed him hard across the cheek. He continued smiling. Two flaring red weals stood out from his flesh.

'Oh, Roger, Roger,' she cried and flung her arms round his neck. 'Roger, Roger. I do love you so very much.'

'I've something to tell you,' said Delphine.

'What?' said Mr Dugdale.

They were standing in the garden by the octopus orchid tree, and its scents were heady and corrupt. Delphine went to open her arms to him. She went to move close into his body. She went to press her thigh into his groin. But she stopped and hung her head.

Mr Dugdale smiled warmly at her.

'You stupid dowdy, dumpy little girl,' he said.

Delphine burst into a thin wail. She stood before him, shoulders drooping, mouth contorted in pain.

Mr Dugdale shook his head, bewildered and hurt.

'Now what have I said?' he said.

Delphine continued to wail.

'What on earth is the matter?' said Mr Dugdale. 'Have I said something to upset you?'

Delphine stopped crying. She stared at him, mouth gaping open, eyes smarting with red rims.

'My dear precious little girl,' said Mr Dugdale. 'I would never dream of saying anything to hurt you. Nothing on earth would induce me to do such a thing.'

He smiled at her. He put his hands gently on her shoulders. He leant forward and kissed her tenderly on the forehead.

She sighed and smiled.

'Halitosis,' he said.

The Doucemain twins had tamed the parrot. Now it spent all its time in the tree house and offered them the back of its head to be scratched.

One evening they entertained Samira and Burnaby, who sat side by side holding each other round the waist.

'Are you going to get married?' said Charles Doucemain.

'Yes,' said Burnaby.

'When?' said Guy Doucemain.

'Very soon,' said Burnaby. 'We're going to elope.'

'Why did you choose me?' said Dolly to Colonel Joubert.

He said nothing. He continued to stroke her thigh and tauten her nipples with the tips of his fingers.

'I thought you'd go for one of the girls. I mean Natasha's absolutely ravishing, isn't she? And Samira's a real sultry oriental beauty. I should have thought any man would just wilt and melt when she looks at him with those smouldering eyes of hers. Mind you, if Margot had been alive, I'm certain you would have . . . oooh, oooh. I do like it when you do that.'

Later she said: 'And look at Mamselle. I should have thought you'd have really gone for her. Two Froggies together? Just the job. I know she's none too clean under the armpits, but . . . ooh, ooh, that's nice. Do it again.'

Later she said: 'I mean even Celia comes into the reckoning. I know she's not much to look at, but at least she's virgin territory and . . . oooh, oooh, eee. Oooh, that's just wonderful.'

Later he said: 'Everything is coming along smoothly, Dolly. Soon we shall have enough for a consignment and then we do business. And then . . . I say, Dolly. Whoever did you learn that from?'

'And so step by step, children, the playwright charts the cause of vanity and melancholy, of inertia and frivolity, of pain and sombre joy and at the end the old servant is forgotten by his masters and his mistresses as they, absorbed in their own self-indulgence and overbearing conceit, say farewell to the house and make for the train which will . . . which will . . . do you know, I rather think I might be falling in love.'

'I can't marry you, Burnaby,' she said.

'Why not?'

'I must marry one of my own kind.'

'Rot.'

'No, Burnaby, it is not. I am already spoken for. My father has chosen the man I must marry.'

'Who is he? I'll punch his teeth in.'

'You would not have a chance, Burnaby. He would kill you. He would chop off your head. Then he would chop off your arms and your legs. And then he would send the bits to your mama and your papa.'

'Rot.'

'No, it is not rot. If he were to find out what we have just done, Burnaby, then he would kill both of us.'

'Would he? Are you sure?'

'Certain. Do you want me to . . .'

'No, thank you. Not just now.'

'Helsinki is the capital of Finland. Wellington is the capital of New Zealand. Christ knows the capital of Abyssinia.'

'I think it's disgusting.'

'So do I.'

'She's walking round all day with a great booming grin like the Cheshire cat. And when he comes round in the evening, she fawns on him, prostrates herself in front of him, abases herself and loses all shame and dignity.'

'And the noise they make in her bedroom.'

'The noise! Absolutely terrible!'

Mr Dugdale entered the drawing room with Delphine. The two women stopped talking immediately. Mr Dugdale smiled at them.

'Good evening, ladies,' he said.

They smiled distantly.

He turned to one and said: 'What a frumpy old baggage. You've a face like a sinkful of anchovies.'

Celia fled the room wailing.

Then Mr Dugdale turned to the other and said cheerfully: 'You smell like a polecat, my dear.'

Mamselle slapped him fiercely round the back of his head with the flat of her hand. Then, chin held high, nostrils curling and snarling, clicker-clacked out of the room.

Mr Dugdale turned to Delphine, held out his arms helplessly and said:

'Now what have I said?'

'I want to know your secret, Roger. That's what's wrong with you. You're bottling it up. Why don't you spill it out? Why were you running away? Why won't you say? Why, why, why?'

'Soon, Natasha. Soon I might tell you.'

'I want to know now. Roger, tell me and all your troubles will disappear.'

'I haven't got any troubles.'

'You have. You're loaded down with them. Tell me everything and you'll feel fresh and renewed and we can behave like normal people in love. We can quarrel. We can bite each other and scratch. We can make love all night long. We can make love all through the day. We can make love in the bathing pool. We can make love on the stairs, on the dining-room table, under the dining-room table, inside the –'

'I've just remembered.'

'Oh Roger, my darling, what, what? What have you just remembered?'

'Addis Ababa.'

'What?'

'Addis Ababa is the capital of Abyssinia.'

When Colonel Joubert arrived at Marchmain's Rest later that evening, he lingered for a while in the garden.

'Superb evening, my dear good lady,' he said to Celia.

'Is it?' said Celia. 'I can't say I've noticed one way or the other.'

He turned away and touched the peak of his cap with a flick of his glove.

'Superb evening, is it not, *ma chère Mamselle?*'

'I haven't the faintest idea what you're talking about.'

He smiled.

'Ah, Natasha, my dear,' he said. '*Charmante.* Utterly ravishing.'

'Bugger off.'

He went into the house and strode up the stairs. He stood aside to let Mr Dugdale pass. The old man smiled and pointed to Dolly's bedroom.

'Remember what I told you, old chap,' he said. 'Take no prisoners.'

Then he chuckled to himself and pottered off downstairs. Curious. He was doing a lot of pottering now. He had never pottered before. He quite liked pottering. He must potter more often. He must devote his life to pottering.

When Colonel Joubert entered Dolly's bedroom she spun round crossly from the window and said: 'What were you saying in the garden?'

'I beg your pardon, my dear Dolly?'

'I saw you talking to them. What were you saying about me?'

The Colonel smiled. He sat down on the edge of the bed and commenced to remove his riding boots.

'You were saying I was too old. You were saying you were growing tired of me. You propositioned Natasha, didn't you? Well? You did, didn't you?'

Colonel Joubert shrugged. He took off his tunic jacket and began to unbutton his shirt.

'Leave it. I'll do that.'

She removed his shirt. He blew into her hair and ran his tongue down her cheeks.

'I'm just as good as Natasha. I'm better. I've more experience. I know how to arouse. I know how to excite. My body is not worn and old. My body is mature and rampant and simmering with desire and boiling with lust.'

'Quite right, Dolly. Quite right.'

She slipped off his breeches. She took off his silk underclothes.

'Ah, there he is,' she said. 'My wonderful friend, so straight-backed, so willing to please, so lithe and nimble.'

She leant forward, parting her lips, and, never taking her eyes off him, she lowered her head.

'Before you start, Dolly, there is something I have to tell you.'

Dolly drew back sharply. Her voice choked. Perspiration streamed down the dark, cool valleys of her body.

'What is it?' she said.

'In four days' time we do the business.'

'Four days?'

'Yes, Dolly. And before that we do a trial run. A rehearsal. We do it tomorrow night.'

'We?'

'We – my friends, myself and you.'

'I?'

'That is correct, Dolly. You.'

Dolly began to rise from her knees slowly. He took hold of her wrist and dragged her back to him.

'But first, Dolly, we have some unfinished business to attend to.'

42

The rehearsal went well.

Dolly enjoyed every minute of it. It was lovely to be at sea again. The cabin cruiser cradled the blackness of the night and its motion soothed her and stimulated her. They headed out to sea away from St David's. Then they stopped engines and allowed the craft to drift in the tropic stream that surged northwards. Then they started the engines again and headed slowly to a winking red light on an unseen shore. They cut engines again and waited. Soon they heard the sounds of oars and the rowing boat crunched softly against the side.

'How long to transfer them when the time comes?' said Colonel Joubert.

'Ten minutes at the most.'

'Make it five.'

'Sure thing, boss.'

Later the boat crunched ashore at St David's on a silver-sanded beach and they drank rum in a palm-leaved shack.

The helmsman threw back his head and roared with laughter. The laughter was loud and long. His whole body rocked with it. He crumpled up with it as he rolled in the sand clutching his belly.

'Hey, nigger,' said Colonel Joubert.

'Yes, boss?'

'Cut the crap.'

'Sure thing, boss.'

'Where on earth were you last night?' said Celia.

'Out.'

'I know you were out. But where?'

'It's no concern of yours.'

'It is, you bitch. It is. Remember what happened last time you disappeared? We found you half-naked grovelling on the floor of a stinking backstreet shed and you were –'

'Shut up.'

'No, I will not shut up.'

Gosh! She was in defiant mood again. Just as she'd been when she'd given Dolly that tremendous bollocking at the Governor's residence. How marvellous. How wonderful. If only he could see her now. If only he could see her in all her glory, he'd abandon Natasha like a shot. She squared her jaw and thrust her face towards Dolly.

'You make me sick with your selfishness. The whole place was in uproar last night. The staff were horror-struck. The shits were terrified. I was going to send out Rodney with search parties, but then Ernestine came in and she was . . . she was . . .'

'What?'

'Nothing.'

'What was she doing?'

'Carrying a dead man's hand.'

'It was wonderful, wasn't it, Louise?'

'Super-duper.'

'What was wonderful and super-duper?' said Jassy.

'The dead man's hand.'

'Dead man's hand! Why didn't you wake me up?'

'Because you'd have fainted with fright.'

'I wouldn't have.'

'You would.'

'I wouldn't. I wouldn't. I wouldn't.'

'Louise did.'

'Did you?' said Jassy.

'Yes,' said Louise. 'It was super-duper.'

'Do you know something?' said Dolly at the staff table during luncheon next day.

'Tell me,' said Mr Dugdale.

'If ever I wanted to disembowel someone without a single excuse, I'd choose a Romanian.'

'How interesting,' said Mr Dugdale. 'I think I'd probably plump for a Bulgarian.'

The language school in Sofia. What was he known as there? Professor Oslear? No, no. That was in Louvain. Dr Constant? No. It wasn't Dr Constant in Sofia. Where was Dr Constant? Trondheim? Arles? Bilbao?

After lunch Dolly cancelled her lessons and retired to her bedroom. When she took off her shoes, tiny grains of silver sand putted to the wooden floor. She could smell the sea salt on her blouse. She could feel the darkness of the night in the folds of her skirt. She lay back on her bed and closed her eyes. Her sleep was deep and untroubled.

The black owl with the blood-red eyes rapped its beak angrily on the shutters. But they would not yield and he had to stay outside fretting angrily.

When she came down to dinner, she felt refreshed and renewed. Her whole body tingled. Her mind was sharp and clear.

'You've been rather silent these past few days, Mamselle,' she said. 'I trust there is nothing wrong.'

Mamselle sniffed hard.

'Nothing that love couldn't cure,' she said.

And she scraped back her chair and spitter-spattered out of the dining room.

'Now what have I said?' said Dolly.

'Oh really! You insensitive old bitch!' said Celia, and she flung down her spoon and left the room. Had he heard her? Had he seen her? Oh, please God, he had, that lovely, lovely Roger.

The others finished their meal.

'Do you think the shits enjoyed it?' said Dolly to Mr Dugdale as they walked slowly to the glacis.

'I think it highly unlikely,' said Mr Dugdale.

'So do I,' said Dolly. 'The trouble is there hasn't been a delivery of fresh supplies for three weeks. We seem to be running out.'

'Not of strong drink, I hope,' said Mr Dugdale.

'Certainly not. What do you take me for?' said Dolly. 'Whisky or brandy?'

'I rather thought I'd take a tumbler of rum.'

Colonel Joubert did not arrive that evening. But Dolly seemed unworried. She passed from chair to chair on the glacis refilling glasses and chatting about the events of the day. She went into the junior common room.

'Good evening, shits,' she said to the three little girls who were desperately trying to conceal from her gaze a limp, drooping, feathery object. She did not notice and boomed out: 'Well, where is everyone?'

'Doing it,' said Polly.

'Oh good,' said Dolly. 'Excellent.'

When she returned from the glacis, Celia looked up from her sewing and said: 'The Colonel's rather late this evening, isn't he?'

'Yes,' said Dolly.

'Perhaps he isn't coming.'

'Perhaps you are right,' said Dolly.

Celia and Mamselle exchanged glances.

Next morning the three little girls found a dead bat on the lawn.

'Oooh,' said Polly.

'Pooh,' said Louise.

'I'll see if Ernestine wants it,' said Jassy.

She ran with the corpse to the kitchen and showed it to Ernestine.

'Have you seen this?' she said.

'Oh yes, young missee,' said Ernestine. 'I seen it.'

The following morning there were three dead bats laid out side by side on the lawn.

'Don't they look angry?' said Delphine.

'They look absolutely livid,' said Mr Dugdale.

Once again Jassy took the corpses to Ernestine. But she was not in the kitchen. She knocked on the door of her room. There was no response, so she pushed open the door softly. There was no one there, but on the old patchwork quilt there was a curving, wooden-handled knife.

Colonel Joubert did not appear that evening.

'He's ditched her,' said Celia.

'She was too old for him,' said Mamselle. 'I knew it couldn't last.'

'Still, she's putting a brave face on it.'

'What a cow!'

'What a bitch!'

Dolly smiled at them. She knew they were talking about her. But she didn't care. Tomorrow was the day. Tomorrow was the real thing. Tomorrow she would sail with Colonel Joubert. But this time she would not return to the school. Oh no. She would vanish from the face of the earth with Colonel Joubert. They would be rich in money. They would be rich in love. It was all arranged. It was all so perfect. God rot the lot of them.

She went to bed in good spirits.

Mamselle sniffed coldly as Dolly left the room.

'These high spirits of hers,' she said. 'Just superficial. On the surface.'

'Absolutely,' said Celia. 'Next thing the black owl will be back again.'

'Black owl?' said Mamselle. 'What black owl?'

'Never mind,' said Celia. 'It doesn't matter.'

As soon as Dolly's head touched the pillow she fell asleep.

Mr Dugdale could not sleep. He summoned Delphine to his room. He bade her sit on the foot of the bed and he said: 'I have something to tell you.'

'Yes?' she said breathlessly. 'Yes? What is it?'

'Wing nuts,' he said, and then he roared with rage and beat his fists on the walls. 'You see, you see? I've done it again.'

'Done what again?'

'Said something I didn't want to say. Good God, I didn't even know I was going to say it. It just plopped out. I had no control over it.'

'Oh dear,' said Delphine.

'And there's something else.'

'What?'

'I keep saying things which upset people. And I haven't the faintest idea what I've said.'

'I know.'

'Oh! You've noticed, have you?'

'Yes. You said something awful to me.'

'Oh my God. What was it?'

'It doesn't matter.'

'But it does, Delphine. It does. Tell me what I said to you. Please, Delphine, please.'

Delphine bent her neck and closed her eyes.

'You said I was dumpy and dowdy.'

Mr Dugdale groaned and, clasping his head in his hands, rocked backwards and forwards.

'Oh, my poor girl,' he said. 'Oh, my poor girl. What can I possibly do to earn your forgiveness?'

Delphine told him.

'Very well then, my dear. You may fall in love with me,' he said. 'I have to warn you, however, that you are not the first. Not by a long chalk. My life has been a constant sequence of young girls losing their hearts to me and falling in love.'

As Delphine cuddled into his side on the bed he began to tell her of that life.

Right through the night and long into the early hours of the morning he unravelled its tangled knots and threads and wove his story with the weft of his compassion and the warp of his vanity.

She was fast asleep by the time that exotic magic carpet was completed. He wrapped himself deep in its folds with contentment and serenity and slept the precious sleep of the unburdened.

And all over the house other people were unburdening themselves.

'I love you, Burnaby.'

'Tremendous.'

'I want to elope with you.'

'Terrific.'

'We'll bide our time. We won't tell anyone. Not even the Doucemain twins. We'll plan and we'll plot. We'll work out the lie of the land. We'll make contacts. We'll leave nothing to chance. We'll cover our tracks. No one will ever find us.'

'Tremendous. But what if something goes wrong and they do find us? What then?'

Samira shuddered. So did Burnaby.

Clink of midnight glasses. Loll and roll of rum.

'I need a man.'

'So do I.'

'But the trouble is, Mamselle, I've never had a man before. Well, not properly. And I mean to say, you've had hundreds and hundreds, haven't you?'

'Not quite as many as that, Celia.'

'The thing is, I know precisely whom I want.'

'Ah.'

'I worship and adore him. I crave for his love. But I know it's impossible. It's hopeless. There is no future in it. There is only bleakness and despair.'

She sighed deeply and took a long, slow swig of her rum.

Then she continued: 'Still, it can't be helped. Life has to go on. Oh yes, Mamselle, it'll go on all right. We shall carry on living this life we lead now. We shall come through an endless succession of futile days and endless evenings. We shall bear patiently the trials that fate has in store for us. We shall –'

'Who is this man, Celia?'

161

'Roger Carey.'

The gecko gulped.

Moth flutter and beetle blunder.

The blonde girl turned and whispered to the young man lying in her arms: 'Tell me, Roger. Go on, my darling. Please, please. Tell me why you had to run away.'

'Because I murdered someone,' said Roger Carey.

Next morning, the day of Dolly's mission with the Colonel, there were five dead bats on the lawn.

They were laid out side by side.

Each one had been decapitated.

The curving, wooden-handled knife was covered with blood.

'You see it, young missee? You see it good?' said Ernestine.

'Yes,' said Jassy.

'Then do not forget it. Tell the other white niggers. Tell them to beware.'

There was a faint rumble from the distant twin peaks. The picture of St Bartholomew rattled on the wall and then dropped to the floor, shattering its glass pane.

Ernestine smiled to herself.

43

All through the day Dolly was agitated. She could not rest. She could not concentrate. She twitched. She jerked her limbs. She started and jumped out of her skin when anyone spoke to her.

'She's cracking up,' said Celia.

'Yes,' said Mamselle. 'Her colonel has flown the nest. He has found another girl more suitable to his lusts.'

'Why couldn't it have been me?' said Celia.

At length it was time for Dolly to set off for her rendezvous with Colonel Joubert. It was a cool, windless evening. The trees were still. Frogs croaked. Swifts screeched, white-rumped and dusky-banded.

She did not look back.

'Bye bye, shits,' she whispered. 'Bye bye, the whole lot of you.'

As on the evening of the rehearsal she was met in the lee of the old sugar mill by the Colonel's black boatman. He greeted her with a flashing smile. His breath stank of rum and he was not too steady on his feet as he led her down the steep valley that wriggled its way to the sea.

It was pitch-black by the time they reached the shack on the strand.

The black man reached out for the bottle of rum standing on the bar counter. The Colonel thwacked his wrist with his riding crop.

'Not now, nigger,' he said. 'Later.'

Then he smiled broadly at Dolly and kissed her hand.

They waded through warm, clear, moon-sparkling water to the boat. Colonel Joubert started the engine. They headed out over the flat-calm, dappled sea. The lights of Port Cedric blazed out shamelessly, flaming the sky and extinguishing the crackling stars. Very soon the Colonel cut the engines and allowed the boat to drift in the stream. He handed the wheel to the black man.

'Okay, nigger, you know the bearing?'

'Yep. No problem.'

The current frizzed at them in the blackness. There were skeins of gulfweed on the stream, and the seabirds worked them, squawking and squabbling.

'You know how to use the rifle, nigger?' said Colonel Joubert.

'Yep,' said the black man. 'No problem.'

Colonel Joubert handed him a quart bottle of rum and he drank the liquid greedily from the neck so that it splashed and splattered down his chest.

'That's enough,' said the Colonel, snatching back the bottle. 'I want you rum-brave. I don't want you useless.'

'No problem.'

'You know what to do?'

'Yep.'

'When we make our rendezvous, and as soon as the transfer is over, you put her ahead and get the hell out of it straight out to sea. No matter what happens, you keep her going flat out. You understand that, nigger?'

'Yep. No problem.'

Dolly was excited. She was elated. She was having an adventure. A real adventure with guns and a dusky Frenchman and a drunken black man. How marvellous. The sea breeze whipped at her scarf and snuckered up her skirts and pranced and cavorted in her loins.

Colonel Joubert was nervy and restless. She could feel his tension. She stretched out her arms to him, but he thrust her away testily.

She smiled. She understood. He was a man preparing for action. And she was a woman waiting for his triumph when she would reward him with the bounties of her thrusting body.

Suddenly Colonel Joubert sprang forward and began scanning the horizon with binoculars. After a few minutes she heard him whistle softly between his teeth.

'Got them,' he said.

He sprang down into the cockpit.

'Start the engines,' he said.

The engines barked and spluttered and then they caught and once more they were underway. The boat sidled its way out of the stream and then in the far distance Dolly saw the two red winking lights.

'Boss,' pleaded the helmsman. 'Please, boss.'

Colonel Joubert handed him the bottle of rum. He took a deep swig from it and handed it back. The Colonel nodded and took a sharp swill himself.

164

Nearer and nearer came the lights.

'Keep your eyes on those lights,' growled the Colonel softly.

The smell of land from an unseen shore.

Dolly tingled and seethed. She was exhilarated. She was beside herself with passion. Her whole body pulsated with anticipation.

'Now,' hissed Colonel Joubert.

The helmsman cut the engines.

'You got that gun, nigger?'

'Yep.'

'First sign of trouble and you shoot. Okay? You understand me?'

'Yep. No problem.'

Silence.

Lap of water against the hull. The wheeze of the black man. She heard the pump of her heart.

'Listen!'

The sigh of oars. The bump.

'Good evening, Captain,' said a voice from the pitchy darkness.

'Come astern and put her broadside,' said Colonel Joubert.

The boats touched again.

The Colonel leant over the stern and said: 'Let me see it.'

'You get half now. The other half you get when everything's on board,' said the voice from the darkness.

'Agreed,' said the Colonel.

He took hold of a packet and took it to the cockpit. He turned on the binnacle light, opened the packet and counted the wad of money carefully.

'Fine,' he said, returning to the stern. 'Bring them aboard.'

One by one six Chinamen clambered over the stern rail. They clutched cardboard suitcases. They wore frail suits. Their shoes were hung round their necks by the laces. On each of their faces was a look of searing terror.

'Get the bastards forward,' said the Colonel.

'Right, boss.'

'Lock them in the cabin.'

'Sure thing, boss. No problem.'

The Colonel doused the binnacle light. In the darkness the bare feet shuffled. There was the click of the key.

'Okay,' said the Colonel. 'The second half, if you please.'

A dark shape skipped nimbly aboard over the stern rail. He handed

Colonel Joubert the package. But this time the soldier did not count its contents. He shoved it into the inside pocket of his jacket.

Then suddenly he leapt forward and grabbed the stranger by the throat. The stranger screamed as the fingers gouged into his flesh. The two men fell to the deck. The stranger thrashed his feet on the deck as the Colonel pressed his knees onto his chest and forced his fingers deep into his neck. The stranger gurgled and hacked and spluttered. And then he managed to move his head a fraction out of the vice of the Colonel's grip. Instantly he thrust forward and took a deep slittening bite into his attacker's cheek. The Colonel fell back and howled with pain and agony. Instantly the stranger sprang to his feet.

Flash of metal. Flash of bullet.

Crack, crack, crack.

Splinter of bone. Spew of gore. Splatter of brain.

Colonel Joubert lay dead in the cockpit.

The stranger fought for breath. His lungs whistled as he knelt over the body and removed the packages from the jacket.

'You,' he said to the helmsman.

'Boss?' said the black man, and his voice cracked and wavered and teetered.

'Over the side.'

'Yep, boss. No problem.'

The black man heaved and he tugged and he cursed and he sobbed. And finally he managed to throw the Colonel's body overboard.

'Have you got rum aboard?'

'Sure thing, boss.'

Dolly did not move. She could not move.

She was beyond terror.

She was far far beyond it.

The rum stenched the air.

There was a battering on the door of the cabin. It grew louder.

'You have a gun?' said the stranger.

'Yep?'

'Bring the Chinks out. Keep the gun trained on them. One false move and you blow their heads off. Right?'

'Right.'

Click of key. Stumble. Clatter. Bare feet pattering on planking. The Chinamen cowered at the stern. The black man's gun never left them.

The stranger put his gun to the temple of one of the men and said: 'Jump.'

Cries of terror. Jabble of voices.

'Jump, you bastards. Jump.'

One by one the Chinamen jumped over the rails.

Faintly the cries of panic. The pleading cries. The lung-clutching cries.

'Right,' said the stranger. 'Let's move.'

The engines roared. The bow lifted. The wake thrashed. The boat made a great snarling arc and, fighting the glutting stream, ploughed its way home.

The stranger lit the binnacle lamp. He smoothed down his greasy hair strand by strand across his naked pate. When he turned to Dolly, his gold tooth flashed.

'Well, Mrs Bradman,' he said. 'Quite an evening's entertainment for you.'

When they reached the silver-sanded strand and beached the boat, the black man and the bartender carried Dolly back to Marchmain's Rest.

She was senseless.

There was no light in her eyes.

44

Dolly slept for seventy-eight hours.

She hardly moved.

Celia was distraught. She sent for the doctor. He arrived on horseback. He examined Dolly. She did not stir. He tut-tutted and twittered. Then he rode away.

Celia consulted Mr Dugdale. He stared at Dolly for several minutes. Then he turned to Celia and said: 'Wing nuts.'

Celia consulted Ernestine. She stood silently at the foot of the bed. Then she said: 'She will live. Or she will die.'

Celia watched her. Her eyes slitted in her coal-black face. They glinted red.

'Obeah,' she said. 'We see what obeah will do. You follow me.'

Celia followed Ernestine to her room next to the kitchen.

'Sit down.'

Celia sat down.

Ernestine reached down behind the press. She pulled out a dead man's hand. She called out. Rodney appeared at once. He was carrying in his hands a bird with its throat slit. Ernestine placed it on her knee and let the blood fall slowly drop by drop into a calabash.

When the flow of blood had ceased, she looked up at Celia, who had not said a word nor moved a muscle.

She stared at her silently.

She held up the corpse.

Then she said through taut-stretched lips: 'The black owl has gone. It is all over.'

When she got back to the house, Celia found Dolly sitting up in bed wide awake, eating plump, velvety, juicy purple plums and drinking beakers of white rum.

'I have had the most wondrous, exciting adventures,' she said. 'Sit down, pour yourself some rum, and I shall tell you all about them.'

She did.

Not a detail did she miss.

Celia's mouth drooped open so wide you could have quartered inside its icy depths a whole colony of black bats with blood-red eyes.

45

Next morning Ernestine presented herself at the door of Dolly's study.

'Ah, Ernestine, my dear,' boomed Dolly. 'Do come in.'

Ernestine entered the room.

'Pull up a chair. Sit yourself down. Have a glass of sherry.'

Ernestine remained standing, back straight, the thin shoulder blades ridging through her black dress.

'Well?' said Dolly. 'And what can I do for you this exquisite, beautiful morning?'

'You are ruined,' said Ernestine.

'I beg your pardon?' said Dolly.

'You will not survive. You have no money. You have no credit. Black niggers know when poverty strikes. They smell it long before white niggers smell it. They wait. They watch. And when that poverty come, they slip away into the darkness. There is no escape. You are doomed.'

And then she turned and slipped away silently.

Dolly summoned Mr Dugdale and told him what Ernestine had said.

He smiled. He nodded.

Dolly smiled and nodded too.

Then she said: 'Correct me if I'm wrong, Mr Dugdale, but did I not appoint you bursar shortly before we set sail from England?'

'Oh no. That was Major Pickavance.'

'And where is he skulking at this time of crisis?'

'He ran off with a harlot. Don't you remember?'

'So he did. Do you think he ran off with the money as well?'

'I rather doubt it. He was rather a duffer where money was concerned.'

'That's probably why I appointed him bursar,' said Dolly. 'Never trust a bursar who knows anything about money.'

'Walnuts,' said Mr Dugdale.

Dolly smiled and said: 'I think it might be a rather good idea if I checked the accounts.'

Dolly did indeed check the accounts. She discovered that the school was in considerable debt. The income from fees had long since been exhausted. There were sheaves of unpaid bills from the traders in town. She discovered three unopened, threatening letters from the bank manager.

Later that day she consulted Celia.

'Oh my God, what are we going to do?' Celia cried. 'They'll come for us. You'll see. Gangs of them will come for us and they'll ransack the house and they'll loot and they'll pillage and they'll rape and they'll . . .'

'Oh shut up, you silly old tart,' said Dolly.

She sought out Mr Dugdale once more and over a large decanter of rum asked his advice.

'Tell them to fuck off.'

'Mr Dugdale!' said Dolly. 'Well, really! I don't mind foul language among the pupils. But I do draw the line, when it comes to a senior and much-respected member of my staff. Really, Mr Dugdale! Really!'

'Now what have I said?' said Mr Dugdale.

They touched glasses and drank more rum.

'Curiously enough,' said Dolly, 'I'm not the slightest bit worried about the situation.'

'Neither am I,' said Mr Dugdale. 'I'm not worried about anything these days. Since I've been cleansed, my life has taken on a completely different meaning.'

'Cleansed! That's precisely what I feel has happened to me.'

Mr Dugdale nodded. He smiled.

Dolly sat in the droopy old rocker pulling thoughtfully at the lobe of her ear.

'I slept so long,' she said. 'How long did I sleep? I don't know. It was so long. And something happened to me whilst I slept. I don't know what. But I feel so different. Did I tell you about the Chinamen?'

'What Chinamen?'

'The Chinamen they threw overboard.'

'Who's they?'

'The nigger and the gangster from SS *Drayman*.'

'Why did they throw the Chinamen into the water?'

'Because the Colonel had been murdered.'

'Which colonel?'

'Colonel Joubert.'

Mr Dugdale screwed up his eyes and tapped his right fist thoughtfully into the palm of his left hand. At length he said: 'No. I don't recall your having said anything to me on those matters.'

'Then I shall tell you now.'

'Thank you. Do you think we might switch our allegiance to port?'

'Of course. Naturally.'

And as they slowly browsed their way like elderly manatees through the establishment's last bottle of port Dolly told Mr Dugdale of her adventures.

He listened intently to every word.

'And now it's all over, I feel no sense of loss, no feelings of remorse or unhappiness or shame. I feel no horror. I can see the blood and the splinters of bone and the splatters of brain, and I feel neither revulsion nor grief.'

Mr Dugdale smiled.

'And thus you are cleansed,' he said.

'Yes,' said Dolly very slowly. 'Thus I am cleansed.'

Mr Dugdale held up the bottle of port to the light of the hurricane lamp.

'Splendid colour,' he said.

'Yes,' said Dolly. 'Splendid colour.'

They drank on in reflective silence. Indeed she was a handsome woman. What a noble body she had. Bountiful. Sumptuous. It reminded him of those pictures he had stored in a tin trunk in the attic of The Marine Hotel. They were photographs of the last days of the Habsburg Empire. How he loved them. The Biedermeier nudes. The naked serving girl, shy and stilted, clutching the shift round her ankles. Countess Zichy, sensuously aloof and wistful and arrogant in her coronation robes. The Viennese society lady at the races, long-legged and slim, buoyant and fleeting. The Viennese housewife on the Naschmarkt, wide-hipped and heavy-breasted, her arms swinging, her thick juicy lips curling, inviting, provoking. Oh yes indeed, Dolly could hold her own with every single one of them.

'And you, Mr Dugdale,' said Dolly. 'What of your cleansing?'

Mr Dugdale told her.

He held nothing back. His voice was soft and mellifluous. His silky silver hair glowed in the light from the hurricane lamp. His fine features stood out firm and bold against the shades.

He told her of Delphine and her visit to his room. He told her of the girl's wish to offer him her love. He told her of his acceptance of that

172

offer. He told her of his life as he had told Delphine when she lay alongside him in his bed.

Dolly was enthralled. Not once did her gaze falter as his sonorous, mellisonant voice soared and ebbed and crooned to her the histories of his life.

'I was born in Riga. Mother was Hungarian. We never knew the nationality of my father. I was a stateless person. So I was given a Nansen passport.'

They replaced the bottle of port with a bottle of claret.

Once they were interrupted when Celia and Mamselle, unaware of their presence, entered the room.

'Piss off, you old crones,' bellowed Mr Dugdale.

All those amours. All those scandals. All those passions.

'But where was happiness?' he said.

He leant back in his chair, stretched out his legs and yawned expansively. Then he said: 'But now I have happiness.'

'Why?'

'Because, dear lady, I have been cleansed of my youth.'

They opened another bottle of claret.

And out on the glacis Celia said to Mamselle: 'Did you see all the empty bottles scattered round their feet?'

'I did indeed,' said Mamselle.

'It's no wonder we've got no money. It's all spent on drink.'

'Yes.'

'Do you know how much liquor the shits get through each week?'

'No.'

'Neither do I. But I do know for a fact vintage burgundy doesn't come cheap these days.'

They sipped at their absinthe.

'What are we going to do, Mamselle? We're trapped here. We can't afford to stay. We can't afford to move. We'll starve to death and years later explorers will find our bleached bones and the withered rags and tatters of our clothes. Oh, Mamselle, what are we to do?'

'We should open a house,' said Mamselle.

'A house?'

'Yes. The girls here are all exceptionally pretty. They'd be very willing and eager I'm sure to please all ages and all tastes. You yourself could be a great source of comfort to the less demanding.'

'I don't follow you,' said Celia.

'Let me explain to you in simple and explicit terms,' said Mamselle.

But before she could continue, Celia jumped out of her chair and shouted: 'Got it!'

'Got what?'

'The answer to our problems. We'll get your gangster to help.'

'My gangster?'

'Yes. He must be loaded with money now.'

'What on earth are you talking about, Celia?'

'I'm talking about your gangster. You know. That awful man on the boat with the ghastly suits and the greasy hair and the stinking breath and the –'

'What about him?'

'Dolly bumped into him one day last week. Didn't I tell you?'

'No, Celia, you most certainly did not,' said Mamselle.

'Right then,' said Celia. 'I'll tell you.'

As soon as she heard Celia's story Mamselle leapt to her feet and stormed into the small retiring room where Dolly and Mr Dugdale were idling their way through a bottle of kümmel.

'Right then, you old cow!' she screamed. 'Where is he?'

'Where is whom?' said Dolly with ornate, tipsy formality. 'Where is whom of whom you are talking about?'

'My gangster,' said Mamselle. 'The man who shot your colonel's guts out.'

'Oh him,' said Dolly, and she turned to Mr Dugdale and said, 'She is talking about whom we are both acquainted of.'

'Wallflowers,' said Mr Dugdale. 'Flowerpots. Potted meat.'

Mamselle took hold of Dolly by the shoulders and commenced to shake her.

'Where is he? Where is he?' she screamed at the top of her voice.

'I haven't the faintest idea, my dear,' said Dolly placidly. 'I've been thoroughly cleansed, you see. I recommend it most heartily.'

Next morning they were refused credit.

And by the end of the week the little girls were begging for food at the kitchen door.

'Little shits!' said Dolly. 'Why can't they make do with rum like the rest of us?'

46

The situation was indeed desperate.

In the kitchen Ernestine and Rodney feasted on goat and wild boar and plump chicken and sizzling, ring-tailed pigeon.

In the dining room the pupils were reduced to lentils and semolina and emaciated, sticky-boned fish and sour grey bread.

Dolly issued increased rations of burgundy and cancelled all lessons so they could tend to their hangovers in peace and quiet.

'You are doomed,' said Ernestine each morning as she padded softly up and down the glacis sprinkling fresh sawdust. 'There is no escape, white niggers. You are faced with the eternity of holy damnation in the great throbbing void where cockerels scream and zombies cavort and beat their drums.'

'Obnoxious little black turd,' said Mr Dugdale.

Ernestine curled her lips and swaggered slowly out of the glacis.

'Now what have I said?' said Mr Dugdale.

Soon they grew too weak to swim in the bathing pool.

The Doucemain twins were able to float but they had no strength to towel themselves and they would lie in the sun like two shards of salt cod drying on a slab.

They were all too weak to make love.

'Shall we have sherry instead?' said Natasha.

'I think I'd rather have the hock,' said Roger Carey.

'It will be all so different when we get away, Burnaby.'

'I hope so, Samira. I hope so. My thing's just like a baby's little finger these days.'

All day long Celia raced hither and thither until she, too, was overtaken by fatigue.

'This can't go on,' she said to Mamselle.

'I know,' said Mamselle. 'That is why I am leaving.'

'Leaving? Leaving?' cried Celia, and she fell on her knees in front of Mamselle and clawed at the hem of her dress and sobbed and blubbered. 'You can't leave us. You can't leave me. What will I do without you?'

'I shall come back for you, Celia,' said Mamselle, stroking her hair. 'Don't worry, love. I'll come back.'

'But when?'

'When I have found him?'

'Who?'

'My gangster.'

'What?'

'If what Dolly told you is true, then he must be living in town. I shall seek him out. All those letters he wrote. You remember? You remember what he wanted from me? You remember what he promised me in return? Well then, I shall find him and I shall strike a deal with him. I've been doing that all my life, love. I'm an expert. I'm a dab hand. Don't bother your arse about me. I'll be back for you soon enough.'

And she left.

Dolly did not turn a hair when Celia told her of Mamselle's defection.

'Common little tart,' she said. 'French? And my backside. Chic? Sheep more like. Mutton dressed as lamb more like. Would you care for a bottle of stout?'

The three little girls danced from foot to foot outside the door to the kitchen.

'Please, Ernestine.'

'Oh, please, please, please.'

'Come on, you old tart. Give us some food. We're starving.'

'Jassy!'

'Jassy!'

'What's the matter? What have I said now?'

Ernestine beckoned them into her room. And there for the rest of the evening she fed them choicest meats and fruits. She fed them from the dead man's hand.

47

Natasha and Roger Carey clung to each other in support as they staggered upstairs. They entered the room and collapsed on their bed.

'Of course I could always cable my guardian for money.'

'Mm.'

'He's got oodles and oodles of money. He doesn't know what to do with it.'

'Mm.'

'Cheer me up, Roger. Tell me again. Tell me why you had to run away.'

'I embezzled money.'

'What?'

'I embezzled thousands and millions and billions and trillions of pounds.'

'But you told me you'd murdered somebody.'

'Did I?'

'You pig! You pig!' she cried, trying to strike him about the body. But she hadn't the strength. She sank onto her back, closed her eyes and murmured: 'I love you so much, Roger. You're such a dreadful shit.'

Burnaby and Samira rarely left their room.

'Soon, Burnaby. Soon.'

'Yes.'

'If we don't escape soon, we shall die.'

'I know.'

'The plans are in a high state of advance,' she said, and then she giggled to herself. She had heard those words spoken before. The customs officer in her father's courtyard. The contraband laid out on the cobbles. The money changing hands. The officer touching the peak of his cap and saluting. Her father rubbing his hands together softly and shiftily.

Burnaby moaned with hunger.

'You are so good to me, Samira,' he said. 'Tell me how the plans are advancing.'

'I have spoken with Rodney. He will arrange things.'

'But how?'

Samira kissed him on the forehead. She kissed him on the temple. She would have kissed him on other parts of the body, but she had not the energy.

The food rations became more severe.

The pleas of the little girls became more strident.

The Negroes gathered on the lawn in full view long before dusk. They stared. They whispered. They cackled. They jeered and sometimes they spat.

'We can't have this,' said Guy Doucemain.

'Of course not,' said Charles Doucemain.

'We're English. They're just a load of niggers.'

'And Father's a general.'

'And Uncle's an admiral.'

'Shall we?'

'Yes. Come on. Action!'

They took the kukri which their father had given them as a parting souvenir. They took the cutlass which the Admiral had presented to them in similar vein. They dragged themselves out of the tree house. They tottered down the rope and they crumpled up on landing on the ground. The Negroes looked on. Someone began to giggle. And then the others joined in. And then they began to laugh. And they clapped their hands and stamped their feet.

'Back, you bastards, back!' roared Guy Doucemain, and he waved his kukri high above his head and advanced slowly on the horde.

His brother thrust out his cutlass and moved slow and menacing at his brother's side.

At first the black people laughed and jeered. But when they saw the purpose in the two boys' mien they stopped their clatter and glanced at each other nervously.

Suddenly Guy Doucemain stopped. He drew back his wicked knife and hurled it with all his might at the Negroes. A shriek of pain. A slim youth fell to the ground, blood gushing from his shoulder. In an instant the crowd howled out in fear. They dragged the wounded man upright and they fled with him into the jungle.

'Well thrown, sir,' said Charles Doucemain.

'Thank you,' said his brother. 'But after all is said and done, they were only a gang of niggers, weren't they?'

178

48

And then the drink began to run out.

First the claret. Then the burgundy. Then the whisky. Then the kümmel.

'We'll have to put the shits on Cointreau,' said Dolly.

No one said a word.

'Come on, come on, what's wrong with you?' cried Dolly. 'Why the gloom? Why the despondency? We're winning, aren't we? We're always winning. That's what life's all about.'

Mr Dugdale shook his head.

'I fear not, Dolly,' he said. 'As far as I'm concerned life has always been an inconclusive draw.'

Dolly organised foraging parties. The Doucemain twins proved adept at trapping cumbersome flightless rails and coots. Burnaby managed to snare the odd toad or two. The little girls showed their worth as diggers of roots and grubs and collectors of acrid berries.

None the less poverty and starvation relentlessly cast their shrouds over them.

From the kitchen the smells of cooking coiled round their noses, and the fizzle and spat of frying and the rumbling and bubbling of stewing thrashed in their ears.

Their skin began to sag on their addled bones. And then it began to flake. The bellies of the little girls began to distend and their legs were like spindles. Celia spent hour after hour in a coma. And then she would wake up, scream and prowl round the house slamming doors and rattling windows and banging her head against the shutters.

The others did not leave their beds.

Slowly and surely death came squirming and slithering out of the jungle and sniffed and snuffled at their unbolted doors.

And then Mrs Otto stepped in.

She had not been seen for weeks.

Suddenly she appeared at the top of the stairs, yawning and clutching the *Speisewagen* close to her chest. She looked all around her. There was not a soul nor sinner in sight. Then she caught sight of Ernestine. She was sitting at Dolly's desk in the small retiring room sipping fastidiously from a glass of sherry.

Mrs Otto lumbered up to her and smashed her flush on top of the skull with her massive fist.

'Up, nigger,' she growled. 'On your feet.'

Ernestine's eyes flashed. The whites were suffused with red. She snarled back her lips. She crouched. She held her arms close to her sides. She began to circle slowly round Mrs Otto on the balls of her feet.

'Less of that,' said Mrs Otto. 'This is no time for ballroom dancing. Where is everyone?'

Ernestine did not speak.

Quite carelessly Mrs Otto stretched at a podgy forearm. She grasped hold of Ernestine by the collar of her black dress and shook her till her teeth rattled.

'What is going on?' she said. 'You tell me now. What goes on?'

Ernestine wriggled herself free from Mrs Otto's grasp.

And she rasped out: 'They have no food. They have no money to buy food. They are starving. They are dying.'

She gobbed hard on the ground at Mrs Otto's feet.

She tossed her head, flaunted her shoulders and whisked out of the room.

Mrs Otto clicked her tongue and turned to her *Speisewagen*.

'Do you hear that?' she said. 'She said they're dying. Right then. We soon see about that.'

She made her way cumbersomely to Dolly's bedroom and, wheezing and panting, lowered herself heavily on the bed where Dolly was lying, her head swathed in cold compresses.

'They tell me you are starving,' said Mrs Otto.

'Do they?' said Dolly.

'There is no trouble,' said Mrs Otto. 'I have the means to help you.'

She held up her *Speisewagen*.

'Oh no. No. No. Anything but that,' screamed Dolly. 'I'd rather carry on starving to death, thank you very much.'

Mrs Otto chuckled.

She opened up the bag and began to root ponderously in its deepest recesses.

Finally she grunted with pleasure and drew out of her bag a wad of notes.

It was an extremely thick wad of notes.

It consisted of currency from twenty-three sovereign states, three over-seas territories and one League of Nations mandate.

It was covered in vestiges of coleslaw salad, beetroot, rhubarb chutney, rollmop herring, Wiener schnitzel, baked beans, brown sauce, noodles, battered haddock, Russian egg and maggots.

'My life savings,' said Mrs Otto. 'They are of no use to me no more. You are most welcome.'

When Dolly counted the money, she discovered that at current rates of exchange it amounted to approximately nine hundred and sixty-three pounds fourteen shillings and tuppence.

She dashed into the garden, turned round to face the house and bellowed full blast: 'We're saved! We're saved! We're back in business.'

And then she scratched her chin and said softly to herself: 'We mustn't squander it. We must be careful. I think I'll abandon the château-bottled stuff for a while.'

49

Dolly decided to throw a ball.

'It will be a *bal masqué*,' she said. 'It will be the talk of the island. Never before in its history will such a spectacle have been witnessed. We shall have Pathans guarding the gates. We shall have Sudanese warriors serving canapés on their beaten-silver scimitars. We shall dress the niggers in crinolines and doeskin breeches.'

'But we haven't got the money left for it, Dolly,' said Celia.

'We shall hire musicians of the finest, most ferocious talent and reputation. We shall engage Klemperer and Chaliapin. We shall summon Sidney Bechet and Josephine Baker. I shall invite Chopin to write a special polka. And as for the food, my dear Celia! Stupendous. Colossal. We shall have whole oxen roasted on spits turned by Berber tribesmen. We shall –'

'But, Dolly, we've no money,' screamed Celia. 'We've spent it repaying our debts. We've only got enough for another week's food.'

'We shall have the choicest, most succulent sweetmeats served from the navels of Persian concubines. We shall have grouse specially flown in from the Scottish moors and caviare brought by submarine from the fatlands of Mother Russia. We shall have . . .'

Celia left the room, shaking her head sadly and muttering to herself: 'Come back, black owl. All is forgiven.'

The money did run out within the week.

The drink stocks had, of course, been lavishly replenished. Once more the pupils were forced to exist on a diet of cream crackers, gentleman's relish and estate-bottled claret.

'Never mind, Burnaby. Not long to go now. It's all arranged.'

'Terrific.'

'Rodney has been an absolute brick. He's arranged everything. He's organised a boat for us. He says the owner's a bit of a rummy but he's very reliable and very experienced in smuggling people off the island. All we have to do now is wait for the tides and the winds.'

'Terrific. But how did you persuade Rodney to do it?'

'I told him that if he didn't help us, my father and my brothers and my uncles and my cousins and their warriors would sail across the oceans in their battle dhows and hang him from the highest palm tree and cut his balls off.'

'Terrific – the sooner the better.'

'Oh yes, Burnaby, oh yes – the sooner the better.'

He squealed in agony of joy as she mounted him.

As the days frittered away, so did the hunger of Dolly's party increase. This time Ernestine did not feed the little girls at the kitchen door. This time the success of the foraging parties was limited. There was a fatal epidemic among the toads who died in their thousands from blisters. The flightless rails and coots had deserted the jungle for more hospitable climes. The berry collecting ended when Louise ate three handfuls of death berries and was rushed off to hospital on the pack cart driven by Rodney. The doctor said she would not survive.

Next morning they found Major Pickavance lying in the front porch.

He was dressed as a choirboy.

He told them he was dying.

'My dear fellow. My poor old chap,' said Mr Dugdale. 'You must take my room. You must take my bed. You must take all my love and all my care and consideration.'

The Doucemain twins bore the Major gently upstairs and laid him to rest on Mr Dugdale's bed.

'There, there, there,' said Mr Dugdale. 'You are back home among loving, caring friends. Oh indeed you are, you useless little prick.'

50

For two days Major Pickavance lingered between sleep and waking.

Mr Dugdale and Delphine gave him their meagre rations. But he was too ill to digest the soya beans and he drank so much sauternes that he fell out of bed three times in a drunken stupor.

Then on the third day he opened his eyes, and they were clear. He raised himself up.

'No, no, my dear fellow,' said Mr Dugdale. 'Take care of yourself. Don't be a twat all your life.'

Major Pickavance smiled weakly. He allowed Delphine to place pillows behind his back. He smiled graciously when she filled his toothbrush glass with a Bernkasteler Ausspaetlese.

'I wish to tell you what happened to me,' he said.

'Oh God,' said Mr Dugdale. 'He's going to bore the living shits out of us.'

'Shush,' said Delphine sharply. 'For heaven's sake, Aubrey. Shush!'

'Now what have I said?' said Mr Dugdale, and he smiled at Major Pickavance and tenderly wiped the beads of perspiration from his brow.

'I had the most wonderful time at Monsieur Willy's,' said the Major. 'Everyone was so kind to me. They were so attentive and loving. They beat me constantly. It was lovely. They debased me and humiliated me. I was ecstatic. They made me serve drinks to the clients dressed in a wig of blond ringlets and velvet pantaloons. It was heaven. Sheer heaven.'

Mr Dugdale smiled and refilled his glass.

'There, there, old man,' he said. 'Don't disturb yourself. Please don't distress yourself.'

'They were kindness personified. And the girls! Oh, what lovely creatures those girls were. Most of them convent-educated, you know. Oh yes. All of them convent-educated except for the Jewess with the tattooed buttocks. I think she came from Dumfries. How delicate they were, those girls. How refined. How elegant. I used to bathe their feet and cut their toenails. Snip, snip, snip. Never in the whole of my life had I felt so happy. Never before had I felt so fulfilled.

'They made me ride a fairy cycle round the gardens attending to the needs of the clients. And those clients! What delightful men! The Monsignor was kindness itself. So thoughtful. So charitable. A real credit to his faith. And the Governor, too, when he wasn't inebriated, could be most considerate. He showed me his cigarette cards once. I could not possibly have lived in greater bliss.'

'I'm sure,' said Mr Dugdale tenderly. 'Let me pour you more wine.'

He uncorked another bottle and refurbished Major Pickavance's glass.

The Major nodded his thanks, sighed, struggled a while for breath and then continued his story.

'And then one morning I fell ill. The doctor said it was a fatal illness. Poor things – they simply hadn't the facilities to deal with a dying man. But they were so thoughtful. They offered to smother me in my sleep or spike my bouillon with cyanide.

'I thanked them profusely for their kindness. I said I didn't want them to think that I was ungrateful, but that I would take it as the greatest possible favour if they would bring me here to die peacefully among chums. And this they did. And I shall be eternally grateful to them.'

He sank back exhausted.

Mr Dugdale mopped his brow again and Delphine fanned him with the hem of her skirt.

'There, there. Sleep in peace. Die surrounded by your loved ones,' said Mr Dugdale.

He stroked his old friend's brow once more.

'You poor, benighted little runt,' he said tenderly.

Two days later the bailiffs arrived and threatened Dolly with eviction unless her outstanding debts were paid within the week.

On the following day a letter arrived from the Governor, informing her that unless the conduct of the school were changed immediately he would be forced to expel them from the island.

Once more they lolled in the torpor of hunger. Their bones rattled. Their skin sagged. The Doucemain twins fought each other savagely for a chicken's foot they found at the back of the kitchen.

That night Samira said: 'Tomorrow night, Burnaby. That's when we bolt for it.'

'Terrific.'

'We mustn't give anything away. We can take nothing with us. I have some money hidden in my shift. It will get us by till we reach Cuba and then I will cable Father for money.'

'Won't he slit our throats, if he finds out?'

'Not if we are strong in our love, Burnaby. Not if we are firm and united. Not if you give me a child.'

'A child?' said Burnaby. 'Terrific!'

Samira kissed him. In the darkness she smiled to herself and wondered what it would be like to drown in an open boat and have one's bones crunched and ground by gnashing sharks.

She was happy.

She was truly happy. She was happier than Natasha. She had never been so happy in the whole of her life.

And then Mamselle arrived at Marchmain's Rest with the gangster and put forward their proposition.

The school was in debt.

They knew how Dolly could repay that debt three times over and still have money to spare.

She should sell Samira to be married.

51

Dolly sat down heavily.

She gasped.

Mamselle smiled.

The gangster probed his teeth with a gold toothpick glinting with diamonds.

'Well?' said Mamselle. 'What do you think to it?'

Dolly turned to Celia.

'Do you think we ought to inform Samira?' she said.

'First things first,' said Celia. Then she turned to Mamselle and said: 'Who is this man who is willing to pay so much for Samira?'

'He's outside in the Cadillac,' said Mamselle. 'Shall we fetch him in?'

'Yes,' said Celia. 'It might help our decision.'

Without turning to the gangster Mamselle snapped: 'Bring him in, Jean-Claude. And quick about it. Shift yourself.'

She smiled at Dolly and Celia.

She was wearing a dress of shimmering silk, nipped at the waist, slit to the thighs. Over her shoulders was a careless mink stole.

The gangster returned with the putative suitor.

He was a gargantuan man of some sixty summers. He waddled, rippling with wrinkled flab. He wheezed. His teeth were stained with tobacco and there was pus in the corner of his right eye. On his head he wore a scarlet turban and a blue silk tarboosh. On his feet he wore curved-toed slippers. On his body he wore a jubbah and Harris tweed knickerbockers.

'Say how do to the sultan,' said Mamselle.

'Good morning,' said Dolly. 'Would you care for a drink?'

'Would he care for a drink? Don't make me laugh, love,' said Mamselle. 'He's been rat-arsed ever since we left town, hasn't he, Jean-Claude?'

'Yes,' said the gangster.

'I'd better fetch Samira,' said Celia.

She left the large drawing room. Mamselle smiled at Dolly and pointed at the sultan.

'Ugly old sod, isn't he?' she said.

'Well I . . .'

'Oh, don't mither, love. He doesn't speak a word of English. All you need to know is that he's stinking rich and he's prepared to shell out thousands to get Samira.'

'But how . . .'

'Listen, Dolly. Listen to me, love. One good turn deserves another. You got me out of that mess all those years ago when I was in dire straits. Right then. I'll get you out of your mess.'

Dolly looked from face to face.

The sultan had plunged his thumb halfway up his nose and was contentedly excavating, grunting and groaning with pleasure.

The gangster smiled at Dolly and winked.

Mamselle pursed her lips, pouted and said: 'I talked it over with Jean-Claude, didn't I, Jean-Claude? I said to him: "Now then, Jean-Claude, who do we know can help Dolly out of her mess?" So we put our thinking caps on, and we came up with the sultan here. He's been looking for a bride for years, has the sultan. So we casually mentioned Samira to him. Well, he almost burst a gasket, didn't he, Jean-Claude? His eyes rolled. His eyes slavered. He was like an otter hound on heat. And when I described her – well, words can't paint the scene, can they, Jean-Claude? I thought he was going to have a seizure. I was convinced of it. We started to talk money and he held up his hand and shook his head. Money was no object, he said, didn't he, Jean-Claude? He said –'

'Hold on,' said Dolly. 'I thought you said he didn't understand a word of English?'

Mamselle turned to the sultan and winked.

He winked back.

'This is the universal language we speak, love,' she said to Dolly. 'Everyone understands that.'

And Celia returned with Samira.

Celia had warned her, informed her and prepared her.

She looked to neither right nor left when she entered the room.

She had eyes only for the sultan. She stood stock-still and stared at him silently.

Dolly coughed nervously.

'You've got to make your decision by nightfall, Samira,' she said.

Samira nodded slowly.

Suddenly she turned on her heels and left the room.

The jumble of voices.

The confusion of voices.

The despair. The anger. The misery. The rage.

'But you can't, you can't, you can't. You just can't.'

'I have my duty to perform, Burnaby.'

'It's idiotic. It's insane. Do you love him? Do you, do you, do you, do you, do you?'

'No, Natasha. But I have my duty to perform.'

'Only you can decide, my dear.'

'Yes, Mr Dugdale.'

'You can't, Samira. You can't.'

'Maybe I must, Polly.'

'No, Samira. No. No. Please don't.'

'Maybe it is ordained for me, Jassy.'

'Don't do it, Samira. We'll find another way out of the mess. I'll sort things out. I can't see you disappearing into the clutches of that odorous, obese, snickering, slavering brute.'

'I shall think it over, Celia.'

'You must not commit yourself on my account, Samira. I am no stranger to disaster and distress. Once I had a black owl. He taught me. He cursed me. He tormented me. He consumed me and engulfed me in the venom from his beak and the fire from his eyes. Oh, how I wish I had him back.'

'I'm sure you do, Dolly.'

'You must do it, Samira. You have no other choice.'

'Haven't I, Delphine?'

'No, Samira, and I will tell you why.'

The two girls were sitting by the bathing pool at the bottom of the garden. They were sharing a crust of bread Delphine had found on the kitchen's rubbish dump. She had beaten back the crows to gain it.

'You don't owe it to Dolly or to the school or to your friends. You owe it to yourself.'

'Tell me why, Delphine.'

'It is your chance to escape.'

'But I'm going to escape with Burnaby.'

'To what, Samira? To what?'

Samira turned her head away. The water in the bathing pool was streaked with blue-grey slime. The octopus orchid tree was bare. The birds did not sing.

'I am dumpy and dowdy, Samira. So I've always lived my life through other people. Princes. Grand dukes, officers of the guards, coachmen, countesses, Mr Dugdale. You.'

'Me?'

'Yes. You are so beautiful, Samira. You are so extremely beautiful. Natasha is beautiful, too. But she is too beautiful. She is too everything. Too happy. Too miserable. Too spiteful. Too generous. Too timid. Too bold. Oh yes, she is beautiful. But she is beautiful of body and nothing more. You, Samira, are beautiful of body and you are beautiful of mind.'

She took hold of Samira's hand.

She pressed it.

She felt the response.

'Marry him. He's old. He's decrepit. He will not want anything from your body. He'll be incapable, Samira. Mr Dugdale has spoken about it, and he says the sultan only wants you as a possession. Nothing more. Nothing less. Mr Dugdale says all he wants to do is ogle you and bask in the admiration shown to you by others. He will give you anything you want. Anything, Samira. Anything you want in the whole wide world. Well then, Samira, use it. Exploit him. That's what Mr Dugdale says. And I agree.'

Delphine leant forward and kissed Samira on the cheek.

'Oh, the things you can do, Samira. The things you could have.'

'Yes.'

'The sledge swishing over the snow, Samira, and you wrapped deep in furs. The bells ringing on the harnesses. The horses plunging. Your lover, reins relaxed in his hands, turns to you. He smiles. He is home from the wars. He is safe. He is well. And he adores you.'

'Yes.'

'You could go to Hollywood.'

'Yes?'

'Of course, of course. You can go anywhere, Samira. You can do anything.'

'But what about Burnaby?'

'You can ride wild chargers in the deserts of Araby.'

'What about Burnaby?'

'You can stalk Sumatran tigers.'

'But what about Burnaby?'

'You can dine with great statesmen. You can flirt with famous poets and playwrights. You can converse with booze-sodden pugilists and holders of the world land speed record. You can make love with holders of the Schneider Trophy.'

'Yes, yes. But what about Burnaby?'

'Who?'

'Burnaby.'

'Oh him.'

Samira smiled. Then she stood up and said:

'Right. I have made up my mind.'

52

The day of Samira's wedding dawned with fat-bellied thunder, lightning, hissing sheets of rain and a distant rumble and grumble from the twin peaks.

Then the sun appeared and the earth and the trees streamed and mist rose from the skirts of the jungle and coiled its way through the silent canopy.

Drums throbbed.

During the two weeks since the proposal and acceptance of marriage, gangs of East Indian coolies had toiled ceaselessly round the clock cleaning and widening the tracks from Marchmain's Rest to the metalled road.

And it was down this newly furbished track that at the crack of dawn Samira bounced and swayed in the back of the sultan's fawn and orange Daimler Light Straight-Eight. She was accompanied by Mr Dugdale, who was to give her away at the civic ceremony, and by Delphine, who was to be her witness and bridesmaid.

The rest of the inmates of Marchmain's Rest waited for their return.

They were decked out in the finery provided by the sultan's bride money.

But their mood was sombre and gloomy.

Dolly sat in the small retiring room drinking cognac.

She had failed. She should have offered herself to the sultan. The poor girl. So frail, so fragile, so innocent. That great podge of blubber floundering all over her, wheezing and panting and dribbling. Oh God above, she had failed most wretchedly.

Celia sat in the small drawing room drinking vermouth.

That poor girl. She had failed her. Of course. Of course. She should have offered herself to the sultan. Of course. Of course. The fat bastard was obviously desperate for a woman. She had all the required attributes of a woman. She could meet his needs. She could satisfy his desires. Urgh! The stench rising from that porcine flesh. The drunken roll and shuffle. Podgy hands clawing at her body. Fume and spittle spraying her face.

Natasha and Roger Carey and the two little girls sat silently on the glacis.

Polly was sobbing softly. Jassy stared out at the garden.

Upstairs in his bedroom Burnaby squirmed and tossed and turned on his bed. The door was bolted. The windows were barred. The Doucemain twins stood guard on the landing.

In mid-afternoon the bridal procession returned.

There were cars, pantechnicons, charabancs, caravans, coaches and outriders with fluttering pennants. There were drums and cymbals, bassoons and trumpets. Tumblers performed their tricks on the lawn. Clowns swayed and jigged through the shrubbery. Porters bore steaming cauldrons and slowly-turning spits to the house. The girls from Monsieur Willy's danced to the pipes and drums of the French marines. Balloons soared into the sky and were borne away to sea on the trades.

Samira stood on the lawn in her simple gown.

There was a garland of orange blossom round her brow.

Her face was expressionless.

The sultan, draped in shimmers of gold and rubies, emeralds, amethyst, peridot, topaz and citrine, swayed backwards and forwards, grinning and leering at his bride.

The gangster took hold of his arm and heaved him towards the house. He stumbled and fell, dragging down the gangster with him. For a moment they thrashed wildly on the grass. Then two Senegalese sharpshooters dashed forwards and helped them to their feet.

The inhabitants of Marchmain's Rest looked on glumly.

'Well, come on, you lot,' cried Mamselle. 'Show a bit of enthusiasm, can't you?'

A Moroccan acrobat grabbed her round the waist and twirled her round and round and she fluttered her eyelashes and pouted her lips.

The Negroes hid in the shrubbery and watched and waited, their eyes rolling, their limbs quivering.

Just before the wedding feast was about to begin Celia took Mamselle to one side and said: 'We've known each other a long time, you and I.'

'We have that,' said Mamselle.

'Right then. Tell.'

Mamselle smiled.

She took off her mink cape, held it at arm's length and let it drop to the floor. It coiled itself softly and silkily and made not a whisper as it caressed the carpet.

'See that?' said Mamselle. 'That's class. Oh yes, Celia, that's class is that.'

She lit a cigarette.

'Right, I'll tell you,' she said. 'Well, when I left here I hitched a lift into town on Rodney's cart. I thought I knew where I'd find him – the nearest dosshouse. The steamiest dockside bar. I was wrong. The first person I asked directed me to his place. Talk about luxury. You name it, he's got it. And he wanted me. So he had me. And as soon as he had me, I had him. Oh yes, Celia, I had him by the short and curlies . . . literally. Little runt he is. Hopeless in bed. But I'd got him. He was mine. Give them what they want, Celia, and you've got them bound hand and foot to you.

'I didn't have to bide my time. I told him what was going on here. I told him. I said: "Jean-Claude, you've got to do something." "Right," he said. "Right, I will." And he did. He came up with the sultan. And Bob's your uncle, Fanny's your aunt.'

'I see,' said Celia. 'And where does he get his money from, this gangster of yours?'

'Oh, search me, love. I don't ask, I just take.'

She laughed and, linking Celia by the arm, steered her back to the dining room. On the way there she said: 'You want to come and see us some time. Stay with us. Stay as long as you like. We get all the programmes on the wireless, you know. We've got stacks and stacks of Victor Sylvester records. I'll get you a man as easy as anything. Well, they're crying out for anything these days.'

The wedding feast was gargantuan. The tables were groaning with mouth-watering food and palate-squirming wines. A string orchestra played melodies from Lehár and Strauss. Later a stout Negress with protruding teeth sang arias from Verdi and Gluck. Tumblers tumbled. Jugglers juggled. Contortionists contorted.

Mr Dugdale excused himself and pottered upstairs to his bedroom. He smiled warmly at Major Pickavance.

'Hello, bacon balls,' he said. 'How are you feeling?'

'Poor. Very poor,' said Major Pickavance. 'I am coming near to my death.'

Mr Dugdale sighed and sat down on the bedside chair.

'Is there anything I can do for you, old friend?' he said.

'Yes,' said Major Pickavance. 'You can tell me about the wedding.'

Mr Dugdale told him. He did not spare any detail. He related his story in calm and measured tones. There was no animation in his voice; not even when he described the sultan's snores and his coughing and retching and the way he stretched his length on the floor when summoned to kneel.

He told him of Samira's mien.

Major Pickavance began to cry.

'Poor girl,' he sobbed. 'Poor, precious girl.'

'We are all poor,' said Mr Dugdale. 'We are all precious.'

'True,' said Major Pickavance.

He was weaker now. His body was whisper-thin. His eyes turmoiled deep in their sockets. There was a hoarse flush to his cheeks.

'I am prepared for my death,' he said.

'Are you really?' said Mr Dugdale.

'Yes,' said Major Pickavance. 'I have decided to die a tepid death.'

'Good.'

'I shall be neither hot nor cold.'

'I see.'

'Just tepid.'

'Excellent.'

'I shall show no enthusiasm for my death. I shall not watch myself die. I shall be content, but not to the point of clapping my hands.'

'Good,' said Mr Dugdale softly. 'Good.'

Major Pickavance closed his eyes, turned his head on the pillow and whispered very softly: 'I shall not answer any more questions.'

And then he fell asleep.

When he pottered downstairs, Mr Dugdale found that the guests had transferred themselves to the ballroom. The girls from Monsieur Willy's were dancing the rhumba. The tumblers and the contortionists were sitting cross-legged on the floor playing dice. One of the Senegalese sharpshooters was dancing cheek to cheek with a blond French mariner.

Samira left the room to prepare herself for her departure.

She paused at the door. She looked round at all her friends. With her hands pressed in front of her forehead she nodded her farewells with each of them in turn.

As soon as she had left Dolly could contain herself no longer. She jumped onto the stage and bellowed at the top of her voice: 'No more. No more. Enough. I have had enough. Do you hear me? I have had enough.'

She screamed out those last few words. She looked around wildly. Her lips were spittled. Her eyes were wild.

'Bugger off,' she howled. 'Bugger off, the lot of you.'

She fled from the room. She stumbled into the hallway. She crashed through the front door and reeled down the flight of shallow steps.

Then she stopped. She sniffed the air and her whole body tensed and her jaws firmed and her eyes narrowed.

Purposefully, staring straight ahead, she strode to the kitchen. She flung open the door. Ernestine was there, crouching over a pot.

'Right,' shouted Dolly. 'Right, you black nigger bitch. What are you doing to us?'

'What I do to you?' snarled Ernestine. 'Why you want to know, white nigger bitch?'

'Give me back my owl.'

'I piss on your owl.'

'I want my black owl.'

'I piss on your black owl. I piss on you, white nigger bitch.'

The two women flew at each other. They crashed into pots and pans and ladles and calabashes. They clawed. They scratched. They ripped. Dolly's breasts twirled and whirled. Ernestine spat and snarled. They screamed. They hollered.

And then they heard the voice.

It was ice-spiked with panic and terror.

'Dolly! Dolly! For Christ's sake, Dolly!'

It was Roger Carey.

'Dolly, come quick,' he cried.

Ernestine squatted on her haunches in the mud and her voice sizzled and festered with hate as she said: 'Go, white nigger. Go and see what black nigger bitch has done.'

Dolly followed Roger Carey.

He led her rapidly to the garden.

It was full of people.

They were all silent.

Guests, inmates, musicians, tumblers, acrobats, contortionists, clowns, soldiers, marines, sharpshooters, coolies, Negroes and Mrs Otto.

All silent.

All standing motionless and staring at the tree which contained the Doucemain twins' house.

From its branches side by side hung the bodies of Samira and Burnaby.

Silence.

And then Delphine said very softly:

'I told her she could go anywhere she wished.'

53

That night after the wedding guests had departed, the Negroes burnt down Marchmain's Rest.

Exhausted, drained, grieving, wretched, frightened and bewildered, Dolly and her army bedded down on the glacis.

'Just like the first night here,' whispered Polly.

'Shush,' said Jassy. 'Let them sleep. They're all worn out, poor dears.'

It was Jassy who first heard the sounds of disturbance three hours later.

She heard a window shatter upstairs. Then she heard voices on the lawn. Before she could rise from the floor to investigate, a stone hurtled through the window of the glacis and showered them with shards and splinters of glass.

Dolly leapt to her feet. Her eyes were still feverish and wild. Her hair tumbled around her shoulders.

'Stand back,' she shouted to them as they staggered to their feet. 'Keep out of sight.'

Another stone smashed through the window.

'Bastards!' shouted Dolly. 'Drunken bloody niggers.'

She threw open the door and stepped outside.

'What do you want?' she shouted. 'What's going on here?'

Another volley of stones clattered on the glass roof and smashed more windows.

Dolly slammed the door. She was pale and there was fear in her eyes, which she tried to hide with the warmth of her smile as she shut and bolted the door.

'No problem,' she said. 'They'll be as right as rain when they've sobered up tomorrow morning.'

And then they smelt smoke.

'Christ Almighty, they've set fire to the back of the house,' cried Dolly.

They looked to where she was pointing. Smoke was billowing through the folding doors of the drawing room.

Natasha screamed. Celia gasped with horror. Mrs Otto snored soundly.

Rodney staggered in with two slopping buckets. When he opened the doors to throw in the water, the flames billowed out and he stumbled backwards and they felt the searing breath of the fire.

Roger Carey felt the same fear that had transfixed him that night when they had brought the wounded men aboard SS *Drayman*.

He fought it. He scratched at it. He swore at it.

And then something in him clicked and snapped open and he shouted: 'Come on. Quick. Let's get out of it. Move. Bloody well move!'

He grabbed hold of Natasha's wrist and dragged her to the door like a sack of turnips. He snatched up Polly and Jassy and dumped them alongside Natasha. He kicked Mrs Otto awake.

'Move!' he shouted. 'Move. Move. Move.'

Celia unbolted the door. Dolly began to usher them outside, when suddenly Mr Dugdale cried out: 'Major Pickavance! He's still upstairs in his bed.'

Before anyone could stop him he blundered into the main drawing room and disappeared into the clouds of rumbling smoke.

'Oh my God,' shouted Delphine.

She struggled free of Roger Carey's grasp and dashed after him.

In the acrid, cloying blackness she could see nothing. She could hear the roar of the flames and the crack of bursting glass and the clatter of falling timbers. She groped her way to the main staircase. She clawed her way up and then halfway up she stumbled over Mr Dugdale and fell on top of him. He was screeching for air. He was gulping for it. He was sobbing for it.

She took hold of him by the ankles and began to heave. He was a dead weight and his shoulder had caught fast in one of the soldiers of the banisters. She heaved and heaved and heaved. It was no use. She could not shift him. She began to wail with rage and frustration and terror.

'Delphine! Delphine! Where the hell are you?'

It was Roger Carey's voice.

'Over here,' she shouted. 'On the stairs.'

She heard him blunder and trip. She heard his feet and his hands skitter-scattering for grasp on the splintering wooden stairs. He tripped over her.

'He's stuck,' said Delphine, choking with the smoke, her eyes stinging and smarting.

Roger Carey grabbed Mr Dugdale by the scruff of the neck and yanked him free.

'Right,' he said. 'Let's get the hell out of here.'

They dragged Mr Dugdale down the stairs. A great ball of fire swooshed out of the small retiring room and snaked and whipped its way over their cowering heads. It hit the main drawing room with a shriek, a roar and a boom.

They burst open the front door and staggered out into the front garden bearing the limp, dangling body of Mr Dugdale between them.

They found Dolly and her charges huddling together and retreating slowly back to the house under the pressure of the mob of Negroes massed on the lawn.

The whole house was ablaze and the night was vicious with sparks. Great flames shot high into the sky from the blazing bamboo. The tree ferns, damp from the rains, smouldered, billowing out choking clouds of sulphurous smoke.

'Don't let them trap us,' shouted Roger Carey, pushing his way to the front. 'We've got to get away from the house.'

'Bastards! Bastards!' screamed Dolly. 'Make way, you load of black shite.'

The mob moved slowly towards them. Their eyes slashed at the night.

Then suddenly they heard the clink and clatter of harness and from round the back of the house came the pack cart driven wildly by Rodney.

'Folkies! Folkies! Climb aboard. Climb aboard pretty damn buggering quick.'

He was quaking with fear and his teeth chattered like castanets.

But they could not reach him. The mob crowded in on them. A stone whistled over their heads.

Someone shouted: 'White niggers. Look at the white niggers shitting themselves. White niggers. White niggers.'

And then the rest of the mob took up the chant.

'White niggers. White niggers. White niggers.'

'Back, you bastards,' shouted Dolly. 'Back off, you vermin.'

But still the crowd pressed forward.

Some of them were laughing. Some of them were yelling and cursing. Some of them carried flaring branches. A stone was lobbed from the back of the crowd. It hit Jassy on the shoulder. But she did not flinch.

She just whispered to herself through tight-gritted teeth: 'Black bastards! Black nigger bastards!'

The horses began to plunge and rear. Rodney screamed at them and beat them with his whip.

'We've got to get to that cart,' said Roger Carey to Celia. 'It's our only hope.'

He tried to force his way through the crowd. All at once they fell silent. They parted. And through the passage of black, sweat-smouldering bodies appeared Ernestine. She wore a new headscarf. It was vivid scarlet. She wore a new dress. It was jet black. The whites of her eyes glared blood red from the flames. She walked slowly up to Dolly. She pressed her nose right into Dolly's face.

'You want your black owl, white nigger?' she said. 'So here it is. Take it. Take it right now. No problem.'

Behind her back she was holding a machete. Slowly she raised it above her head.

And then the voices rang out.

'Black pigs! Here. Over here, black pigs.'

It was the Doucemain twins.

They were standing at the foot of their tree house. They did not hold weapons of war in their hands. They held the weapons of abuse and contempt and mockery.

They directed them at the mob.

'Black pigs,' they shouted. 'We piss on you. Black pigs.'

The mob bayed. The mob cursed and howled. It turned to the twins. Ernestine was deserted as the Negroes pushed towards the tree house. The Doucemain twins scrambled up into its highest branches and mocked them again.

'Right!' screamed Roger Carey. 'The cart!'

They scrambled aboard it. Delphine, with the help of Jassy and Mrs Otto, scrambled aboard the dead weight of Mr Dugdale. Celia snatched up Polly. Dolly clambered up beside Rodney. He cracked his whip and the horses reared again.

'Natasha!' bellowed Roger Carey. 'Where the hell's Natasha?'

'There, Roger, there,' cried Jassy.

Natasha was standing rigid and motionless in the lee of the octopus orchid. Flames were snaking and sputtering up its trunk.

'Natasha! Natasha!'

Roger Carey leapt down from the cart and sprang towards her. He grabbed hold of her arm. But he could not move her. She was leaden with fear. He tugged. His feet scrabbled at the earth as he tugged and tugged. But she would not budge.

Suddenly he drew back his feet and punched her flush on the point of the chin. He flung her senseless body over his shoulder and jumped back on the cart as Rodney whipped the horses into action.

The whole garden was ablaze now. The cart rocked and swayed crazily as it rattled through the barriers of fire. Everything was burning. The house was burning. The golden ferns, the silver ferns, the orchids, the roses, the hibiscuses, the magnolias, the honeysuckle, the jasmine, the clematis, the quince and the jew's mallow – all were burning.

And the tree house was burning, too.

In its fiery death the Doucemain twins cowered and hugged each other tightly and in their eyes was the look of triumph in their defeat of their parents.

And the parrot screeched at the top of its voice: 'Black nigger bastards. Black nigger bastards!'

And then it was engulfed by the flames.

And Roger Carey said to himself:

'I'm sure I've seen this all before.'

PART THREE

54

'The Governor isn't in residence at the moment,' said Colonel Ryder. 'He seems to have tootled off somewhere. God knows where. Still, not to worry. I dare say something will turn up in due course. Anyone care to inspect my collection of beer mats?'

They were quartered once more in the Governor's residence.

The days passed.

Jassy decided it was time for her to assert herself.

She was proud of her conduct during the fire.

She had not shirked her duty. She had been steadfast and brave. It was as though the flames had consumed her shyness in the same way that they had consumed the tree house and the flaring bamboos.

She decided that the cooking was execrable and the standards of hygiene deplorable. She established herself in the kitchen and with Polly as a surly, unwilling assistant, re-arranged the menus, supervised the cooking and the ordering of provisions and endeared herself to the entire kitchen staff whose boils, rashes and pustules disappeared within ten days of her establishment of the new regime.

Mr Dugdale was blissfully happy and content. He had not spoken a word since his rescue from the inferno of Marchmain's Rest. He lay in his bed peaceful and silent, gently simmering in the devoted care and attention of Delphine.

How dumpy she was. How dowdy. Yet her beauty shimmered through and matured as each single minute passed by. How he adored watching the progress of her ageing. She had long since outstripped Natasha. Soon she would catch up on Celia. And then for Mrs Otto!

How wonderful. They would grow old together.

How wonderful, too, to be wanted. How wonderful to be fussed over. He had always hated fuss. The nursemaid had fussed over him. The doctor had fussed over him in his sickly boyhood. His mother had fussed over him when he got his Nansen passport. He'd loathed it. But now Delphine was fussing over him, and he loved it.

The look in her eyes was so tender. The touch of her hands was so subtle. How lovely it was to be growing old. How fulfilling to have abandoned youth and virility and passion and anguish. Yes, he was a deeply contented man.

And so he spoke.

For the first time in two weeks he spoke.

'Rivers are roads and march and carry you where you wish to go,' he said.

'What's that?' said Delphine. 'What's that you said?'

He turned his head to her and smiled. He had not meant to speak. It had just popped out. That was the best way to communicate. He would devote his whole life to letting things pop out.

Delphine stroked his cheeks.

'You spoke,' she said delightedly.

Pascal. It was a quotation from Pascal. He had seen it years ago on a London Transport poster advertising the charms of Hampton Court Palace.

He closed his eyes. He could see the poster vividly. The motor launches on the river. The skiffs. The swans. The high chimneys of the palace clawing at the sky.

Ah, a man could indeed die happy with visions so clear and sparkling in his mind's eye.

Creative old age, he said to himself.

Long live creative old age.

Delphine swatted contentedly at the bumble of a flying beetle.

Dolly was not content.

She sat with Celia in the garden watching the major-domo's wall-eyed Boston terrier waving its stunted tail and wafting the flowers as it limped down to the carp pond.

'Do you know where I'd love to be at this very moment, Celia?'

'No. Where?'

'Riding on the Romney, Hythe and Dymchurch Railway.'

'How lovely, Dolly.'

'The wind roaring across the marsh. Smuts from the loco smarting in our eyes. The prospect of crumpets.'

'The prospect of crumpets! Ah, how lovely, Dolly.'

Dolly took another lazy sip at her rum punch. Hummingbirds flashed iridescent in the soothe of the sun. Dragonflies hovered lazily over the carp pond.

'I want the chill back in my life,' she said.

'Do you, Dolly?'

'I want bleak winds and dampness. Dampness in your bones. Dampness on the sheets and in the pillows. Dampness in the pit of your vest when you put it on in the morning. Dampness everywhere.'

Celia did not speak. She wanted to agree, but she could not help remembering their visits to Mamselle and her gangster's residence. The memories were warm and soothing. Dancing to the records of Geraldo and Roy Fox. Smoked salmon and goat cheese. Mazawattee tea and chocolate digestives. Robinson Cleaver on the wireless all the way from London.

'My God, how I hate the niggers,' said Dolly.

'Mm.'

'A land free of niggers – that's what I want, Celia. That's why I can't wait to get home.'

Roger watched them from his bedroom window.

He turned to Natasha. She was lying on the bed, staring into space.

'Speak to me,' he said. 'Say something.'

Nothing. She moved not a muscle.

'Why are you doing this to me? Why do you behave like this? One minute rapturously happy. Next minute crumpled up in misery and despair. Why? Why do you do this to me? One minute talk, talk, talk. Next minute total silence. I can't cope with it. I can't be expected to cope. I never know where I am with you. There's no method in your behaviour. There's no sanity. Speak to me. Tell me what's going on.'

She said nothing.

He strode angrily out of the room slamming the door behind him.

She did not move. Her face remained expressionless.

She thought she felt the draught of a black owl's wings as it fluttered tentatively above her shoulder.

But she could not be sure.

Roger Carey bumped into Celia in the hall.

'Ah, Celia,' he said. 'And how are you this lovely day?'

'Very well, thank you.'

He paused. He hesitated. Then he said: 'I'm going to walk into town. I thought I might have a spot of afternoon tea. Would you care to join me?'

Celia blushed and flustered.

207

'Well. I . . .'

'Good. That's settled. How very nice.'

And he took hold of her arm and directed her to the door. On the driveway they bumped into Louise.

'Ah, Louise,' said Celia, pointing at her suitcase. 'Where have you been? Anywhere nice?'

'I've been in hospital,' said Louise. 'I got poisoned by berries. I was at death's door for days and days and days.'

'Oh dear,' said Celia. 'What a nuisance for you.'

They sauntered down the hill to the centre of town. It was a fresh day. The shacks and the shanties did not look so cowed or forlorn. The curs did not snap and growl. The flies did not cluster round their sores. There was no stench from the abattoir. There was no gore in the gutters.

He's holding my arm. Gosh, how delicious. How delicious it would be to walk arm in arm through a marshland storm. The gale turning the umbrella inside out. The rain flackering at our waterproofs. Our wellingtons squelching. Water cascading from the brims of our sou'westers.

Mind you, it could be just as nice as dancing cheek to cheek to the music of Chappie D'Amato.

'I hope this suits,' said Roger Carey.

He led her into a tearoom and seated her in the bay window overlooking the harbour. There were potted palms. The furniture was white. The waiter was Indian. Roger Carey ordered sardines on toast, scones with cream and blackberry jam, and Darjeeling tea.

The water in the harbour was not oily and scummy. It sparkled. The bum boats were jaunty. The old tramp that hopped the islands pottered good-naturedly out to the open sea.

'How is Natasha?' said Celia.

Roger Carey grunted.

Trouble again. There always will be trouble. A beautiful girl. But wilful. Moody. A torrent of jumbled passions. Too complex to handle. There would never be a happy end to her life. Never, never.

'You seem to be preoccupied.'

'Do I?'

He *was* preoccupied.

Celia. He had never seen her in this light before. Honest. Fresh. Wholesome. Modest. Generous. Gentle. Handsome.

Yes, she was a handsome woman. What lay beneath those frumpy clothes? She had a generous body. Not plump. Generous. A generous body designed to please. Her skin was fresh. Her eyes were fresh.

She was womanly. Womanly – that was the word.

'You're such a mystery to us all, Roger,' she said.

'Am I indeed?'

'Oh yes. A real mystery.'

Should he tell her? Should he lean across, take hold of her hand and tell her the whole story?

He ordered fresh tea.

She felt his interest. She felt the intrigue of his emotions. She blushed. He was younger than herself. But did it matter? She had things to offer a man. She had things to offer specifically to him. She could love him. She could delight him. She had no experiences in these matters. But she could always mug it up. In any case surely there must be a natural instinct. Surely they weren't descended from chimpanzees for nothing.

Arm in arm they walked back up the hill.

Did he deliberately press himself into her when they moved to dodge the mound of dog dirt? Did he squeeze her hand just a bit too tightly when they stepped over the dead cat?

'Well, Celia, I enjoyed that.'

'So did I.'

'We must do it again. Will tomorrow be convenient?'

'Oh yes. Tomorrow will be lovely, Roger.'

And the day after.

And the day after that. And the week after that. And the month and the year and the decade and the century and the millennium.

Later that evening Mr Dugdale turned over in bed.

Yes, Delphine was still there. As always she was lying alongside him. As always her sleeping attire was unruffled. As always she was innocent of carnal pleasures. Her only pleasures were service and self-sacrifice.

He grunted with pleasure.

'All, everything that I understand, I understand only because I love,' he said.

It just popped out.

55

Two items of note occurred on the following day.

First, Natasha spoke.

Secondly, Colonel Ryder proposed marriage to Dolly.

Natasha first:

It was mid-morning.

As usual she had not responded to Roger Carey's blandishments. He had brought her breakfast in bed on a tray – melon, grapefruit, figs, two lightly boiled eggs, croissants from Port Cedric, fresh Viennese coffee. She had not touched the tray. He had sat on the foot of the bed telling her of Louise's return from hospital, of the Sikh major-domo's varicose veins, of the dead rat they had found in the carp pool. She had not responded. Not a word did she utter. Not a movement of muscle. Furious, he had charged out of the room.

A little later she felt again the draught on her shoulders. She shivered. She rose from her bed. She walked along the corridor and threw open the door of Mr Dugdale's bedroom.

The old man was sitting in a deep armchair, sipping at a glass of dry sherry and puffing at a long, slim cheroot. Delphine was squatting at his feet reading the morning newspaper to him.

'Ah,' cried Natasha. 'How lovely to see you both. And particularly you, Mr Dugdale. How well you look. Doesn't he look well, Delphine? And how handsome. You're more handsome than ever, do you know that, Mr Dugdale? In fact, I'd go as far as to say that you are the most handsome man I have ever met in the whole of my life. No. Really you are. No wonder you look so happy. It's no wonder he looks so happy, is it, Delphine?'

'Out!' screamed Delphine. 'Out, out, out.'

Never before had she raised her voice in anger. Never before had she lost control of herself. Never before had she struck another person.

Natasha reeled away clutching her nose.

She staggered along the corridor bumping from wall to wall. But when she removed her hand from her nose, there was a smile of triumph on her face, and her eyes flashed wickedly.

'I was furious when Natasha told me what she'd done. I was incensed.'

'I'm not surprised, Roger. It was a wicked thing to do.'

'Wicked, Celia? It was stark, raving bonkers.'

Stark, raving bonkers? She had used those very words herself. But when? And about whom? She couldn't remember. And she didn't care. She didn't care one single jot.

They were sitting in the tearoom again. They were eating tomato sandwiches sprinkled with fresh-cut basil.

The Danish sloop was tied alongside in the harbour.

He told Celia that he had ranted and raved at Natasha. He told her of Natasha's indifference to his rage. He told her of the taunting look in her eyes.

But did it matter? Did it really matter? Was it jealousy that made him so angry? No. No, it wasn't that. Was it the distress she was causing Delphine? No. Not really. He had always quite liked Delphine. He had always quite liked Mr Dugdale, too. No. As you were. He was extremely fond of Mr Dugdale. But that wasn't why he was furious. So why? What was going on? What was she doing to him?

He looked across at Celia.

She had changed the style of her hair since yesterday. Was there the faintest touch of powder on her cheeks? She was wearing a white blouse tied at the throat with silk cords. He would love to stretch out his hands and gently pull those cords apart.

'It's greengage jam this time.'

'What's that, Celia? What did you say?'

Celia laughed.

'I said it's greengage jam they've given us with the scones this time.'

Her arms were bare. They weren't fleshy. They were firm. They were soft and generous. He wanted to lean across the table and stroke them.

Natasha? What did he care about Natasha? Bugger Natasha. But, my God, she was beautiful. My God, the way she could use that beautiful body. The way she could . . .

'It was very nice.'

'Sorry, Celia? What was very nice?'

'The greengage jam.'

They walked slowly up the hill back to the Governor's residence.

He was preoccupied. With her? No. Not with her. That was too much to ask. He had been off hand with her today. It was Natasha that had dominated all his thoughts. Little cow. It was obvious what she was up to. Trouble-making. She wanted to be the centre of attraction again. She always did. She wanted to dominate. She wanted everyone to fall under her sway. Attention had to be paid. Regardless.

And she had succeeded.

Roger was caught completely in the tangle of her web.

He hadn't noticed her today. She had taken the pins and tortoiseshell combs from her hair and let it hang free. She had brushed it till it glowed. She had put the faintest whisper of powder on her cheeks. She had worn the sleeveless blouse. She had let the cords at the neck hang loose. But he hadn't noticed. He had been totally obsessed with Natasha. Bitch! Bloody self-centred, self-obsessed bitch she was.

'Shall we have tea tomorrow?' she said diffidently.

'What? What's that you say?'

They were greeted at the front door by Jassy.

'Now mind you wipe your feet before you come in,' she said. 'I'm not having people tramping dirt in all over the hall.'

Celia looked at Roger Carey. Roger Carey looked at Celia.

Dear Jassy. Dear shy, retiring Jassy. Not timid. Just retiring. Sitting unobtrusively, observing, silent, smiling her enigmatic smile.

And now?

'Now I've taken over the housekeeping. Everything is far and away too slack. There are cockroaches everywhere and I don't think the lightbulbs have been dusted for half a century.'

They looked at each other again.

They wiped their feet on the mat.

Meanwhile in Dolly's sitting room?

56

Meanwhile in Dolly's sitting room Colonel Ryder was adjusting his watch strap and preparing to address Dolly. He plucked at his moustache. He plucked at his eyebrows. And then he said: 'I wonder if I could ask for your attention, Mrs Bradman?'

'Certainly.'

'I have something to impart to you, which I feel might be of some interest to you.'

'And what is that, Colonel Ryder?'

'I wish to marry you.'

Dolly gasped, but in an instant recovered her composure and said sweetly: 'And may I ask why, Colonel?'

'I'm not sure really,' said Colonel Ryder. 'I haven't given it much thought, to tell the truth.'

Dolly smiled.

'Well then, Colonel, perhaps you could set out your stall,' she said. 'Convince me why I should marry you.'

'Well, it's a bit difficult really,' said Colonel Ryder. 'The truth is that I'm not a particularly prepossessing sort of bloke.'

'You must have some virtues.'

'Can't think of any at the moment.'

'Are you a passionate person?'

'Not really.'

'Are you kind and considerate? Are you romantic? Are you a lover of the pleasures of the flesh? Are you a man of experience in matters of the heart and the bed chamber?'

'I think you'd better ask my sar'nt major. He's rather more qualified to answer that than I. He's a positive mine of information, the sar'nt major. What he doesn't know about head lice is –'

'Are you financially secure?'

'No.'

'Are you fun to be with?'

'No.'

'Have you got a keen sense of humour?'

'Certainly not.'

Dolly gazed at him. There was a half-smile on her lips. In her eyes there was a look of amused confusion.

He smiled at her and began to drum with his fingers on his Sam Browne belt.

'Don't do that,' snapped Dolly. 'I can't stand people who drum with their fingers.'

'Sorry.'

He began to tap on his teeth with his thumbnails. Dolly winced.

Presently he smiled and said: 'You see, Mrs Bradman, the thing about me is this – I might look placid and easy-going on the surface, but by nature I'm an extremely truculent and argumentative sort of bloke.'

'I see,' said Dolly. 'So, all in all and summing up, would you describe yourself as a good catch?'

'Oh dear,' said Colonel Ryder. 'You've got me stumped there.'

Shortly after he departed, promising to return in the evening to escort Dolly on 'a night on the town'.

When Dolly told Celia about the Colonel's proposal, her niece threw back her head and bellowed with laughter.

'What's so funny?' said Dolly. 'What's so comical?'

Celia stopped laughing at once.

'You're not taking this seriously, are you?' she said.

'Why not?'

Celia gazed at her dumbfounded.

'I could do worse for myself,' said Dolly. 'I could do far far worse. In many ways he's the perfect sort of man.'

'How?'

'He wouldn't make any demands on me.'

'And?'

'There's nothing else – he wouldn't make any demands on me.'

At seven thirty sharp the Colonel presented himself at the Governor's residence and escorted Dolly to the rear of the open-topped staff car.

The driver tossed his cigarette into a ceanothus bush and said: 'Wotcher!'

The car started.

The Colonel leant round from the front seat and said to Dolly: 'I haven't much experience of entertaining ladies. I thought perhaps you might like to visit the asylum and look at the lunatics.'

'That would be very nice,' said Dolly.

They were greeted by the superintendent of the asylum. He was a Dutchman. He had a stubbly chin and spindly teeth.

'How are you, old boy?' said the Colonel, clapping him vigorously on the back.

'I am without hope,' said the Dutchman. 'My mother is dying in Groningen. I have the grippe. There are termites in my bedroom. I have a constant metallic taste in my mouth.'

The Colonel clapped him on the back again and said: 'Now he's just the sort of chap we'll have round regularly to dinner when we get married.'

They inspected the lunatics.

'Not fearfully amusing, are they?' said Colonel Ryder. 'Last week they had a chappie who thought he was Dame Edith Sitwell. Now that was really amusing.'

When they left the asylum, the Colonel said: 'I'll take you for dinner. I'm not all that interested in food myself. I find chomping a rather tedious business. Still, we might witness a few cases of food poisoning to cheer us up.'

To Dolly's surprise she was taken to a small harbourside restaurant, where the seafood was simple and delicious and the wine elegant and beguiling.

Under its influence Colonel Ryder began to unburden himself.

'I suppose the most powerful influence on my childhood was the frog on the terrace.'

'What?' said Dolly.

'It was a very dry summer and Mother put out terracotta pots on the terrace. She didn't plant them with flowers or anything like that. She filled them with water so the birds wouldn't go thirsty. Little bastards never showed any gratitude. They just used to fly down and guzzle their fill and then bugger off as to the manner born. Anyway, one autumn day I went to fill the pot by the honeysuckle and, jigger me, do you know what I found in it?'

'No.'

'A frog. I found a frog there. It had taken up residence. I didn't tell anybody. It was my secret. I used to spend hours there watching the frog. Sometimes he'd be underwater with his arms and legs spread out.

He looked rather like an elderly Central European gym instructor who'd grown too ancient to perform his tricks. Sometimes he'd have the tip of his nose sticking out of the water. And he'd stare at me. And he'd look so resentful, so bad-tempered, so ill-humoured with the world. Yes, he made a profound impact on me, did Master Frog.'

He ordered more wine. He drank in silence for a while. Then he said: 'Do you know what I always wanted to be?'

'No. Tell me.'

'A duke.'

'How interesting. Why?'

'Because I think I'm cut out for it. I'd love to organise bonfires for the estate workers on occasions of national rejoicing. I'd love to visit aged nannies when they're sick and cheer them up doing card tricks and making silhouettes. I'd love to cast my vote in the House of Lords in promotion of the welfare of chimney sweeps and laundry workers. I'd love to prowl round the grounds of my palace in the early hours of the morning cracking my stock whips and terrifying the housemaids. Yes, that's my greatest ambition in life – to be elevated to the peerage and have a son and heir to carry on the traditions.'

Dolly dropped the cheese knife with a clatter.

'And that's why you want to marry me?'

'Now I come to think of it – yes,' said the Colonel, and then he pointed to the cheese and said: 'When you've finished with the mousetrap fodder, would you care to visit the jail and inspect the prisoners?'

Half an hour later the governor of the jail was leading them to the women's section, when they turned a corner and bumped into Jassy and the other two little girls.

'Jassy!' cried Dolly. 'What on earth are you doing here?'

'Seeing to the prisoners' comforts.'

'You what?'

'I told you before,' said Jassy. 'I'm taking charge. The adults are making such a bollocks of things, it's high time the shits took over.'

'It's awful,' said Polly.

'I hate it,' said Louise.

'Oh, shut up moaning,' said Jassy. 'Let's go and distribute these apple cores to the child molesters.'

She led them off to the men's section.

'A pleasant child,' said the Governor. 'Exceedingly popular with the arsonists.'

The first person they saw when they entered the women's section was Ernestine. She was crouching on all fours on the floor of her cell. When she saw Dolly, she drew back her lips and growled. She darted forward and hissed. And then she turned and lifted her skirts to expose her bare buttocks. She cackled and darted into a dark corner and snuffled in the dust.

The next person they saw was Mamselle.

Her hair, unkempt and undyed, was matted and streaked with gashes of coarse grey. Her face, unpainted and free of unguents, was lined and wizened. Her tunic was rancid and ripped.

'Thank God you've come,' she sobbed. 'I knew I could rely on you to get us out. Jean-Claude is in shackles in the dungeon. You must help us. You must. You must.'

She stretched out her hands through the bars to Dolly.

Dolly could not help herself. She recoiled and stumbled backwards into the Colonel.

'I say. Steady on, old girl,' he said.

Dolly turned to the Governor and said: 'This woman. What is she doing here?'

Before he could reply they were summoned upstairs urgently to his office.

There they found the residency major-domo bearing a message for Dolly. It informed her that Sir Graham had completed arrangements for them.

They were to present themselves at the customs shed at six thirty prompt next morning.

'Oh crumbs,' said Colonel Ryder. 'Does this mean . . . ?'

'I'm afraid it does,' said Dolly softly.

'Well, never mind,' he said. 'The sar'nt major would never have given his approval.'

57

The flying boat brooded listlessly at its moorings.

It seemed out of humour with the world. It seemed care-worn and haggard.

It lay lopsided in the water. Its fuselage was agued and patched. Its wings cowered. Its back drooped. A brown pelican sat on one of the ragged floats preening its back.

'You want us to go on that?' exclaimed Dolly to the boatman.

'Them's my instructions, missus.'

The launch chugged fussily across the harbour.

The boatman spat into the water, adjusted the damp dimp in the corner of his mouth and said: 'A good little flier she is, missus. Once she's up, she don't want to come down.'

'It looks to me as though it needs a jolly good dusting,' said Jassy.

'Oh, shut up,' said Polly.

It was a calm day.

Frigate birds loitered.

The Sikh major-domo had fussed over them as they boarded the launch and burst into floods of tears when it slipped away from the quay.

Two customs officers sat on a bench outside their shed, warming the soles of their feet in the sun and drinking contraband gin.

To her surprise Dolly was disappointed that Colonel Ryder was not at the quay to see them off.

A nice man. A nice word, nice. Much abused. Much scorned. She did not use it often. She was not accustomed to treating with nice things or nice people. Yes, a nice man, Colonel Ryder. A really really nice man. They could have had a nice time together.

And what about her skipper? What about her handsome French colonel? Were they nice? Certainly not. They would have made constant demands on her.

She no longer liked having demands made on her. That's why she had ceased owning dogs even though she loved them dearly. They kept making demands on you. On and on and on. More and more demands. It wasn't nice. Bugger dogs. Let them fend for themselves. Her shoes were pinching her again. More demands.

The boatman brought the launch alongside the flying boat's mooring buoy. He sounded his klaxon. There was no response.

'Probably pissed,' said the boatman.

He took out his boathook and worked the launch round to a door in the side of the fuselage. It flapped to and fro wearily in the faint sea breeze.

'Hoi! Anyone at home?'

No response.

'Hoi! Wake up, you bastards. I got the rum you ordered.'

This time there was a response.

A man appeared at the door. His shirt was undone to the waist. His flies were undone. He wore open-toed sandals and an aviator's peaked cap.

He gazed at them blearily.

'I got your rum, mate,' said the boatman.

The man nodded.

The cases of liquor were handed across to the aircraft.

'Ta,' said the aviator and he reeled away from the door and disappeared.

'Hoi!'

'What?'

'I got your passengers, too.'

They climbed aboard. The aviator struggled with the door, cursing and swearing. Before he could close it he was hailed from outside.

Dolly recognised the voice of Colonel Ryder. She went to the door, pushed the aviator to one side and gazed out. Colonel Ryder was standing at the wheel of the harbour master's launch. He was alone.

'Just thought I'd nip across to say goodbye.'

'Goodbye,' said Dolly.

'Goodbye.'

Colonel Ryder smiled and saluted.

Dolly smiled. Her eyes filled up with tears. She felt weak at the knees. She blew him a kiss. She was just about to retire into the flying boat's interior when the Colonel called out to her.

'There's something else,' he shouted.

He looked round rapidly and then stuck up his thumb. Immediately

Mamselle and the gangster appeared. They were shivering with terror.

'I almost forgot,' said Colonel Ryder.

Roger Carey helped Dolly drag them aboard. They blubbered and wailed. They sank to the floor and tried to kiss Dolly's hands and ankles. They were as frail as a watercolourist's wrist.

'Don't ask me how I got them,' said the Colonel. 'Don't ask me how I got the boat. Trade secrets, what? Well then, Mrs Bradman, have a pleasant trip. Oh, by the way, have you by any remote chance got an answer to my proposition?'

Before Dolly could answer, the aviator pushed her to one side and with a colossal heave and a gargantuan volley of curses slammed shut the door.

Colonel Ryder's boat chugged away placidly.

Dolly whispered to herself: 'Yes. You poor old booby, the answer's yes.'

The aviator buttoned his flies and wiped the back of his oil-clotted hand across his mouth. He swayed gently. He grinned, showing a mouthful of splintered teeth.

'Look at me,' he said. 'Drunk as a skunk. Don't worry. I'm not flying the kite. I leave that to Carlos up front. You'll be relieved to know he's not Venezuelan.'

He turned to enter the cockpit.

Dolly called out: 'Just one minute, if you please.'

'Yes?'

'Where are we going?'

The aviator shrugged.

'Search me, missus,' he said. 'I'll ask Carlos when he's got a minute.'

He turned to the cockpit again. Its door was flapping to and fro.

'You have to tie it down from your side once I'm in,' he said pointing to a length of rusting chain and a large brass padlock.

He grinned, waved his hand and stumbled into the cockpit. They heard the sound of glass being trampled underfoot. Voices were raised. The aviator's peaked cap came flying out of the cockpit and skittered along the cabin floor. The petrol fumes rose round their knees. The cockpit door banged and slammed like shutters in the frenzy of a storm.

Roger Carey secured it with the rusting chain and the coffin-sized padlock.

The flying boat began to move.

The noise of the engines clamoured at the roofs of their mouths and battered and flailed deep inside their skulls. It hammered at their breastbones and clattered up and down their spines.

The vibration set them shaking like victims of a plague.

They clutched at the sides of the seats desperately trying to keep themselves steady.

The seating accommodation was varied.

There was a row of old tip-up cinema seats. There was a church pew clamped to the side of the fuselage. There were cane chairs and stacks of unopened striped canvas deck chairs. Mr Dugdale sat on an ornate, beetle-bored carver.

The flying boat gained speed.

The spray swished past the windows. The engines screamed. Every rivet and every bolt was straining and rattling. The noise was deafening. The juddering ached in the marrow of their bones. They sat forward on their chairs, fists clenched, willing the craft to rise from the water.

It didn't.

With a great sigh and a groan it flopped back in the water and the engines chucked and chuttered.

Delphine stroked Mr Dugdale's arm. He smiled at her. He was happy. He was content.

And it just popped out.

'Better drowned than duffers. If not duffers won't drown.'

'What?' said Delphine. 'What's that you said?'

The engines roared again. The water swished and snarled. Fumes. Smoke. A deck chair hurtled across the cabin and slammed against the door of the cockpit.

'Golly,' said Louise.

'Gosh,' said Polly.

'Oh, shut up,' said Jassy.

On the third attempt they succeeded.

How strange. How curious.

As soon as they were airborne all their terrors and their tensions vanished. They were rocked and cradled. The noise was so great they could not speak to each other. But in their eyes were happiness and excitement and anticipation and love.

Natasha's eyes betrayed nothing.

Mamselle clung tightly to her gangster. He stroked her matted hair. His hands trembled.

The sea was blue.

White clouds scudded.

Time passed by.

A chain of islets ruffling the surf. The deep purple of the stream.
Slow, coiling carpet of bleached weed. A schooner under slapping sail.
Sand spit of cays. Egrets and raft of pelicans corralling the fish.

The plane dipped its wings and circled the island. Its mountain was
covered with jungle to the top of its summit. Smacks and pinnaces
bobbed in the harbour. Cattle grazed in lush green meadows. The sun
shone.

Slowly the plane descended. It swayed and it shivered. Once it
dropped and turned their stomachs over. Then in a long skimming glide
it touched down on the water and came to a stop, bobbing and curtsying
to the town.

The engines stopped.

They stood up and stretched themselves.

Celia looked out of the window.

'It looks very nice,' she said. 'It looks a bit like Felixstowe when it
isn't raining.'

There was a furious knocking and hammering on the cockpit door.
Roger Carey unlocked it and the aviator stepped out, blinking, yawning,
belching, rubbing his eyes and scratching his armpits.

'I see we got here then,' he said.

He began to jerk at the handle of the door in the fuselage. He heaved
at it. He kicked it. He put his shoulder against it, cursed and beat at it
with his fists.

A small, dapper young man stepped out of the cockpit. His skin was
the colour of milky coffee. He had a soft, downy black moustache. He
saluted them and smiled. Then he pushed the aviator aside and with a
swift, dexterous movement of his right wrist opened the door.

There was a gig waiting for them.

Four blond young men with ruddy cheeks and clear blue eyes were
at the oars.

They helped the passengers aboard with care and tenderness.

One of them fondled Delphine's bottom. Another made an indecent
suggestion to Natasha.

They rowed with style and vigour to the waterfront.

The helmsman invited Dolly to sit on his knee. She declined. The
oarsman once more assisted the passengers as they disembarked. The
quayside was lined with young men. Most of them were blond and

tanned. They looked at the girls and licked their lips and nudged each other.

'I don't see a single nigger in sight,' said Dolly.

'You won't, missus,' said the helmsman. 'We shot them all years and years ago.'

58

It was an overnight stop.

They were quartered in an old isolation hospital.

They were told that the island was inhabited by the descendants of French Huguenots.

'Isn't that interesting?' said Dolly.

They had roast porcupine for dinner.

They were told it was a speciality of the island's cuisine.

'Isn't that interesting?' said Dolly.

They went to bed happy, exhausted and replete.

Natasha shared the bed of the dapper young man with the downy black moustache.

They took off from the island at first light the following morning.

Natasha sat rigid beside Roger Carey. She did not look out of the window. She refused food from the hampers provided by the authorities on the island. She never took her eyes off Mr Dugdale.

Delphine glared at her threateningly.

They reached the mainland coast and landed in a long, lazy lagoon, in which they bathed nude and shameless.

They spent the night in a hotel with wide, creaking verandahs and yawning balustrades.

They were told that the town had once been owned by the Swedish Crown.

'Isn't that interesting?' said Dolly.

Mamselle was restored to high spirits.

She told Dolly of her escape from prison.

'Such a charming man, Colonel Ryder,' she said. 'So gallant. So chivalrous. If it hadn't been for Jean-Claude, I would have fallen in love with him on the spot.'

Later in the bedroom Dolly said to Celia: 'Mamselle! Bloody Mamselle! She really gets on my tits.'

They ate vast juicy steaks and golden chips, crisp on the outside, white and fluffy on the inside. They drank pale beer, ice cold and sharp.

'If you keep on staring at Mr Dugdale like that, I'll knock your teeth in,' Delphine said to Natasha.

Mr Dugdale said: 'I cannon off the cushion. I pot into the middle pocket.'

Dolly turned to Celia and said: 'And he's another one who's sticking up my nose.'

Next morning the flying boat crashed.

They did not have time to unlock the cockpit door before the aircraft sank. They saw the dapper young man banging frantically at the windscreen. The drunken aviator raised his bottle in a gesture of fond farewell.

Roger Carey and the gangster managed to drag out the dinghy.

It was by far the newest item on board.

It had been stolen three weeks previously.

It inflated itself within a minute and they all clambered aboard.

'Well, all we can do now is hope and pray,' said Roger Carey.

Dolly whispered to Celia: 'And he's another who's getting on my wick.'

59

Night fell.

The seas were sullen and muddy.

'We can't be far from shore,' said Roger Carey. 'Look at all this mud. I bet it's silt brought down by a great river.'

That's me now, thought Mr Dugdale. My whole being consists of silt brought down by a great river. All my life's work, all my joys and all my sorrows are silt. And the sea disperses the silt and there is nothing left save for a distant scar on an untroubled sea. He smiled.

'Czechs make good coachmen, nothing else,' he said.

But no one heard him.

Delphine, exhausted by her efforts in dragging him from the sinking aircraft and establishing him in the dinghy, slept with her head resting on his lap and her mouth sagging open.

Next to him sat Natasha. Her head rested on his shoulder. Her eyes were closed and there was a smile of wistful malice on her face.

'We mustn't fall asleep,' said Jassy. 'We've got to keep awake. Let's have a singsong. What about "The Drunken Sailor"?'

Before she could begin to sing Dolly stretched forwards and clipped her sharply round the ears.

'Shut up, you little cow, shut up!' she screamed. 'I'm sick and tired of your bossing and your bullying. I'm in charge here. Not you. You're just a little shit. Do you understand that, madam? I am in charge here. Not you. Understand?'

And with that she boxed Jassy's ear once more. The little girl cowered away from the blows and began to sob piteously.

'Serve her right,' said Polly.

'I feel sick,' said Louise and she squirted out a stream of vomit over Mrs Otto's *Speisewagen*. The old lady did not budge. Her steady snores did not miss a beat or break a rhythm.

Celia dozed. The night was warm. She felt Roger Carey's body next to hers. Oh, how she wanted him. What plans she had for the two of them. They would join forces and become market gardeners. She could

226

run a teashop and he would have a workshop at the bottom of the garden and carve and whittle and turn things on a foot-pumped lathe. They could breed springer spaniels in Wales.

No. No use. They were doomed. She knew it. There was no escape. They would die. Their flesh would be pecked by scavenging seabirds. Their bones would be bleached white by the sun. They would whirl and twirl in the dinghy in a slow waltz of death.

So long since they had left the marsh. So much had happened. She had found herself a man. And now she was going to die.

Dolly, too, knew they were going to die. She was haunted by visions of what happened in Madeira all those years ago.

Dawn came and they found themselves in a vast, deserted sea. No sign of land. No birds. No ships. Mist at first, chill and damp. Then it was burnt away by the sun and they scorched and frizzled in its cruel and cunning rays.

They had no water. Roger Carey had managed to stow aboard one of the cases of liquor taken on at St David's and those who were awake supped at the bottle of rum passed from hand to hand. Roger Carey had rigged up a shelter over the stern of the dinghy. He had moved Mr Dugdale there. Delphine had helped. She had hissed at Natasha and shoved her to one side when she tried to take hold of Mr Dugdale's arm.

Dolly had refused the offer of accommodation.

Why bother? They were doomed to die. Just as the little boy was doomed to die in the dove-pink mansion high in the hills above Funchal.

Would she die happy? Yes. Yes, she would. Such a dear man, Colonel Ryder. A nice man. They could have had a nice life together. They would have lived in a stone cottage by a beck. Or maybe on a houseboat with a bent-stemmed chimney and striped awnings and a pug dog yawning in the sun. What fun they would have had. She would have made him walk the plank.

And then she felt the presence of the black owl. Her whole body stiffened. She heard the soft beat of its wings. She heard the skitter of its talons. She felt the heat from its blood-red eyes. But it did not land on her.

Where was it?

Where was that bloody owl?

It landed gently on Natasha's shoulders and began to preen itself.

Natasha smiled to herself.

Yes, it landed on her and now she knew for certain what she had always suspected – she was mad. She'd known it ever since she was a little girl. The hysterical happiness. The convulsive misery. The white mouse died from a lump on its back. Misery. Despair. Locked in her bedroom for days. Her guardian bought her a dormouse. Bliss. Radiant happiness. So it went. So it went. I love you, Lance. I love you, love you, love you. I love you, Roger. I love you, love you, love you. Mr Dugdale, I love you. I really really really love you. Madness!

Roger Carey, attempting to fashion a paddle from the lid of the liquor case, stole a swift glance at her.

The sun rose higher and the heat blistered down on them.

Mamselle and the gangster, wrapped in each other's arms, did not move.

Mamselle thought of coolness. Not of cold. Not of chill. She thought of coolness. The cool evenings on the lazy, lonely Moss. The cool hands of Mr Mazarene. The cool touch of the lino in her mother's bathroom. The coolness of the tow horse's breath as it nuzzled her cheek. The coolness of her life cooling away to nothing.

The emergency ration box contained no food. It was stacked with miniature bottles of liquors.

'I'm hungry,' wailed Louise.

'So am I,' said Polly. 'I'm absolutely starving.'

It could not be avoided.

It had to be done.

Roger Carey crawled under the awning where Mr Dugdale and Mrs Otto slept side by side. Gently he prodded her awake. Diffidently he pointed to her *Speisewagen*.

'But of course,' she said. 'It is my great pleasure.'

Very slowly Roger Carey undid the clasp of the *Speisewagen*. He opened it even more slowly. His companions looked on shivering with awe, fear and revulsion.

He drew out a portion of roast porcupine. Louise snatched it out of his hand and gobbled it in an instant. He pulled out a porcupine drumstick. He offered it to Mamselle who smiled and proceeded to share it with the gangster. The first four or five layers of food were reasonably palatable. But as Roger Carey excavated deeper and deeper into the seams of rancid, rotting comestibles, the stench grew stronger and the maggots more active.

'Throw it overboard,' cried Dolly. 'For Christ's sake get rid.'

'No,' said Roger Carey. 'It might be the only thing to keep us alive.'
It was.

The *Speisewagen* was their only source of food throughout that night
and the following searing, sun-spitting day.

Once they saw a warship on the distant horizon. Roger Carey stood
up, took off his shirt and waved it furiously. He was not seen. The
warship's upperworks dodged away out of sight. Once they heard the
drone of an aircraft, but they could not bear to look up into the stinging
skies.

The black owl nested peacefully in the crook of Natasha's neck. She
smiled. At last she had a real friend. Someone who understood her.
Someone who cared for her. Mr Dugdale! Oh, how she loved him.

The rum burnt deep into Dolly's lips. That night in Madeira. She
should have been on duty. But she was not. She was writhing in the
bed of her lover. And the grandson was killed.

The sun. That bloody sun.

The island of whites. Arrived there in the old days long long ago.
Why? No niggers. All shot. Blond men. What about them? Who cares?
We're going to die. Dugdale won't go first. He's far too tough an old
bird for that. It'll be someone we least expect. Delphine? No. The
gangster? Possibly. Jassy? Yes, that's it – Jassy. Yes, Jassy'll be the first
to go. Serve her right.

She screwed up her nose, closed her eyes tight shut and thrust into her
mouth a mould-encrusted green-glistening, perspiring, writhing sausage.

Delphine pressed herself closer to Mr Dugdale under the awning.

This is how they would die. They would die together, he with a smile
on his face, she with her head resting on his lap. She could wish for
nothing more. Her life fulfilled. Dead before her love was drained. Such
a long time. Such a long long time she'd nursed the dying soldier. Night
after night, day after day, she sat by his side and tended to his every
need. The flight from Moscow. The long exile in the country. His death.
And now the soldier had returned and now she lay by his side. He
would die. She would die. Perfection. If Natasha moved one muscle,
she'd kick her teeth in.

Roger Carey huddled in the bow and kept a long and lonely vigil all
through the night. There were no stars. The moon dragged back the
veil of clouds to gloat and leer. Once the waters parted and he thought
he heard the songs of whales.

Who was that walking across the water to him?

She had dark crinkly hair. She held out her arms to him. She was garlanded with empty, creaking shells and she wore a shroud of rotting seaweed. Running away? Yes. Why had he done it? Did it matter now? The fatal illness sucking away her juices. The screams of pain. Pleading, pleading. So he did it. Just for her. Her last sad look. The crumple of her mother. Her father's tears. Running away. Running away. What did it matter now?

The first sneak of the sun.

The mist, damp across his shoulders, sliming at the neck.

He would be the first to go. Why not? Dead easy. Just slip over the side now. No one to see him. No one to hear him. Scarcely a parting of the waves. Why not? Just disappear from life like the woman with the dark, crinkly hair. No problem, boss. No problem.

The mist parted and he saw them.

Four men in a narrow, low-slung smack.

60

Roger Carey shouted. He bellowed. The noise awoke the others. They joined in, shouting and waving. The smack turned and headed towards them. It seemed to take an age before it drew alongside. They were Indians with Mongoloid eyes and pock-marked skin. They held rifles at the ready. They had shawls round their shoulders. One wore a brown bowler hat. They looked at each other. They muttered and scowled. There was an argument. Roger Carey saw stacks of ammunition boxes laid out on the deck of the boat. One of the Indians intercepted his gaze and the arguments grew more animated.

'They're going to kill us,' said Roger Carey.

'Show them the girls,' said the gangster.

'What?' said Roger Carey.

The gangster pointed to the girls. His gestures were too explicit to be misunderstood by the Indians. They conferred again. Then after much discussion the man with the brown bowler hat indicated that the women should come aboard. He smiled at them as fearfully and stiffly they transferred themselves from the dingy to the smack.

And so slowly the overloaded smack, towing the men in the dinghy, made its way to the shore. It was at the mouth of a wide river, whose distant opposite shore was not to be seen. The Indians helped the women ashore. Roger Carey, wading waist-deep in the warm, yielding water, carried Mr Dugdale on his back.

The Indians stood in a circle round the little girls and licked their lips.

'Leave this to me,' said the gangster.

And with that he walked to the Indian in the brown bowler hat, smiled at him and extended his hand. The Indian smiled and extended his hand, too.

Before they could make contact the gangster flung himself into the air and kicked the Indian hard and flush in the testicles.

He howled and rolled in the sand.

The gangster smiled at Roger Carey.

'The universal language of love and tolerance,' he said.

And then out of the jungle there stepped a figure whose appearance made them gasp.

He was exceedingly tall.

He was exceedingly thin.

He had a bald pate, but lank grey hair curled over his shoulders and hung down his back. He had a long grey beard.

He wore a stained and tattered white smock.

He was carrying an aged and emaciated teddy bear.

When he opened his mouth to speak, he said: 'I fear you find me in somewhat straitened circumstances.'

He never spoke to them again.

61

The man with the teddy bear beckoned to them to follow him.

He led them through the jungle.

After a short while they came to a clearing.

In the centre was a vast, roofless crumbling church with vampire bats hanging from its rotting timbers and its cloisters embowered with weeds.

There was a cluster of half-derelict native huts. There was a single-storey concrete building with corrugated iron roof and smashed windows. Out of it hobbled an elderly friar.

He bowed to them wearily and winced with pain.

His accent was the accent of polders and gables and long, lonely mud-choked strands where waders piped and fluted and the twisting creeks made riddles in the sands.

'Brother Matthew is very weak,' he said pointing to the concrete building. 'He is dying by the hour. We have few provisions. The ship is late coming. What we have, we will share with you. We shall try to sustain you until they come for you.'

Then he bowed again and hobbled back to the infirmary.

The tall man with the beard and the teddy bear smiled at them and whispered himself into the jungle.

Evening came and they established themselves in the more habitable of the native huts. The thatch was ragged and many of the walls had caved in. None the less in the flicker-black shadows of the campfire and the swaying beam of the storm lantern they were inviting and comforting and secure. Spiders patrolled the dust-ridden floors.

The Indian with the brown bowler hat lay by the campfire bathing his swollen testicles in a thick, sticky, greenish-purple liquid. He bore no malice against the gangster. Every time the gangster passed by flashing his gold teeth, the Indian would point to his genitals and nod his approval.

The other Indians lolled by the fire drinking the same liquid from a calabash passed round with indolent resignation.

Dolly sat at the door of her hut with Celia. It was the largest hut in the whole encampment.

'I wonder what this place is?' she said.

'It's a mission,' said Celia. 'It's where the Brothers care for the natives and teach them about the love and mercy of God the Father.'

'Stupid buggers,' said Dolly. 'They're flogging a dead horse there.'

In a hut on the furthest fringes of the encampment Roger Carey propped himself up on one elbow and gazed down on Natasha. She stared back at him.

'I hate you,' he said.

She smiled at him.

'You fooled me. I thought you were full of love. I thought you were gentle and kind. I thought you were full of happiness.'

Another smile.

'You're mad. You're bloody mad. And you're evil, too.'

She snuggled down and blew softly on the nape feathers of the black owl with the blood-red eyes.

In the morning the old Friar brought them a pot of thin gruel and ladled it out onto enamel plates.

'I wish I had more,' he said. Then he shrugged his shoulders. 'Maybe they will provide you with more when they come for you.'

'Who are these people who are coming for us?' said Dolly.

The Friar shrugged his shoulders and hobbled back to the infirmary.

Meanwhile the three uninjured natives returned from their marauding expedition in the jungle clutching in their fists huge fat white grubs.

'Scrumptious,' said Louise. 'Let's see if they want to swap.'

She took them to Mrs Otto's *Speisewagen* and showed them the maggots crawling in the last fragments of fermenting goat's cheese and chocolate fudge. The Indians whooped with delight. They scooped out the maggots and rammed them into their mouths so that their cheeks bulged and their eyes rolled and whirred with delight. They handed over the white grubs to the little girls, who bolted them back with glee.

Celia cast a furtive glance at Roger Carey.

Oh, those enchanting afternoons when she had taken tea with him. He had looked at her with desire. Not lustful desire. Nothing dirty or carnal. Just a desire to be with her. A desire to be privy to the pleasures of her body. Useless. Bloody useless. She looked at him again. He was sitting next to Natasha. Yet there was no warmth in their closeness. She could see that. The only thing they had in common was their frenzied scratching against the flies.

Everyone scratched. Their skin was red raw and blotched and swollen. They had been bitten by cabouri fly, sucked at by leeches, burrowed at by ticks and gorged on by *bêtes rouges*.

Who would want to take her to bed in a state like that? Even the little bandy Indians with their pot bellies and their pitted faces would draw the line at that.

At midnight the Friar and two elderly pap-breasted native women brought them strips of dried fish and plates of farina.

Each of them in his and her own way was happy.

They had been rescued from the seas.

What next?

Who cared?

The stupor of the jungle closed around them and they sat round the campfire drinking miniatures of kümmel, Benedictine and white rum.

Mr Dugdale lay in his hut and allowed the night to lap around him. He did not feel pain or exhaustion. He just felt that he was dying. He was dying of happiness. He looked forward to the torpor of his dying. He welcomed the happiness of his demise.

Once he had thought that happiness was the screech of ecstasy and the pump of frenzy.

Once he had thought it was drinking coal-black strong beer in a gas-lit arcade.

Once he was convinced it was walking along a cliff top with a romping retriever and ships bleating in the Channel and the two Holms snoozing and the logs in the parlour fire crackling and his bottle of port glowing his belly and mellowing plump on his palate.

Now he knew that real happiness was here.

It was now.

The screech of howler monkey. The scream of forest birds. The croak of frogs. The crashing of timber. The cries of fear from the hunted and the snarls of lust and triumph from the stalkers. The presence of the girl lying beside him.

Yes, she had made it. At long last she had reached her goal. She was as old as himself.

Very slowly the words slipped out without warning and without delib-
eration:

'Life's slipped by just as if I'd never lived at all.'

Next morning the soldiers came for them.

62

Six men burst into the clearing just after dawn.

They wore navy-blue uniforms buttoned high at the neck. Each uniform was identical. Their headgear was varied. One wore a sombrero. Another wore a Basque beret and another wore a French army tin helmet. The leader wore a battered bush hat. He was a large man with a blue stubbled chin.

The men were of all nationalities.

The blood of Indian, African, Caucasian, Mulatto and Semite flowed rich and motley through their veins; ancient, knowing, deceitful.

They carried carbines and bandoleers of ammunition and leather belts hooked by grenades.

They announced their arrival with a hail of bullets.

They crashed through the huts dragging the occupants outside and lining them up against the wall of the infirmary.

Bush hat talked to bowler hat. There was much smacking of lips and leering of eyes and brooding throaty chuckles.

'Right! You! Move!'

Bush hat thrust his carbine into Dolly's back and prodded her roughly. She stumbled forward and fell to her knees. No one moved to help. Dolly turned. Her eyes blazed with anger. The soldiers silently made a circle round her and thrust out their weapons.

She stood up. She dusted herself down, never taking her eyes off the man with the bush hat.

'You wait,' she snarled. 'Just you wait. Bastard!'

Six safety catches clicked open.

They released their spitting bullets round Dolly's feet. She screamed and jumped and jigged as the dust spurted about her and clods of earth and jagged splinters of rock flew in all directions.

Silence.

Dolly burst into tears.

'Right! Move!'

They stumbled along the jungle track to the strand, where they had come ashore.

A slice-bowed, powerful-thighed motor launch was anchored in the shallows next to the smack.

The soldiers forced Dolly and her charges to wade out to the launch and climb aboard. They made no attempt to help Roger Carey and Delphine haul Mr Dugdale on deck.

The engine of the launch sneered into life. The smack putt-putted and sent out a skein of pungent blue smoke.

And so they set off upstream into the interior.

No one spoke.

The soldiers smoked cigarettes. They drank bottles of beer from the neck and ate plump chicken legs and fiery red sausages.

They offered nothing to their captives.

They made no attempt to protect them from the sun.

They did not speak.

On the smack the Indians were full of animation. They were excited. They sniffed the air and pointed upstream and jabbered.

What was in store for them?

Execution? Slavery? Rape?

Dolly didn't care. She really did not give one jot. Her war was over. She had been defeated. She was prepared to surrender unconditionally. They could do what they liked with her. They could do what they liked with any single one of them.

Phut, phut, phut! The bullets had sprayed about her feet. She had jumped. She had jigged. And then she had burst into tears. Defeat. Her war was over.

Mr Dugdale was deeply contented. He had always loved rivers. The Danube at Ulm. The Rhine at Koblenz. The Wusong at Shanghai. The Thames at Hampton Court.

Lovely, lovely Hampton Court. The Mole slinking into the main stream below the lock. Number 4 trolley bus from Wimbledon Station via Raynes Park, Malden and Kingston. Or you could take the Number 67 tram from Hammersmith Station. How he loved those old-fashioned, flat-topped, double-decker trams. How they rocked and swayed and pitched and tossed. Galleons of the open road he'd called them. Slow and stately the Number 67 from Hammersmith Station via Kew Bridge and Twickenham. Rivers were indeed roads and marched and carried you where you wished to go. Good old Pascal.

In the mid-afternoon the river began to narrow and the current grew swifter. The trees closed in on them and the overhanging branches clawed at their faces.

And then they came to a gorge and a run of fast-flowing rapids. The boats were drawn into the bank and the soldiers motioned with their rifles that they should disembark. They did so and watched in a bedraggled huddle as the Indians unloaded the ammunition boxes from the smack.

'Right! Move!'

The soldier with the French army helmet led the way. It was a steep, twisting track. They slipped and they slithered. They held on to each other and cowered under the muzzles of the carbines.

'Come on, Jassy,' said Dolly. 'Give me your hand.'

Timidly Jassy held out her hand and Dolly took hold of it warmly.

Yes, this was indeed defeat.

Delphine and Natasha each had hold of Mr Dugdale's elbows and Roger Carey pushed him from behind. Delphine could not have refused Natasha's offer of help. But she glowered and glared at her. How she loathed her. How she hated her. How she detested that saintly smile and the wistful look in her eyes and the lilt of her neck and the composure of her tread as the other slithered and scrabbled.

The jungle heat beat down on them.

The flies were remorseless.

The soldiers refused their requests for rest.

The Indians had shed their clothes as they hauled the ammunition boxes up the track. They were naked and cascading with sweat. For the sake of modesty and the sensibilities of the squeamish their leader had covered his malformed private parts with his brown bowler. He groaned and whimpered with pain. But never for an instant did he shirk or slack.

Louise began to cry. Polly took hold of her arm and dragged her ever onwards and upwards.

And then quite suddenly it was all over.

They reached the summit.

They looked down and once again gasped at what they saw.

A long, wide, flat-bottomed valley. Towering cliffs on either side. A lake shimmering and glimmering. Cattle. Sheep. Fields tended and tilled. Wood smoke piercing the cloudless sky.

The bush-hatted soldier smiled.

He pointed down into the valley and said: 'Bandito land. Territory of The Man. He mighty big bandito. He mighty savage killer.'

And then he drew his finger across his throat and commenced to chuckle.

63

They were allowed five minutes to rest.

And then they were ordered to their feet and they were on the move once more.

'Move! Move!'

The road to the valley bottom was skittish. It was hidden from above by the thick canopy of trees. Monkeys swung and howled. Gawdy birds blundered and shrieked. Small flying mammals glided through the twining branches.

It was humid and sticky.

No one spoke.

Presently the road levelled off and after a final twist and turn they came out into the valley bottom. They had just time to take in a field stilted with sunflowers, and three women staggering with laden yokes on their shoulders, and then they were ordered to halt.

They saw a stone building with narrow, slit windows tightly barred. Two men in blue tunics stepped out, yawning and stretching. They conferred with bush hat. They nodded. One of them looked over his shoulder at Natasha. When he turned back to his colleagues, there was a coarse cackle of laughter.

Bush hat and his colleagues left them without a glance or a comment. The taller of their new guards pushed Roger Carey roughly in the back and propelled him through a door unlocked by his companion. He motioned for the others to follow. They did so and the door was clanged shut behind them and they heard the slamming of bolts and the clanking of keys.

'I hate the people here,' whispered Louise.

'Yes,' said Polly. 'They smell of dead horses.'

In the distance beyond the valley walls they heard the sound of heavy artillery and a plane flew overhead, its motors snarling and clattering.

They had been numb with exhaustion. Now the fears and terrors returned and once more they felt the snuffle of death at their ankles.

Celia gulped. With a great struggle she composed herself and then

241

in a voice slightly high-pitched and snatched said: 'Well, come on, everyone. Let's make ourselves at home, shall we?'

They looked around them.

It was a high-vaulted building. At one end there was a flight of wooden stairs leading to a balcony laid out with iron bedsteads. The floor had been freshly swept and strewn with sweet-smelling sawdust.

The windows that ran along each wall were narrow but plentiful and gave good light to the room. Through one set of windows they looked out onto a small, sluggish brook and a pond full of squabbling ducks. The other side looked out over a meadow grazed by thin, spindly cattle and enclosed by a gap-toothed dry-stone wall.

In the room were long trestle tables and benches. There were jugs of cold water on the table and rough-glazed earthenware tankards. They drank greedily. There were chunks of unleavened bread and bowls of radishes, endive and plump cloves of garlic. They ate ravenously.

On the opposite wall to the gallery was a small stage on which was a lectern. Roger Carey, munching on a chunk of bread and radishes, examined it.

There was a book on the lectern. It was newly bound in the finest and softest Moroccan leather. On its cover was the monogram G. E. Its title was *Cold Comfort Farm*. Roger Carey opened it. On the flyleaf was a hand-written inscription. The writing was spidery and went thus:

> *Hic liber est meus.*
> *Testis est deus.*
> *Si quis furetur.*
> *Per collum pendetur.*

'I've seen that somewhere before,' he said to himself. 'How very curious.'

After they had finished eating, their heads began to nod and their eyelids to droop heavily.

Roger Carey examined one of the stanchions supporting the balcony. There were names carved into the wood. Some were very old. Some were quite recent. Among the more legible were 'Leo', 'Nancy' and 'Captain Flint'.

Roger Carey rubbed his chin thoughtfully.

'How very odd,' he said. 'How exceedingly curious.'

They dozed fitfully, some on the floor, some on the straw palliasses on the iron bedsteads on the balcony.

The afternoon loitered.

Duck quack. Goose gobble. Chatter of women's voices. Trudge of feet. Swallows swooping in through the slit windows and feeding their brood in the nests on the rafters.

After three or four hours the door was unbolted. The two guards entered, carbines at the ready. And then six women came in bearing bundles of clothing.

The clothing consisted of the navy-blue tunics worn by everyone in the valley they had met so far – men, women, soldiers, workers.

The guards indicated to them that they should remove their clothes and put on the tunics. The women went up to each of them and with a shy smile handed over the uniform. Each one was near perfect in fit. Each one was faded and much patched. But each one was crisply ironed and smelt fresh and pure.

It was a relief to rid themselves of the slime and stench and tatters of their own clothes.

The women did not speak, but their eyes were friendly and it seemed that they sought to reassure the captives with the softness of their move-ments and the quietness of their manner.

They brought in fresh jugs of water, bowls of cucumber, chillies, celery and scallions and a huge iron pot steaming and gurgling and seething with chicken and hares and kids and peppers and garlic and rice and dumplings and grated cheese and pungent roots and tubers and olive oil and deep purple red wine.

With smiles and fluttering hands they motioned for them to eat.

And then they retired.

The guards bolted the doors and rattled the keys.

Dolly and her army threw themselves upon the food and gorged themselves.

Then after an hour they were let out one by one under guard to use the privies in a small cobbled courtyard walled off from view of the duck pond.

Night came and there was no light given to the room. There were holders for lamps and rushes, but nothing was brought to them.

One by one they fell asleep.

But Roger Carey remained awake.

He had seen this all before. Where? He had heard it all before. Where? The Man? Who the hell was The Man? Why had he brought them here? What had he in store for them? Celia relaxed in her sleep. He looked down on her. Yes, there was real beauty in her person and in her soul. She would be a comfort. How marvellous to have the talent to comfort. The most precious gift of all.

Once Mr Dugdale stirred in his sleep and said: 'Sailing in half an hour.'

Roger Carey had heard that before, too.

Odder and odder.

64

Distant gunfire.

Howitzer and mortar.

Night-sky flashes. Flickers.

Silver glint of aircraft high in the sky.

Duck quack. Goose gobble.

'What's going to happen to us?' said Celia.

'I don't know, Celia.'

'We've been here three days and –'

'Four days.'

'Four days! Is it really four days?'

'Yes.'

'And nothing's happened to us.'

'I know.'

'I don't like the feel of things, Roger. I think we're in for something absolutely ghastly.'

'So do I.'

She could see it vividly. The whole lot of them on their knees in the dust, hands tied behind their backs. A roll of drums. The scrunch of boots. The sobs. The wails. The screams. The cries for mercy.

Then one by one they are beheaded.

The two guards ushered in the women, who raked the floor and sprinkled it with sawdust. Then they brought in fresh water, jugs of wine and bowls of olives and crispy bread.

What new book had they brought for them this time? thought Roger Carey.

Each day they had brought in a volume, exquisitely bound in the choicest of leather and printed on the most luxurious of paper. Already they had the complete works of Wilkie Collins, *The History of Myddle* and *Bulldog Drummond Stands Fast*.

The women smiled and bowed silently as they left. Roger Carey picked up the new book and read its title.

First Steps in Field Surgery.

245

He decided not to show it to Celia.

Meanwhile the little girls pranced and frolicked, although from time to time Jassy would hide herself in a corner and sob herself to sleep. Mrs Otto snored and slumbered. Natasha sat apart from them, smiling and whispering soft endearments to her black owl. Mamselle and the gangster never left each other's side and Dolly brooded with vacant eyes and listless bosoms.

Mr Dugdale observed these actions with the deepest, most profound satisfaction. A high barn with swallows nesting on the rafters and fresh, sweet-smelling sawdust on the floor. Perfection! It was the simplicity of it all that engaged and enthralled him. His life had never before been so simple, so straightforward. It had never before been so beguilingly austere. The routine, the order, the predictability, the security lulled him and lullabied him.

How swift the change in his circumstances. The anguish of waiting for Natasha on the quayside at Cardiff. The fury of his couplings with Mrs Banks. And now this. Old age. Infirmity. Approaching senility. All achieved in an instant. Without effort. Without foresight. Without planning.

It was like Delphine's prince laid low by a grenade on the field of battle. One moment in the full vigour of his manhood, virile of mind and body, full of hope, full of confidence, and arrogant for the future.

And then the smash and the splinters, and the suppurating of his wound. And then the peace and the comfort of the sick bed. No pain. No regrets. The slow rhythms of death. The longing for it.

He looked across at Natasha. Yes, she was a fine young woman. Had he really lusted after her? Had he really felt panic at her absence? Had he really felt devastated by her indifference to him?

He looked down on Delphine. Was it possible? Was she now really older and wiser than he? And was it really possible that in her joyous gallop towards extreme old age she would become infirm of mind and body and thus become entirely dependent on him? How could he cope? Would he want to cope? No. He'd bung her in a home and let her die.

He looked across at Natasha. She saw the movement of his head and the roving of his eyes. She smiled at him.

Delphine saw that smile.

She resolved to act at once.

She turned to Mr Dugdale and whispered into his ear.

'I love you. I want you to marry me. Will you? Will you, Mr Dugdale?'

246

He patted her hand.
He kissed her on top of the head.
Then he said:
'Thrist! Thrist, my dear! The funeral baked meats
'Did coldly furnish the marriage tables.'
He hadn't the faintest idea why he said it.

65

'On your feet! Move!'

The guard with the bush hat and the blue-stubbled chin stood in the centre of the barn, feet spread wide, carbine at his hip. His three companions adopted a similar stance. The women who had tended them hurried out of the room silently, heads lowered, shoulders bowed.

'Move!' snapped bush hat. 'Move!'

He indicated that they should form a line by the door.

They did so and then his men attached chains to their wrists and ankles and tied them together in single file.

'You can't do that to Mr Dugdale,' cried Delphine. 'He's an old man. He's not well. He's –'

One of the men trod hard on her foot, and she screamed out with pain.

'Move! Move!'

Roger Carey was in the van of the file. He was followed by Celia. Dolly and Jassy brought up the rear.

'I'm frightened, Dolly,' whispered Jassy. 'I'm terrified.'

Dolly reached out her hands and rested them lightly on the little girl's shoulders.

'There, there, Jassy,' she said. 'I won't let them harm you. I love you, my darling. I love you.'

And she did.

Defeat! Surrender! Total capitulation!

They plodded in shuffling single file. In the eyes of each one of them except Natasha and Mr Dugdale there was a tortured look of rampant terror. In the eyes of the old man and the young girl there was calm and contentment.

The valley widened out. The dry-stone walls disappeared and were replaced by hedges of fuchsia and honeysuckle and the roadside ditches were a turmoil of sweet-scented flowers and blossom-laden bushes.

The fields were neat and well-tended. They passed a fish farm. There were oxen in a paddy field. A shepherd passed them by with a flock of dusky-fleeced, teetering-toed sheep. The people were all dressed in tunics of navy blue. They did not look up from their labours when the straggled band passed by.

Bush hat called a halt just before noon. They had reached the shores of the lake. They saw a man in a long, narrow punt fishing with cormorants. There was a squat, single-storey house painted pink with a roof hanging low over bulging windows like a hat pulled low down. Their chains were loosened. They sank down on the springy green turf. They heard the faint throb of aircraft engines and the clump, clump of heavy artillery.

Three young girls appeared from the squat house bringing jugs of wine and corn cobs and spicy crackers.

The guards squatted against the walls of the house, smoking bedraggled cigarettes. They spoke in low voices roving their eyes from girl to girl. Presently one got up, walked slowly to Natasha and offered her a cigarette. She smiled and shook her head. The guard narrowed his eyes and nodded. His companions snickered and he flushed livid red and scowled.

Delphine put her hand over her mouth and from behind it whispered fearfully to Mr Dugdale: 'Are you all right? Are you coping?'

'Shut up!' yelled bush hat. 'On your feet! Move! Move, move, move!'

Their chains were secured. They plodded off.

The cliffs towered above the valley. Vultures soared and circled. Small falcons dashed. Herons stabbed and strutted. The afternoon dragged at their shackles. Sometimes they stumbled over ruts in the road. Sometimes they stumbled in the ruts of their memories.

The retriever flattening the cliff-top wind with its ears.

The coolness of the autumn moss. The jet-black soil. Crooked coppices. The lamp in the bedroom window.

I can't cope with it. I'm sorry. But I cannot cope. And he fled from the girl with the dark crinkly hair and the cancer eating away her life.

The houseboat crackling the ice in the winter lake. The bent-stern chimney rumbling at the red-hot stove. Measles! That's it – they'd get measles. Poor skipper. Poor gallant French Colonel. Poor slouch-eyed English Colonel. Measles could be quite fatal for men of their age.

There were great gashes of cave openings in the cliff face. Fires flickered. People trudged up the winding, sheer and rocky paths.

They rested again at the roadside. A formation of men with carbines slung over their shoulders marched past by them as they lay in a dappled glade drinking beer and eating apricots. Three lorries with rocket launchers chugged past and scattered clouds of dust. There were no flies. There were neither ticks nor leeches.

Celia glanced across at Roger Carey and he shrugged his shoulders helplessly.

She looked across at Jassy. The slim young neck. The fair skin. Unblemished. Smooth. Soft. Swish, goes the axe.

'Right! Move!'

They turned off the valley road and commenced to climb a path clawing its way up the great, soaring ridges of cliff. The drop was sheer. They were petrified. They dared not look down. The breeze whispered at their ankles, wheedled them to open their eyes and gaze down into the searing, spinning drop. They pressed themselves hard into the rock face and their hearts pumped and the bile was sour and stinging in the back of their throats.

Quite suddenly they squeezed their way round a buttress in the cliff and there it was. The opening to the cave protected from view of the valley bottom by the great shoulder of rock.

The soldiers pushed them inside.

They cried out in astonishment.

The cave's entrance was small. The cave's interior was vast. It was high. It was wide. It was long. It was labyrinthine. Scores of subcaves and corridors led off the main thoroughfare.

There were masses of people. Soldiers cleaned their weapons. Smiths worked at their bellows. Dressmakers sewed. Cooks cooked. There were small wooden galleried houses set into the rock. There were shops and bars. Dogs yapped. Chickens scraped and scrapped. Then the cave pinched its waists and they were faced by a huge wooden wall with guardposts on stilts at either side. There was a gate topped by spikes and wreathed in barbed wire.

It was opened.

They passed through.

Waiting for them was an extremely small man with a club foot and jet-black dyed hair swept straight back from his forehead.

A mulberry-red welted scar seared his left cheek and puckered in the corner of his eye. He had thin lips and protruding teeth. From the right cuff of his navy-blue tunic jacket there protruded a white and pink lace handkerchief.

He ordered the guards to unchain their prisoners and then dismissed them.

'I apologise for the stench of the men,' he said to Dolly. 'It is, I fear, the stench of the barbarous and the uncouth.'

He had a German accent and a slight lisp.

He beckoned to them to follow him, gently taking hold of Dolly's arm.

This part of the cave was a blaze of light. There were streetlamps. Strings of bright-lit bulbs twining the walls. Soft lights coy in dark corners. A generator throbbed contentedly and a clear, sparkling stream spluttered and flurried.

They came to a small, cobbled courtyard. There were lines of birds in bamboo cages. And they were all singing at the tops of their voices. And each song was distinct to itself. Yet each song blended with the other.

The dwarf smiled.

'Charming, don't you think?' he said. 'They are sublime on hot toast in the morning.'

The courtyard stood in front of a long thin wooden building. The dwarf led them inside.

'The bathhouse,' he said. 'You have precisely one half-hour to bathe and cleanse yourselves.'

He pointed to a row of new uniforms laid out neatly on a marble slab.

'Purest cashmere,' he said. 'Your host insists on the very finest for those who are shortly to meet their deaths.'

66

In precisely half an hour the dwarf returned with a party of guards.

This time he did not bow. He did not touch Dolly.

His manner was brusque. He organised Dolly and her companions into pairs. He instructed two of his men to assist Mr Dugdale.

'But I do that,' sobbed Delphine. 'That's my job.'

A heavily mustachioed guard cuffed her on the back of the neck. But unseen by the dwarf he cast a swift look at the gangster and winked jauntily.

They were all transfixed by terror.

Natasha's black owl shivered uncontrollably. She tried to console it, but she could not speak. Her voice seemed to be clogged with the gurgle of slow-seeping blood.

They blundered on deeper and deeper into the cave.

You bitch! It's all your doing. You got us into this mess and now you've washed your hands of us. You bitch! You lousy bitch!

Celia glared at Dolly through the red mist of her anger and her fear.

There was no hope for them.

Garrotting. That's what it would be. The ligature wound round the neck. The iron twisted in the heart of the knot. Tighter and tighter. The eyes bulging. The veins bursting. The blue tongue swelling out through blackening lips.

'Wait,' snapped the dwarf.

They were standing outside the entrance to a small side cave. There was a spike-studded gate. It was guarded by two men with tommy guns. They opened the gate and the dwarf disappeared inside.

The mustachioed guide sidled up to the gangster and whispered out of the side of his mouth: 'I know you, don't I?'

'Do you?' said the gangster.

Before the guard could reply the dwarf appeared at the gate and ordered them inside.

The floor of the cave was tiled peacock blue. There was a flute-voiced fountain in its centre. There were crystal chandeliers and marble benches. There were doors with jewel-encrusted handles.

The dwarf opened one and they followed him through.

'Welcome to the Chinese drawing room,' he said.

It was a cluttered riot of Chippendale carving and porcelain and lacquer and painted hangings. In the centre was a vast canopied tent, a bed of twisted gilt and velvet columns, and silk draperies and plumes of dried feathers rising from gold-mounted ostrich eggs which crowned the billowing canopy.

And in the bed propped upright by three great pillows was an old man. He was a frail old man. His eyes watered. His cheeks were feverish red. He wore a leather jerkin and a muffler and a cloth cap.

He made a small weary gesture of greeting with a large, droopy bandanna handkerchief. Then he sighed and closed his eyes.

The dwarf bowed to Dolly.

'Sir Graham Egerton instructs me to bid you all welcome,' he said.

67

'I have come home to die,' said Sir Graham Egerton.

It was forty minutes since they had been ushered into his bedroom.

The dwarf had instructed them to sit round his bed on small, flat-seated, inhospitable heraldic chairs arranged by the dying man's Swiss valet.

They had gazed at him silently, not moving a muscle.

'His sickness is up and down,' whispered the dwarf. 'One day, sometimes for several days, he is strong and lucky. And then he is down and is ready for death.'

Silence.

The dwarf whispered again.

'Mrs Simister deserted him. She ran away with an aviator. It broke his heart. So he came home here to die of a long word.'

And then Sir Graham awoke.

His valet moved forward to adjust his pillows.

Sir Graham smiled at them and pointed to the heavy clothing he wore.

'I had forgotten how cold death can be,' he said.

Then he called for afternoon tea.

When they had finished he said: 'I have come home to die.'

They said nothing.

The fever had left his cheeks. His eyes were unclouded. His lips were no longer deathly pale.

'Tomorrow I shall get up,' he said, and smiled. And then he smiled again and chuckled. 'I have such entertainments and diversions lined up for us.'

Two maids removed the tea things.

Sir Graham watched them with twinkling eyes.

Then he sighed deeply and said: 'Once I had a son.'

They all stiffened.

The rills of fear. The baying of the hounds of dread. The black owl tackering its beak.

'Did you know my son?' he said. 'Did you?'

Silence.

'I had such plans for my son. I had such plans for his death.'

A long pause.

'Those plans were foiled. Such a pity. Such a dreadful pity. Such a dreadful pity.'

He sighed again, closed his eyes and slid down his pillows.

The dwarf put his finger to his lips and led them outside.

And then he took them to their quarters.

They all agreed it was an adorable room.

Its proportions were exquisite. Its furnishings were sumptuous. It was simple yet elegant. It overlooked the square with the peacock-blue tiles and the flute-voiced fountain.

'I have seen this before. I have. I have,' said Roger Carey to himself.

He looked round the room. There were low divans bedecked with silken quilts and finely woven rugs. There were loom chairs and sofas and chaise longues. There were ripple-fronted closets for the new clothing they had found waiting for them. There were screens for the modest and cabinets of drinks for the bibulous.

They could not take stock of their emotions.

Oh the relief. Oh the joy. Oh the happiness.

Oh the horror, the dread and the dismay.

The little girls romped and giggled.

Mamselle and the gangster clung tightly to each other.

Dolly drew in deeply on a fat Egyptian cigarette and sipped Bombay gin.

Mrs Otto snored. Mr Dugdale twitched. Delphine's face was deathly white. Natasha stared ahead expressionlessly.

There was a gentle pat on the door.

Roger Carey looked across at Celia.

She nodded.

He padded softly across the room and carefully opened the door.

The mustachioed guard stepped inside.

He put his finger to his lips, looked out of the room from side to side and then closed the door. He turned to the gangster. He smiled. He strode purposefully towards him. He tore him from his lover's grasp. He hugged him to his bosom and smothered him with kisses.

'Jean-Claude. Oh, Jean-Claude,' he sobbed.

The gangster looked at him blankly.

The guard clasped him even more to his bosom.

'It's me. Juan,' he cried. 'You remember me? Barcelona, 1936. The Uprising of July. We stole an ice-cream cart.'

The gangster gasped. He shoved away the guard at arm's length and examined his face thoroughly. Then he burst into tears and slumped to the floor.

'Juan,' he sobbed. 'Juan. Juan.'

And he grasped the guard round the calves and began to smother his feet with kisses.

When their emotions had subsided, Mamselle said: 'Well then, you boys. I think explanations are in order, don't you?'

The two men were only too willing to talk. They all gathered round as the gangster and his friend began to recount their story.

The little girls were enraptured at the tales of gunshot and knife thrust.

Celia was appalled by the stories of reckless driving and total lack of concern for the welfare of their fellow human beings.

When the story had been told they all turned their attentions to the guard. They flung questions at him. Why was Sir Graham Egerton here? Why all the soldiers? Why the cattle and the neatly tilled fields? Why the guns and the aircraft? Why was the dwarf here? Why was the valley here? Why was the cave here? Why this? Why that?

The guard licked his lips. His eyes darted. His shoulders grew furtive. Small nerves shot ripples over his cheeks and up and down his neck.

He refused to say a single word of explanation.

But they did not have long to wait for the answer to their queries.

Very early next morning they were roused from their slumbers and summoned to present themselves at Sir Graham's private quarters.

68

They found him in a school room.

There were rows of desks. The inkwells were full. There were set squares and compasses laid out with blotting paper and pencil sharpeners. The blackboard had been freshly dusted.

'I'm feeling so much better today, so much much better,' said Sir Graham. 'Please will you all be seated?'

They looked at each other, alarmed. The little girls giggled. Mr Dugdale grunted with pleasure.

'Are you all seated?' said Sir Graham.

'Yes,' said one or two listless voices.

'Come, come, you can do better than that,' said Sir Graham with a rigid smile. 'Shall we try again? Of course. We'll try again. Are you all seated?'

'Yes,' they bellowed in unison at the top of their voices.

Sir Graham smiled and clicked his fingers one by one. He was wearing a black frock coat and pin-striped trousers. Around his neck was a silk stock.

'I am a man of great power,' he said.

They said nothing.

He stared at them, and his smile was rigid.

'I have never hesitated to use that power,' he said. 'I have used it to gain whatsoever I wanted in life.'

They said nothing.

His smile flickered.

'And now I have you,' he said.

The chill struck them all in the smooth glades of soft skin behind the ears. They could not take their eyes off him. He revelled in their fear and their curiosity. He laughed.

'I propose to tell you something about myself,' he said. 'It is only polite, don't you think?'

They said nothing and he barked: 'I said, it is only polite, don't you think?'

'Yes,' they bellowed in unison at the top of their voices.

He nodded his approval and once more clicked his fingers one by one.

After a while he said: 'Once the territories outside the cave stretched as far as the eye would see and much further than that. My father conquered and ruled them as a state within a state. No government dared to challenge him. They called him the White Sultan. His enterprises prospered mightily. Those who tried to oppose him were eliminated swiftly and without mercy.

'I was born in these territories in a house by a lake in a valley many many miles away from here. It was an enchanting place, that winding valley. The river was damned to form three lakes, one a mere wet slate among the reeds. There were oakwoods and beechwoods. There were fallow deer and Père David's and muntjac. And the house. Oh that lovely lovely house.'

He paused to wipe a tear from the corner of his eye with his bandanna. He smiled sadly.

'All gone,' he said. 'All squandered. All plundered. And now the civil war which rages throughout the land will finally destroy it and I shall have truly earned my death.'

He closed his eyes. The dwarf and the Swiss valet looked at each other with alarm. But neither moved. They watched his movements like pointers held tight and expectant in their traces.

Suddenly he opened his eyes and a great radiant smile of happiness suffused his features.

'Splendid. Absolutely splendid,' he said. 'And who shall be marmalade monitor?'

Silence.

'I shall explain just once,' he said, and this time there was an ice crackle of menace on the surface of his voice. 'At this time every morning I am accustomed to taking Earl Grey, lightly toasted pikelets and thick orange and brandy marmalade.'

He rang a small silver handbell.

Instantly the door was opened and three young maids entered bearing trays. He dismissed them with a swish of the cane he held across his knees.

'It is the marmalade monitor's task to distribute these goodies. Do I make myself clear?'

A ragged splutter of 'Yeses'.

'Do I make myself clear?' he snarled.

'Yes,' bellowed the voices as of one.

'Good. Then who is to be marmalade monitor?'

'I will.'

Natasha rose from her desk, walked lightly to the head of the school room, smiled long and lingeringly at Sir Graham and presently began to distribute the comestibles.

Sir Graham watched her sinuous, sensuous movements with approval and with pleasure.

They ate and drank in silence.

After Sir Graham had rung for the maids to remove the trays, he turned to the gathering and said: 'And now for my plans for you. I can assure you you will find them totally adorable. You will be my guests. And I will be your teacher. I will teach you the rudiments of physics. We shall study the ancient texts. We shall write compositions on matters of import and matters of no consequence whatever. We will translate Proust and Turgenev. Am I understood? Do I make myself clear?'

They all turned to Dolly.

She shrugged her shoulders and shook her head in a gesture of total indifference.

They turned to Celia.

She took a deep breath and said: 'Thank you, Sir Graham. You make yourself perfectly clear and I must say your plans sound perfectly delightful. But how long will it last? When shall we leave?'

'Leave?' said Sir Graham. 'Leave? Who in their right mind could possibly wish to leave circumstances so conducive to the pursuit of knowledge? My word, I do declare, who could possibly wish to leave here?'

69

And so the lessons commenced.

The routine was rigorous.

Assembly at seven fifteen. Marmalade and lightly toasted pikelets at eleven. Half-hour lunch break at one fifteen. Half-hour physical training at three. Milk and biscuits at four thirty. Evening meal at seven. And then homework.

'Homework!' said Dolly. 'Urrgh!'

Celia glared at her. How she hated her. If she had a cleaver in her possession, she would hack off her head. She would disembowel her and scatter her pulsating tripes to the ornamental fowl that pecked away the tiles of peacock blue.

Sir Graham provided them with a specially designed school uniform. The men wore high-winged collars and bum-starver jackets. The women wore gym slips and straw boaters.

'It's so demeaning,' said Louise.

'Oh, I don't know,' said Mamselle. 'I think we look rather fetching.'

And she pouted her lips and flickered her eyelids.

The curriculum was catholic and relentless.

Latin, Greek, Motor Mechanics, History, Geography, Economics, Domestic Science, English Literature, Physics, Zoology, Mathematics, Comparative Religion and Dressmaking – and each week something new was added to the syllabus.

The little girls loved it. They adored watching the despair and the humiliations of the adults. They revelled in studying the intricate details of the St Bartholomew's Day Massacre.

Throughout it all Sir Graham's health waxed and waned. Sometimes his eyes would sparkle and he would bounce up and down on his toes and scamper up and down the rows of desks chiding, scolding, praising and mocking. Sometimes they would not see him for days and the dwarf, with heavy heart and downcast eyes, would take over his duties. Sometimes they would be summoned to the Chinese drawing room and recite their lessons to the old man as he lay stricken and fighting for breath from the oxygen cylinder by the side of his vast bed.

And throughout it all the little girls prospered and flourished.

How they tittered and giggled when Dolly and Mamselle spent hour after hour in the corner of the school room in their dunces' caps. How they jeered when they watched the other adults struggle wearily with their homework.

Sometimes Jassy would sneak up to Dolly when no one was looking and help her with her Geography.

'No,' she would whisper. 'You've got it all wrong. That's not a gneiss. That's a ventifact.'

Mamselle and Celia were terrified of facing Sir Graham in the morning after they had handed in their homework.

'No, no, no,' he would scream, twitching at his cane. 'You are so uneducated. You are so ignorant. What on earth am I going to do with you? Take one hundred lines.'

However, he was all sweetness and light on his dealings with the gangster, who had developed a considerable dexterity in dissecting tree toads and ornamental carp during Zoology and had made giant strides forward in his History studies.

His opinions on the roles played by Mazzini and Gioberti particularly delighted Sir Graham, and he was ecstatic about his analysis of the origins of the Schmalkaldic League in 1531.

Natasha flitted and floated, tossed her golden hair and beamed and tinkled her laughter.

'I'm so happy,' she sang. 'Lucky, lucky me. I'm so deliriously, radiantly happy.'

'A most exquisite beautiful child,' said Sir Graham. 'And coming on in leaps and bounds with her Motorcycle Maintenance.'

On and on. Day after day.

Sometimes very very faintly, as though from a far distance, they heard the sound of heavy guns and the scream of bombs.

On and on. Day after day.

'I can't stand this much longer,' said Celia. 'It's driving me out of my head.'

'Never mind your head,' said Dolly. 'Does anyone know who this bloke Jenkins is?'

'Jenkins?'

'Yes. Apparently some silly buggers had a war over his ear.'

'Isn't that just typical of history?'

More subjects were introduced.

Political Science, Accountancy, Fine Arts and horticulture.

On and on and on. Day after day. Week after week.

Once for a whole month they saw neither sight nor light of Sir Graham.

'I fear the end is close,' said the dwarf, and he brushed his cheek against Dolly's breasts and lingered his fingers on the back of her neck as he corrected her composition on 'My Favourite Uncle'.

'Take your hands off me, you little turd,' screamed Dolly.

Celia looked across the school room at Roger Carey. He was stumbling with his German vocab. Oh, how she wanted to shout out across to him:

'*Die Unwissenheit*, Roger. *Die, die, die*. Not *das.*'

But she held her tongue as she saw the cane twitching in the whitening knuckles of the dwarf.

Next day Sir Graham appeared in the school room in robust health and high good humour.

Mr Dugdale, untroubled and content, smiled at him benignly. He took no part in the proceedings. He was just happy to be in the company of his fellow men. Delphine's presence, of course, was essential to his happiness. As for the rest of the gathering, for all he cared they could be members of the Moravian Brethren or Norwegian speedway riders.

Sir Graham patted him tenderly on the shoulder and said: 'Ah, Mr Dugdale. My dear old chap, what are we to do with you?'

'Have me measured for a suit of clothes directly,' he said.

'Such wisdom,' cried Sir Graham. 'Praise be for the sage and the sophist.'

Next day he did not appear in the school room and they were ordered to the Chinese drawing room.

They found him sitting high in bed, propped by his pillows and labouring for breath.

The gangster commenced to read him extracts from *The Water Babies*.

After only a few moments he waved his hand weakly and croaked: 'Not now. Later. One day in the summer.'

Later in the evening Juan visited them in their room when they lay on their beds exhausted after the rigours of their homework. He would often pay them such visits, bringing them snippets of news from the outside world.

'The government army, eh? They send out scouting party in the valley. We catch them. Slit their throats one by one, eh? They squeal like pigs.'

Or:

'The rebel army, eh? They make raid last night. They take five of our women. Yi, yi, yi! Soon we start fucking the chickens.'

On this night:

'Things bad. Things go mighty bad. They bomb us. They shell us. Trouble, eh? Mighty big trouble.'

'This can't go on,' said Dolly, after he'd gone.

'Well, do something about it,' screamed Celia.

They looked round the room. Roger Carey was crunched up on his bed, twitching his legs ceaselessly. Mamselle lay haggard and drawn on her bed. Delphine and Mr Dugdale were deep in sleep. Mrs Otto snored. Even the little girls were stricken by exhaustion. They lay huddled together on their divan, their faces pale with fatigue.

Natasha, as usual, had disappeared with Juan.

'Right,' said Dolly firmly. 'Right. I'll do something.'

Next morning Sir Graham reappeared in the school room. There was no hint of the previous day's sickness. He chided his pupils on their slovenly mien and their languor and listlessness. He tore into Mamselle for her deficiencies in Woodwork. He ranted at Roger Carey and screamed at Delphine. But he beamed with joy when the gangster came to the front of the class and commenced to speak.

'The way I look at it is this,' he said. 'Tolstoy was a toff. Gorky was a prole. Tolstoy scorns him. Right? He ain't Russian, he says. Right? His writings are imagined, artificial, mighty sentiments, heroic and false. Right? Well, I for one do not agree. In my opinion –'

'Oh, shut your hole,' shouted Dolly.

They all turned to her, gasping with horror.

Sir Graham's jaw hardened. His lips grew pale.

'I beg your pardon, Mrs Bradman,' he said. 'You were saying?'

'I was saying I don't give a shite about Tolstoy or Gorky. What I care about is us.'

'Us, Mrs Bradman? Us? Don't you mean We?'

'No, I don't mean We, smart arse. Us is the accusative case and in this context it is . . . oh, bollocks to grammar. Just you listen to me, you rancid, snot-encrusted –'

And then the bombs dropped.

Faintly they heard the roar of low-flying aircraft. And then they felt the thud of bombs directly above their heads. The whole room shook and vibrated. More explosions. More hammer thuds. The globe on Sir Graham's desk toppled to the floor and shattered.

The dwarf burst into the school room. There was panic in his eyes.

'I am sorry to intrude, Sir Graham,' he cried. 'But I have to inform you that we are under attack.'

'Please do not bother me with such irrelevances when –'

More explosions. Three vivid flashes. The clank of metal. The smell of cordite.

Sir Graham wrinkled his nose and clucked his tongue with irritation.

'Mrs Bradman,' he said, 'you will report to my quarters at eight thirty sharp this evening. Please, I beg of you, do not be late. You are no doubt aware of those memorable words spoken by Louis XVIII?'

'Haven't the foggiest.'

'Anyone oblige?' said Sir Graham raising his eyebrows.

Mrs Otto did not look up from her *Speisewagen* when she said: '*L'exactitude est la politesse des rois.*'

A mighty thud and the earth tottered and chunks of rubble fell from the roof and clattered at their feet.

And the ink slopped out of the wells and chalk dust rose all around.

'My dog eats nuts,' said Mr Dugdale.

70

Dolly presented herself at the door of the Chinese drawing room at eight thirty precisely that evening.

The dwarf eyed her up and down slowly and licked his lips.

She had soaked in the bath for at least an hour, her shoulders massaged by Celia, her feet squeezed and stroked by Delphine, her hair sudded and rinsed by Jassy and Polly, and her neck caressed by Louise.

When she had finished her toilet, she stood naked in the middle of the room and with her legs wide apart and her arms held high above her head was dried in rich red Turkish towels by the gangster and Roger Carey.

She lay on her bed and her body was covered in unguents and perfumes by Mamselle and her buttocks pummelled by Mrs Otto.

Celia tended to her hair, coiling it and burnishing it and sprinkling it with sparkling dust of silver and gold and ruby and amethyst.

Delphine helped her into her dress, adjusting the cord at her waist and aligning the slit which ran from her ankle to her hip bone.

It was a shimmering, diaphanous gown of purest white. Beneath it her mighty breasts swung free and her nipples surged.

The dwarf's eyes roved all over her.

Then he led her into the room.

Sir Graham was propped up in bed. His skin was pallid. The fever flush suffused his cheeks. His eyes watered. His frail hands trembled on the counterpane.

'Better this morning. Worse tonight,' he said. 'Much worse.'

He motioned for Dolly to sit on a stool next to his bed. He struggled for breath. His valet handed over the oxygen cylinder. He breathed in deeply. The gas hissed. He closed his eyes and sighed.

Then he said softly, 'I am ready to hear what you have to say, Mrs Bradman.'

'We want to leave,' said Dolly simply and boldly.

Sir Graham nodded.

'You are tired of the learning?' he said.

'Yes.'

'So am I.'

'What?'

'I am tired of teaching you. It wearies me. It tires me. I have had enough.'

The valet presented him with the cylinder once more. The dwarf handed him three pills on a silver tray. He took a sip from his wine and swallowed the pills.

Dolly waited for a few more minutes then she said: 'I plan to leave here tomorrow. I plan to lead my colleagues and my pupils out of this establishment and restore to them the safety and security for which I as their headmistress am fully responsible.'

He opened his eyes and smiled at her.

All her calmness had disappeared. Strands of hair, unloosened from her coiffure, hung down at her temples and flapped and fluttered in the violence of the breath spurting from her nostrils. Her eyes blazed. Her upper lip glistened with the juices of her anger. Her breasts plunged and reared.

'We're leaving. Do you hear me? We're leaving and that is that,' she roared.

'Oh no, Mrs Bradman. Oh no.'

He took another sip of his wine. He drained his glass and had it refilled by the valet. He eased himself in his bed, stretching out his legs and snuggling his back against the pillows. He smiled.

'I have other plans for you, Mrs Bradman.'

'Oh yes!' she said. 'Oh yes?'

He paused to admire once more the violence of her passion and the sumptuousness of her body.

Then he continued: 'In ancient China it was the custom when the Emperor died for his courtiers to bury with him his servants and his horses. As you see, Mrs Bradman, I have no shortage of servants.'

A pause. A smile. Another sip of wine.

'I intend you and your friends to play the part of the horses.'

71

Dolly did not return that night.

There was no sign of her the following day. They were not summoned to the school room. They were not summoned to the Chinese drawing room. They were left to their own devices.

'Where is she?' wailed Celia. 'Where's Dolly?'

'Never mind Dolly,' said the gangster. 'What about my essay on Hobbes? When am I going to read it out?'

Juan came in that evening just as the mountain howitzers began to open up.

'Is bad. Is terrible,' he said. 'They get nearer and nearer. Both armies. The bombs, they kill the women in the fields before they can shelter. The shells, they burst the dams and break the terraces for the vines. There is no hope. No escape for us. We die where we stand.'

A roar. A whoosh. Eardrums addled and raddled.

'I must go. My Natasha, she very frightened. She not like to be left alone.'

Next day there was no school.

'She's done a bunk,' said Mamselle. 'The bitch has done a bunk on us.'

Celia sighed. She walked slowly to where Roger Carey was lying on his back on the bed, his head resting on his hands.

'May I join you?' she said.

He nodded and patted the side of the bed.

She sat down.

'Well?' he said.

'What's happening to us, Roger?' she said.

'I don't know, Celia.'

In truth he did not. His thoughts were elsewhere. The storm at sea. The old ship writhing and squirming. Was she writhing and squirming now with Juan? Natasha! One minute wretched. Next minute ecstatic. Sparkle of eyes. Sneer of eyes. The welcoming wink of her backside. The rebuff of the point of her knee.

'Where's Dolly? Where the hell is she?'

'I don't know, Celia.'

She could have done so much better with her life. She could have been a kennel maid. She'd always had an empathy with greyhounds. They looked so miserable and resentful. But everyone said they made excellent pets. Affectionate and desperately anxious to please. Just like her.

The guns. The shells.

Nearer and nearer and nearer.

She could have been a librarian. She'd always liked books. There was so much reading matter in books. Especially the ones with lots and lots of pages. She could have been a cartographer. She liked maps. Particularly maps of the Lincolnshire Wolds. She would draw a map of Roger. She would draw it in all its intimate details and take it to bed with her and cuddle it and caress it. Oh, the things she could do with his unmanned level crossings. The joy she could bring to his high-tide marks and his deepest, darkest, most secret cuttings.

She turned to him. He had rolled over onto his side and was fast asleep, curled up and sucking his thumb.

She kissed him softly on the nape of his neck.

She could have been a libertine.

The days passed. The attacks continued. So did Dolly's absence.

Bombs crunched. Shells screeched. The floor rocked and the roof juddered violently.

'I don't want to stay here,' wailed Jassy. 'Where's Dolly? Where is she?'

Celia tried to comfort her, but she was inconsolable. Polly and Louise cowered in the corner, their eyes wide with torment. Mamselle hugged the gangster and sobbed.

'We'll never get out alive,' she howled. 'I know it. I just know it.'

Mr Dugdale observed their panic. It did not disturb his equilibrium. His response was unruffled.

Bombs? He had seen bombs. Shells? He had seen shells. Memories of an old soldier. The road with screens of corn stalks and straw matting on both sides and more matting on top. The brickyard.

The long stilting beams of the searchlights. The shell bursting short near the river bank. The one he did not hear until the sudden rush. The flash and bump of the burst. The singing of the fragments of shell and the rattle of falling brick. He had been calm then. Now he was aloof. How lovely to be aloof. That was what he had lived his whole life for, he realised now – to be totally and completely aloof.

He gazed at Delphine as she poured out wine and cut up slivers of juice-squirting melon. For him. All for him. For him alone. Did he feel aloof from her? He didn't know. How he wished he knew.

But Dolly knew.

She knew what she had done. She knew what she had to do now.

The floor of the cave was tiled peacock blue. There was a flute-voiced fountain in its centre. There were crystal chandeliers and marble benches. There were doors with jewel-encrusted handles.

The dwarf opened one and Dolly followed him into the room.

Sir Graham lay in his great canopied bed propped up by three podged-up pillows. The oxygen cylinder hissed. The mask was clamped tightly to his mouth. The dwarf dismissed the Swiss valet and motioned for Dolly to sit beside the bed.

The old man's eyes flashed from man to woman. They were flecked with panic and then seared with terror as he saw the expression on the face of the dwarf. He clutched at the mask but he could not remove it from his mouth. He tried to raise himself from the pillows but he was too frail.

He turned his eyes to the dwarf once more and now they were full of pleading.

Dolly looked on.

The stories he had told her since she had been imprisoned in his quarters. His childhood in the vast territories once ruled by his father. He had been suckled by wet nurses from the Balkans. He had been weaned on to quails' eggs and champagne by eunuchs from the lands of the Ottomans. He had a troupe of Armenian dwarfs to entertain him as he cooed and slobbered in his cot.

'I had three Shetland ponies and a squadron of Sikh light cavalry to protect me and guard me. Once I had a Belgian nanny who displeased me. Father had her beheaded on the spot.'

'Fancy.'

'I had tutors from all the great universities and ancient places of learning from the heartlands of Europe to the remote fastnesses of Asia. By the time I was six I could speak Swedish, classical Persian, sixteen dialects of Urdu and a fair smattering of demotic Tibetan.'

'Fancy.'

The old man stirred feebly in his bed and turned his eyes to Dolly. The pleading grew more intense. Dolly moved forwards in her chair. The dwarf coughed sharply and she withdrew. The old man's chest fluttered weakly and he took three sobbing gasps at his mask and the oxygen cylinder hissed its contempt.

The stories he had told her! The adventures he had had! Fighting off pirates in the South China Sea. Slitting the throats of headhunters in the Matto Grosso. Traversing the vastness of the Empty Quarter with naught for company but a white she-camel and a slim-buttocked Berber boy. Piloting his sea planes in the Schneider Trophy. Driving his snarl-throated roadsters in the Mille Miglia. Breaking his back at polo. Breaking the bank at Biarritz. Breaking the hearts of women of every shape, hue and creed.

He had told her these stories as she lay beside him in the great canopied bed and he fondled her breasts and nuzzled at her neck.

'Samoans were the most pliant lovers. So soft and silly. Hungarians were full of passion and pride. The Japanese were dainty and dexterous. Parsee ladies gave themselves relentlessly. The Bulgars were reluctant. The Swiss were repulsive. The Irish were unspeakable.'

'Fancy.'

The old man struggled once more with his oxygen mask. Once more Dolly moved forwards in her chair. Once more the dwarf coughed sharply and she withdrew.

His father had died. His empire had waned. But Sir Graham refused to return home to claim his inheritance.

'So beautiful yet so squalid. So sensuous yet so brutal. How could the intellect flourish? How could the groves of Academe be watered?'

'I've no idea.'

And so he had stayed away from his birthplace and travelled the world and savoured its delights to the full. He had dined with Hitler and breakfasted with Zola. He had fought under Pétain. He had fought under Hindenburg. He had sparred with Carpentier and wrestled with Garbo. He had played quoits with Stravinsky and badminton with Freud. He had gathered raspberries with Poulenc and made bicycle tours of Picardy with Chaliapin. He had shared lovers with Noël Coward and Grock.

'A full life, Mrs Bradman. A full and voracious life. Never once did I catch the clap.'

'Fancy.'

And then mortal illness had struck.

'Quite suddenly, my dear Mrs Bradman. Quite without warning.'

'Fancy.'

He had returned to the great warren of caves in the valley to die.

'I was full of content, Mrs Bradman. I wanted nothing more from my life. I was happy with my death. And then you came along, my dear. Oh yes, you came.'

He had placed his hand tremulously on her thigh. She had guided it to its chosen destination. He had sighed. And he had wept.

'And now you will stay here for ever and keep me alive. Oh yes, my dear, you will keep me alive. It is your destiny. If you try to escape, I shall swallow you and spit you out like a great flat-bellied boulder.'

But that was several days ago.

Now he looked at her piteously.

There was a great, aching, tearful hollowness at the back of his eyes.

The dwarf coughed.

Dolly did not move.

The dwarf coughed again. He motioned with his head. Dolly stood up slowly. Slowly she moved towards the bed. Sir Graham's eyes welled with tears of joy and expectation. He stretched out his frail arms to her. And then suddenly he realised what she was about to do to him. With a massive effort he heaved himself from the pillows. He clawed at her. It was in vain. She brushed him aside. He crumpled back into his pillows. The horror and terror had left his eyes. Now there was only sad bemused resignation there as with a swift twirl of her wrist Dolly snapped shut the tap on the cylinder of oxygen.

They watched him die.

It took fifty-seven minutes.

When Juan visited them that evening he had a blood-stained bandage wrapped tightly round his head.

'Kaput,' he said. 'Everything's gone. One army at one end of the valley. The other at the other end. Now they strangle us. Bombs! Shells! Yi, yi, yi! It is all over, my friends.'

He slip-slopped out, limping and wincing with pain.

'That's it then. We're dead,' said Mamselle.

And it was at that precise moment that Dolly returned.

They noticed that she had scratches on her cheeks and bruises on her neck.

The dwarf stood by her side and looked extremely pleased with himself.

72

The little girls flung themselves at Dolly, hugging her and kissing her.

'Bugger off, you little shits,' she shouted. 'You know I can't bear being kissed by small children. They always bring you out in cold sores.'

The dwarf continued to beam.

'I have some news for you,' she said.

'Are we leaving, Dolly?' cried Jassy. 'Oh, please tell us we're leaving.'

Dolly took hold of her arm and pressed her into her bosom.

'You all leave. I stay.'

'What, Dolly? What's that you say?' cried Celia.

'You lot go. Tonight. It has been arranged.'

'But –'

'Tonight. Get yourselves ready.'

She nodded to the dwarf and he bowed and silently left the room.

There was silence for a moment and then there was a babble of cackering voices.

'You can't stay, Dolly.'

'Yes, she can.'

'No, she can't.'

'If you stay, Dolly, I stay.'

'But how did you swing it?'

'Why have you got bruises on your neck, Dolly?'

'Silence,' thundered Dolly. 'Silence.'

They fell silent.

She surveyed them.

Mr Dugdale and Delphine lay side by side on their bed. Mamselle's eyes were flashing. The gangster's were lowered. Mrs Otto was munching. Natasha, unwanted by Juan that evening, was staring at the wall. Celia's eyes were distraught, full of pleading, overflowing with misery.

'I'll say this only once,' said Dolly. 'It has been arranged. There is no going back. Prepare yourself to leave. Then I shall say my farewells to each one of you in turn.'

And that was that.

Celia attempted to dissuade her. She would not budge. Jassy sobbed her heart out and said she would stay with Dolly through thick and thin till the end of time. Dolly patted her on the head and then pushed her away.

Then midnight came and it was time for them to take their leave of Dolly.

To the gangster she said: 'I like you. You're a clip.'

To Mamselle she said: 'I don't know about you. You're a total fraud, I know. But I think I like frauds. You know where you stand with them. You've got good legs, too.'

'Thank you.'

'Don't mention it.'

To Natasha she said: 'You are a thoroughly wicked woman. You will come to a most dreadful end.'

Natasha smiled.

'Would you like your owl back?' she said.

'No, I would not,' screamed Dolly.

To Mrs Otto she said: 'You saved our lives. Thank you.'

Louise and Polly giggled.

'Guess what I've just done.'

'Ugh! Pooh!'

To them she said: 'Polly, you will grow up to be a beautiful woman. You will charm men. You will frustrate men. You will give them happiness. You will give them misery. You will wind them round your little finger. You will have many many lovers. You will have four husbands. You will be unfaithful to each one. You will neglect your children and be loathed and hated by them. You will be content and utterly self-centred, a beauty still worshipped and adored by men of every age.'

'Golly.'

'And as for you, Louise.'

'Yes, Dolly?'

'You will become even fatter. You will grow fatter and fatter and ever fatter as the years go by. You will waddle and wheeze. You will pant and perspire. You will probably marry a Hungarian.'

'Thanks awfully, Dolly.'

'Don't mention it.'

To Delphine and Mr Dugdale she said: 'Well then? What have you to say to me?'

'Mr Dugdale is going to marry me,' said Delphine. 'We're going to live on a cliff top. We'll buy a golden retriever. We'll keep a scrapbook. I shall read to him. We'll listen to the heave of the sea. I shall look after him when he begins to fade. I shall never leave him. I shan't wear black at his funeral. I shall be joyous. I might even sing a silly song to myself.'

Dolly nodded and kissed her warmly on the forehead.

She turned to Mr Dugdale.

'And you, old friend?'

Mr Dugdale smiled.

'We shall find peace,' he said.

She cradled Jassy in her arms silently for quite a time.

'Jassy,' she said.

'Yes, Dolly?'

'I rather think you will grow up to be like me.'

'Will my tits be as big?'

'Oh yes.'

'Goodie, goodie.'

She clasped Celia tightly to her bosom.

Then she said: 'I've nothing much to say. We know each other too well, don't we?'

'Yes, but . . .'

'The dwarf will turn a blind eye. Please don't ask me to tell you why.'

'I understand.'

Dolly nodded towards Roger Carey.

'Look after him.'

'Yes.'

'Make him happy.'

'Yes.'

'Bye bye, Celia.'

'Bye bye, Dolly.'

She did not speak to Roger Carey.

She just blew him a kiss.

Then she opened the door.

Juan was waiting there with bowler hat.

The Indian smiled at them broadly. His testicles were restored to their normal size. He opened his trousers to show Dolly.

'Very nice,' she said. 'Now put them away and bugger off.'

Before anyone could speak she turned on her heel, dashed into her room and slammed the door behind her.

The dwarf looked on and smirked and smacked his lips.

275

73

The sky was overcast.

'Good,' said Juan.

They had squeezed themselves through the escape hole in the very furthest recesses of the cave. They had to heave and tug at Mrs Otto. She almost did not make it. She pleaded with them to leave her. But then bowler hat bit her on the bottom and she shot through the gap like a shell from a mountain howitzer.

There was dampness in the air and their footsteps were muffled as they climbed the sheer path up the cliff face.

'Good,' said Juan. 'Good.'

The climb was long. It was arduous.

They gritted their teeth and thought of home and what they would see and what they would do when they got there.

Mamselle dreamt of Coq d'Or chocolate biscuits. Celia felt the chill of the attic bedroom overlooking the marsh. The gangster thought of forged ration books.

Far away on the other side of the valley a red Very light coiled itself into the night sky. There was a brief flicker of tracer bullets. Then nothing.

'Good,' said Juan.

Delphine thought of the Lundy-bound steamer buffing back the waves. Polly thought of Jack Buchanan. Louise thought of fig pudding.

They paused. They rested, pressing themselves close to the steel-hard, shiny rock face.

'Don't look down,' said Juan. 'You look down – poof!'

Natasha looked down. She *would* be happy. She would, she would, she would. She'd find herself a man and she would make him happy. She would, she would, she would. She would be his slave. Totally. Completely. She would abase herself. She flung the black owl off her shoulder. Down it plunged, its wings pinioned, its talons desperately flailing in the thin cold air. It hit the ground. Splat!

She turned to Delphine and whispered, 'I love you, Delphine.'

It was time for them to move on. Their limbs were weary. They were bruised and gashed.

'Not long,' whispered Juan. 'Keep going, eh? No fall back.'

Tiny stones clattered.

And then Mrs Otto stumbled. Clean as a whistle she fell over the edge. She did not cry out. She fell and twirled and billowed and bumped and bounced on the rocks below. And her *Speisewagen* landed gently on her great contented belly.

Ten minutes later they reached the top of the cliff. They could not speak. They could not move.

'Move!' shouted Juan. 'Move. No time to rest. We move quick now. Not far to go. We move quick, eh? We make no noise. No noise, eh? Now move!'

They moved quickly through the scrub. Sometimes they slipped. Sometimes they sobbed. Their minds were numb. Thorns clawed at their clothes. Night birds clackered their alarm. They smelt thyme and oregano.

Juan found the track. It twisted into the jungle.

'No noise. You watch your feet. No treading on wood. The army all around us. Make noise and they shoot. You understand. Quick. No noise. Not far to go.'

Mr Dugdale was unruffled. He was completely aloof.

He dreamt of the salt-spit whaler lolling on the swell. The Nansen passport and his mother's pride. The smell of cabbage and bacon. The East Sea's bitter tang. The lines of dunes and the twisted groynes.

And Jassy? Jassy dreamt of . . .

'Stop,' snapped Juan. 'Stop. Gather close.'

They drew themselves up around him. He pointed to a clearing ahead of them.

'We cross,' he said. 'Horses for us on other side. We reach horses and then we ride to our safety. Understand?'

They nodded.

'No noise. Army all around. They shoot. They hear us. They see us. They shoot. Poof! You understand?'

They nodded.

'Okay. We dash across. Quick. One by one. Okay? I go first. I signal you when you come. Okay? You understand?'

They nodded.

Juan glanced all around. He sniffed the air.

'Okay?'

'Okay,' they all whispered.

Their hearts pumped and their knees trembled.

Juan stood up, sniffed the air again and then, swift and silent, darted across the clearing. He crouched in the bushes. He looked from side to side and then stuck up his thumb.

Jassy sped across the clearing.

She was followed by Louise and Polly.

They smelt the horses.

After a while Juan raised his thumb again and Mamselle dashed across followed by the gangster and Celia.

'No noise,' hissed Juan. 'For Christ's sake. No noise.'

He raised his thumb again.

Very slowly Mr Dugdale appeared out of the jungle, supported by Delphine and Roger Carey. He had a broad, contented smile on his face.

'Jesus! Jesus!' whispered Juan.

Painfully slowly they hobbled across the clearing. When they reached the other side everyone, except Mr Dugdale, was drenched in perspiration.

He looked at them and smiled radiantly.

'Gardening boots,' he said.

Swift and sure brown bowler crossed the clearing. He was shaking. He grasped hold of Juan's sleeve.

'She no come,' he whimpered. 'She no come.'

They looked across the clearing. On the other side stood Natasha. She was making no effort to hide herself. She was looking around and smiling.

'Christ,' hissed Mamselle. 'Christ.'

Slowly, delicately, almost jauntily Natasha commenced to cross the clearing.

Delphine grasped hold of Mr Dugdale and whispered: 'I love you, Aubrey. Whatever happens to us. I love you.'

And then the guns blazed.

The bullets whizzed and spattered and pucker-puckered.

Natasha screamed. She stumbled forwards onto her hands and knees. She began to crawl towards them. The bullets spat again. She sank to the ground. Blood was gushing from her neck.

No one could stop Mr Dugdale.

He stood up and stepped into the clearing and began to walk towards her.

Delphine screamed.

Roger Carey and the gangster pounced on her and pinned her to the ground.

The bullets thudded into Mr Dugdale. He spun. He pirouetted. His legs flailed. His arms flapped. He collapsed.

Slowly he stretched out his hand to Natasha.

But her head was turned away from him. And as he watched, her whole body was convulsed with silent writhing and all he could see was the bleakness of her back.

He stretched out his hand to her.

He whispered: 'Why is it so dark in the shadows, Natasha? Tell them to turn up the lights.'

His blood oozed and stuck together the pages of his Nansen passport.

74

Six months later they arrived in New York.
  'Aren't the skyscrapers high?' said Polly.
  'Yes,' said Louise.

75

The small biplane circled the marsh timidly. Its engine sputtered. The sun glinted on its cockpit.

Roger Carey, headmaster of Lygon House Private School for Progressive Young People, surveyed it from the window of the pinch-shouldered common room.

His wife, Celia, stood by his side, suckling their infant at the breast.

The matron, Delphine, sat silently in a corner reading. Her old prince was about to die yet again. She sighed.

Mamselle was away visiting her gangster in Walton Jail. The head girl, Jassy, was playing poker with Polly and Louise.

Small boys and girls chased each other through the grounds or sat in their dormitories sobbing.

It was Sunday afternoon. The war had ended.

The biplane banked, circled the school and then shamefacedly and rather diffidently it discharged a parachute. It opened and drifted and swung in the sharp sea breeze. The onlookers rushed out to greet it.

It landed smack in the middle of the playing fields.

They gathered round the parachutist, goggled and helmeted and leathered. The figure scrambled to its feet. It ripped off its goggles and helmet and smiled.

'Hello,' said Dolly. 'And how are the shits today?'

They stood motionless.

She smiled. She beckoned them. She set forth for the school. She stopped. She turned. They were still standing motionless.

'Well, come on then,' she said. 'Have I got a story to tell you.'